D0344404

THE ISLAND DWELLERS

THE
ISLAND
DWELLERS

STORIES

JEN SILVERMAN

RANDOM HOUSE
NEW YORK

Published in the United States by Random House, an imprint and division of Penguin Random House LLC, New York.

RANDOM HOUSE and the HOUSE colophon are registered trademarks of Penguin Random House LLC.

A different version of "Mamushi" was published with the title "Blood Winter" in *The Ledge*. A different version of "The Pike" was published in *The Gettysburg Review*.

LIBRARY OF CONGRESS CATALOGING-IN-PUBLICATION DATA

Names: Silverman, Jen, author.
Title: The island dwellers: stories / Jen Silverman.
Description: First edition. | New York: Random House, [2018]
Identifiers: LCCN 2017011348 | ISBN 9780399591495 (hardcover: acid-free paper) | ISBN 9780399591501 (ebook)
Classification: LCC PS3619.I55235 A6 2018 | DDC 813/.6—dc23
LC record available at https://lccn.loc.gov/2017011348

Printed in the United States of America on acid-free paper

randomhousebooks.com

987654321

First Edition

Book design by Diane Hobbing

To my parents, Mark and Sue,
and to my brother, Chris

CONTENTS

THE ISLAND DWELLERS

GIRL CANADIAN SHIPWRECK

When I was younger and I heard about anybody trapped anywhere, my first response was always just: why don't you leave?

Trapped in a job? Leave.

Trapped in a place? Leave.

Trapped in your car under a river? Crank the window open and swim to freedom.

It was a great and simple solution that I alone had come up with, and I didn't understand why nobody else had managed to grasp the concept. Among my friends, I was the Messiah of this movement. I said things like: "If that apartment sucks, just move." And: "If you need to fuck a lot of people, just leave him." And: "Study abroad!" My friends said things like: Oh and Wow and Hmm and It's Not That Simple, and You Make It Sound So Simple.

When I grew older, however, it wasn't so much that I learned that I was wrong (this is still a philosophy that, intellectually, I sub-scribe to), but rather that there were scenarios I hadn't thought of. For example: imagine an island. You are on this island. You are alone. There is nobody else with you. Leave! you might say. Okay. But you need a boat. There is no boat on your island, so you need to build a boat. Build a boat! you might say. Okay, but you don't know how, and there is no Wi-Fi on your island, so you can't look it up on YouTube—but okay, you can guess how to build a boat. It involves chopping down trees and hewing them and fastening them and— fuck it, you'll build a raft. But you need tools. You need sharp tools that will chop through wood. You have no tools. And you're so tired. This entire attempt has made you tired. So what are you going to do? Well, you don't know, and you haven't given up on the idea of leaving, but you're just going to sit very still for a time. You're just going to sit very still and not move at all, and try to filter the right answer out of the shadow that is descending from the canopy of uncuttable trees that loom over your head.

You see, *there* is a scenario in which you can't just Leave.

Now imagine that there are a hundred of these islands. And on each island is a little person, crouched down on the ground, trying to filter sense out of shadow, without a boat. Now you have a hundred people who can't just Leave.

And so it goes.

SOMETIME IN JUNE, I GO see Camilo perform. We've been dating for two years, and as Camilo's girlfriend, it's my duty to attend his first performance piece in all that time. He's so excited that I can't tell him my deep personal failing: namely, that I don't like performance art. I think either you're performing, or you're making art. I think that performance art is something that people do because they're not good enough actors to just perform, and they're not skilled enough artists to just make art.

But I don't say this.

On my way to the venue, a basement in deepest Brooklyn, I talk out loud to myself. I practice telling Camilo that I love his work, without sounding like I'm lying. It's harder than you think, but I find that it relies more on tone of voice than words, and by the time I get there, I sound convincing.

Camilo's friends Ev and Keira meet me on the sidewalk outside.

Ev has been a lesbian, but Ev is about to transition into being a man. Ev's current gender pronoun of choice is *E*. Ev says that certain things are inherent, that E identifies as gay before E is a gender, and therefore when E fully becomes a man, E will have no choice but to date men. I understand the idea of inherence. As in: this person is *inherently* skilled. This person is *inherently* clumsy. I am concerned because Camilo is inherently clumsy with things like words and money and other people's feelings. He loses his socks and he interrupts you. If you are inherently clumsy, chances are slim that you will make finely tuned work.

We crowd into the basement. Keira keeps her sunglasses on. Keira is only here for Camilo, she wants that to be clear. Keira is the friend you talk to when things go wrong in your life, because things are constantly wrong in hers. She is very good at telling you it is not your fault, when quite possibly it is your fault. This is a good friend for you to have, but not a good friend for your girlfriend, because you will only ever mention her to Keira when you are angry and sad.

Sometimes I make Camilo sad, and this is the first thing Keira knows about me. She knows that I once said that I didn't understand how Camilo's friends could protest the death penalty and then walk by homeless people on the street—*if* you believe all human life has value (which I do not), then shouldn't you act accordingly at all times? Camilo wouldn't speak to me for a day after that, nor would he articulate which part of my statement upset him the most.

What Keira does not know about: The time Camilo and I skipped work, took the Metro-North outside the city to Dia: Beacon, and ate picnic sandwiches in the grass. The time we read the entirety of Roald Dahl's *The Twits* out loud on the subway, during a trip from the top of Manhattan to the tail of Brooklyn. The time Camilo had a brief but intense nervous breakdown, after a prolonged phone call with his mother, and I stayed up the whole night talking him through it.

These are not the things you would ever tell a friend like Keira, even if they are also part of the map of your relationship. Keira has one map, and the friend to whom you tell all your good things has the other map, and you just have a jumble of chicken-scrawl on a napkin. And that is why your friends always think they know where you should be going, and yet you yourself are so often lost.

For the past two years, I have been dating Camilo, and not leaving. I moved to the large brownstone co-op in which he lives, where things like books and plants and people go missing, slide between the cracks of the ancient and splintering floorboards. There are whole countries that have gone missing inside this house. There are people who emerge from doorways and their faces are unrecognizable faces, because they are faces that have gone missing as well. In this way, Camilo and his house together are not unlike the island of Doctor Moreau.

Now we're in the basement. We are invited to line the walls, standing or kneeling, creating an open rectangle in the center. There is a microphone, waiting at the end of the open rectangle. The concrete floor is cool under my knees, and it feels good after the humidity outside. As the last people trail inside and settle into a hush, Camilo walks out. We are silent, eyes trained on him. He is wearing a white T-shirt. The armpits are stained. The elastic of his black sweatpants is too old, they're sagging dangerously at the waist, and his long hair is loose. I can't tell if he looks like an Artist or a serial killer. I hope everybody in the room is thinking he looks like an Artist. I hope they're thinking about how authentic he seems, how unfettered by societal norms. I briefly hate myself for even letting the thought *serial killer* slip across my mind. Ev, Keira, and I arrange our faces to look encouraging. Keira makes a little "yeah" noise, a little "go get 'em tiger" noise, but Ev is completely focused. Ev also identifies as a performance artist, and is Taking This Seriously. Regardless of why we're here, we all want him to succeed. We desperately want this to be good. The better it is, the less lying we will have to do.

Camilo starts to windmill his arms. I think he's stretching, he's working up to something, he's preparing for takeoff. He keeps windmilling. Any minute now, he's going to stop, shake himself off, and begin something that requires very loose shoulders. He keeps windmilling. Now two minutes have passed and Camilo is still very vigorously windmilling his arms. I sneak a sideways look at Keira. Her sunglasses are still on and you can't see her eyes and suddenly I'm jealous that I didn't think of wearing sunglasses. Now it's three minutes. I am starting to be concerned for Camilo's rotator cuffs. My best friend is in med school, and she has told me about rotator cuff injuries and how often they require surgery. She has told me that you may think cartilage is tough, but actually in certain situations it tears like paper, and then you're fucked. Camilo's cartilage might be tearing this very second, and for what? Now it's four minutes. Keira's sunglasses reflect a small and determined Camilo, glistening with sweat, churning his arms in circles.

Ev gets up. For one shocked moment, I think E is going to leave. E has decided that This Is Not Art, and is going to leave! Is this a gesture of great friendship, because of the depth of its honesty? Should I, as his girlfriend, be so honest as well? The idea is wild and liberating. Then Ev walks to the microphone stand, and I realize that Ev and Camilo must have agreed to this ahead of time. There is a piece of paper taped to the stand. E lifts it up. E begins to read.

As Camilo windmills his way up and down the room, Ev reads a series of sentences about Camilo's mother. These are recollections from when Camilo was a child. His mother is cool and brutal and absent. The sentences all seem to begin "I am six (or eight or four or ten), and my mother . . ." and then they finish badly. She frightens him. She chastises him. She abandons him, for days or weeks at a time. Ev's voice seems to incite Camilo to a more vigorous windmilling. Ev stops mid-sentence, replaces the paper, and walks offstage. A moment. We are hushed. Is it over?

But no. Keira jumps to her feet. Now she understands what is being asked of her, of all of us, as audience members and participants. She darts into the open space and picks up the piece of paper, with great purpose. She reads from the paper in a big voice. Camilo's mother once locked him in a closet. Camilo's mother threw away his diary. Camilo's mother hangs up the phone before he is finished talking.

Some are stories that I knew already, but I thought they were private quiet stories told late at night, and now they are stories being told in big voices in a big basement with mid-afternoon light soaking through the street-level windows. This changes the stories. I don't want it to change the stories, but it changes the stories.

Keira stops mid-sentence, the way Ev did, and returns to the wall. We wait through a long painful silence. The look on Camilo's face is a frown bordering on ecstasy. He's a little biplane, propelling itself forward and backward. His shirt has ridden up now, his sweatpants have slid down. The crisp curl of his stomach hair is visible, and the partial curve of an ass-cheek. *Art is messy*, I think defensively, in case anyone in the crowd is thinking that he looks insane. *Art is not put-together.*

A man that I don't know goes up to the microphone stand. He takes the paper hesitantly. He is older than we are. I don't know if he wandered in here by accident. I like to imagine that maybe he did. Maybe he is a Brooklyn Dad, and he was Wandering By, and he noticed the crowd through one of the street-level windows, and he wanted to see What the Kids Were Doing. He has a decent face. He reads some sentences, but now they have looped back on themselves, they are repeating. Camilo makes the same gestures and the man reads out loud the same stories that Camilo told me late at night, that are the same sentences that Ev and Keira just read out into this dog-damp basement, that are the same sentences anyone will read for however much longer this performance lasts—and I have a moment of pure and unflinching comprehension:

This is Hell.

I never thought there was such a thing as Hell, but this is it.

Here I am, Trapped in Hell.

I have been a bad human.

I have been a bad girlfriend.

I have lied and said I didn't get texts that I actually got but didn't want to reply to.

I have lied and said I had plans, when I just wanted to be alone.

I have lied and said "Yes that was good" after we had sex and it was bad and he asked if it was good.

I have lied and said that it's okay that he's stopped using shampoo because he doesn't believe in shampoo anymore, but actually I don't think it's okay, I think people should wash their hair.

I am a judgmental person, a cynic, a capitalist, someone who does not share with Camilo and his friends their fervent, delirious belief in the life-changing potential of political protest and art.

I am a sad lonely person with conservative values and a crippled soul who cannot appreciate performance art.

And this is my punishment. Here, in Hell.

And, what's more, I know what Dante once knew: Hell consists of many rings. The outer rings are things like the Subway, Times Square, Brokers' Fees. The inner ones are things like Taxes, Grant Applications, Performance Art. Once you get past those, there is only one ring left, the innermost ring of Hell. And that ring is not this basement. That ring is what happens after this basement. That ring is the space of deceit and guilt that will be created the moment Camilo stops waving his arms. That ring is the thing that lies just ahead.

AFTERWARD, WE GO TO A bar down the street. Camilo's friends are abuzz with excitement, in part because we're finally out of the basement, mostly because we're day-drinking. Camilo lets them talk to him about poignancy and the truths of the body, and then he turns to me. His eyes are wide, guileless, depthless. This is the moment he has been waiting for. Every cell of his body strains toward me. "What did you think?" he asks, desperately casual.

I smile at him. I force every cell of my body into an upward position. I try to radiate. I am thermonuclear.

"It was so interesting," I say. "It was really really interesting."

I meant to say good. I meant to say good. Why couldn't I say good! I'd silently practiced the word *good*.

"Interesting?" Camilo asks. His cells sag. His eyes are sad eyes. His mother once locked him in a closet and I just told him that his work was *interesting*.

"Good," I say, taking a swallow of my mid-afternoon Jameson. "Very *very* good."

OTHER THINGS I DON'T UNDERSTAND: How we stop dreaming about ways out and places to go because we stop believing there is anywhere to go at all. What happens after we sit down in the shade and try to rest from all of our mad spinning plans about boats and sharp tools and hewn trees. What happens when the weight of our bodies pulls us down to the mud, and we curl up against the earth. What happens when we grow roots downward. What happens then?

GINA IS HAVING A FOURTH of July party on the rooftop of her Brooklyn studio. She invites Camilo and then me, by way of Camilo. I tell Camilo I don't want to go. He's instantly upset, although he would use the word *concerned*.

"How come?" he asks.

"You guys slept together," I say. "I don't feel comfortable."

"We're not sleeping together any*more*." Camilo points out a flaw in my logic. "I'm sleeping with *you*."

"Sure," I say. "But you slept together at a time when you were *also* sleeping with me, and when I was led to believe that you *weren't* sleeping with her. Or anybody else."

Camilo looks sad. It's hard for him to have this conversation. He wants to focus on positive things like love and trust and rebuilding. We always seem to be rebuilding. Whenever he mentions "rebuilding" I imagine a small shack that keeps falling down. Goats graze near it. Grass grows over it. And yet humans keep coming back and propping it up.

"You have to know that I never would have done it if I knew it would hurt you," he says. "I thought at the time that we shared similar values. And Gina would never have done it if she didn't think you'd understand. I mean, we were at an *artist colony.*"

"*You* can go," I say. "I'd never tell you not to go." I deeply don't want him to go.

Camilo frowns. He is disappointed in the smallness of our minds, "our" as in Human, as in the entire species. He is disappointed in the way we rope ourselves in with feelings of jealousy, insecurity, resentment. There is a whole landscape of human experience. Camilo doesn't understand why we are not out there on the ridgeline of that landscape, arms spread to the wind, embracing it all. Camilo wants me to know that he is not disappointed in *me* specifically because he knows that I am trying as hard as I can to grapple with the limitations produced by my upbringing, but nonetheless, he wonders if this is a learning opportunity for me. Maybe, in this moment, I can push myself. I can challenge myself. I can go to Gina's rooftop party.

I want to be better than I am.

I want to be open-minded, and spiritually free, and I don't want to be the sort of person who is psychologically fettered in the way that (the more time I spend with Camilo and his friends) it becomes clear I am fettered.

I go to Gina's rooftop party.

IT'S ON THE ROOF OF an old rectory that became a warehouse that became a ward for the mentally ill that is now a series of artist studios, or some lineage in some order. Ev comes with us. He is using male pronouns now, instead of *E*. There is a fine peach-fuzz starting on his upper lip. He's embraced cut-offs and sleeveless tees, and he gives me a bro-nod when we meet on the street corner below the rectory-cum-warehouse-cum-insane-asylum. "Where the party at," says Ev. I don't think I've ever before heard him construct a sentence that starts "Where the party," and ends with the dangling preposition "at," but Camilo doesn't seem to notice.

"Hey!" Gina's voice drifts down to us. We direct our attention up to where she leans over the edge of the roof. "You guys!"

"Hey!" Camilo yells back. I can count his teeth in his grin. He is waving both hands: one is no longer enough.

"I'll come down!" yells Gina, and she vanishes from the roof edge.

"Good times," says Ev, who has never before used the phrase "Good times."

Gina appears on the sidewalk. Her hair is dyed red and she's wearing a translucent white tee and blue cut-offs. "Red white and blue!" she says, in case we didn't make the connection.

"Oh wow," says Camilo, who normally can't witness nationalistic displays without discussing immigration reform, but who is now suddenly amenable. "Wow, yeah."

Gina gives him an extra-long hug. Then she gives me an extra-long hug, for almost exactly the same number of seconds. It's not like I was counting, but it's also not like I *wasn't* counting. She isn't wearing a bra and she presses against me, close. "It's *so* good to see you," she says, her breath warm on my cheek.

Camilo introduces her to Ev, and they shake hands. I catch Ev staring at her tits through her T-shirt. Gina leads us up the narrow winding stairs, giving us the brief guided tour: studios down that dim hall, more studios down the next one, bathrooms on this landing, we have to climb the fire ladder to the roof, nobody's scared of heights, right? I'm trying to figure out what it means that Gina gave me the same number-of-seconds hug that she gave Camilo. Does this mean she doesn't want to fuck him anymore? Does it mean she wants to fuck me? Was it an apology or a come-on? If she wants to fuck me, and if I say yes, does that mean that I'm sexually liberated too?

Out on the roof, Gina's primary and secondary partners are drinking PBR. She introduces us: Frankie is her boyfriend, but she says "primary partner," and he's a DJ. They've been together for five years. Macey is her girlfriend, but she uses the phrase "secondary partner." They met on Tinder last week. I watch Camilo's face. He's impressed. Frankie shakes everybody's hands, little tight-handed minor eruptions of a shake. Macey is sprawled out in the shade, all loose bare legs and cut-off jeans. She's sexy as shit, and she doesn't get up for anyone.

Gina urges us to help ourselves to PBRs and hot dogs. Frankie the DJ is running the grill, and Ev takes over helping him. They grunt to each other as they flip mighty burgers and prod engorged hot dogs, wiping sweat off their foreheads in masculine solidarity. Gina, Camilo, and I join Macey in the shade. Macey chews gum at an alarming speed. Gina tells us about the sculpture she's working on down in her studio—it might look like a chair but it's more than just a chair, she's incorporating it into a dance piece about hysteria and misogyny.

"Doctors used to masturbate chicks," Macey offers. "It used to be, like, part of their treatment. Getting fingered."

"It did?" Camilo asks, interested.

"Macey went to Barnard," says Gina. "She's Canadian."

"I dropped out," says Macey, and elaborates no further.

Gina tells us about the other piece she's been working on, at an artist residency in Dubai. Well, she started it there, but then continued working on it at a subsequent residency in Berlin, and now she has a residency coming up in Beijing and she hopes to finish it there. We never get to what the project is, because Ev and Frankie call us over to the grill. Camilo tells Gina over his hot dog that he's so impressed with her drive and ambition and dedication, and that he personally is feeling lost. Gina sympathizes that it's so important for artists to feel lost, because then you can incorporate that lost-ness into your artwork. Camilo offers that he thinks the root of his problem lies with his mother; she makes him feel incapable and re-sentful for days after he has had to talk to her. Gina muses that maybe Camilo should continue developing the performance piece about his mother that he'd shared when they first met, at the artist colony. Then there is a meaningful silence between them, in which they jointly recall all that they shared at the artist colony.

Frankie chomps on his burger, completely unthreatened, calm and secure because he is an Artist with Similar Values, and he doesn't care that Gina fucked Camilo for three days in a variety of positions, some of which Frankie himself may never have imagined. Macey chews a hot dog while storing her gum in her cheek, com-pletely unthreatened because she is as dumb as two rocks rubbing together. Ev continues to eye Gina's tits. I find myself laid bare to the vast realization that I am three seconds away from flinging my-self off the edge of the roof. In the moment, this feels less like hy-perbole than fact.

Gina invites us all to come down to her studio and see her perfor-mance womb-chair. Ev and Camilo are eager, and they follow her down the fire ladder, with Frankie trailing behind. I don't make a move and am unnerved when Macey doesn't either. She just stretches out her long legs and moves her gum from the inside of her cheek back to the central chewing-area of her mouth. She's done with the hot dog. The air is thick and damp with heat, and we both glisten even in the shade. Macey smells like sweat and sugar, even from a few feet away. Barnard, so: no deodorant. But Canada, so . . . maple syrup?

"I don't give a shit about art," says Macey.

"Excuse me?"

Macey tucks the gum under her tongue and enunciates, even though I heard her the first time: "Fuck. Art. Who cares? You care?"

"I don't know," I say.

"You an artist?"

"Not exactly."

"Whaddayou do?"

"Theatre," I say, like I'm confessing to a crime. "I work in the theatre."

"That's not art," Macey absolves me, and for the first time I like her.

"Why's it not art?"

"Actors and prostitutes used to be the same thing," Macey says. "'Art' is like: What *is* that shit? You don't make money."

"You don't usually make money from theatre either," I say, determined to come clean.

"Broadway," says Macey, unconcerned. "*Wicked.*" She spits her gum out over the edge of the roof, pops another piece in. Works at it with her tiny jaws. Offers me a piece, I take it but then don't know what to do with it while I'm drinking PBR. "You know Gina?"

"We've met," I say. "Camilo knows her better though."

"Yeah, they fucked." Macey darts her eyes over me. "You and Gina?"

I don't know if I should say no like "absolutely not," or no like "not yet," so in the end I just try for a very casual shake of the head accompanied by an equally blasé "huh-uh."

Macey jerks her chin toward the exit where our compatriots vanished, implicating them in her question. "You having fun?"

I'm going to volley a bright "Yes!" and then I hear myself say, "Not really."

"So go home. It's Independence Day. Be fuckin' independent."

I don't know what compels me toward honesty, but I say: "Camilo wants me to have a good time."

Macey's mouth quirks. She works the gum extra hard for a second. Then she says: "You know what I'm gonna do? I'm gonna get off this rooftop. And I'm gonna get some iced coffee. And you know what I'm *not* gonna think about? Motherfucking art. You wanna come?"

I stare at her. I don't move. I am a small bird caught in the eye of a hawk. Or a spotlight. Or a storm. Macey gets up. She scratches herself right where her thigh meets her underwear.

"Yeah or no?" she asks.

"Yeah?" I say.

"Great," says Macey the Girl Canadian. "Let's get the fuck outta here." And she climbs down the fire ladder. I wait five seconds, a respectful distance between a worshipper and her sudden pagan god, and then I climb after her.

MACEY DOESN'T HAVE ANY CHANGE and the coffee shop won't take a credit card, so I buy Macey's coffee. She doesn't apologize for this. She doesn't apologize for anything. She says, "Cool, thanks," with genuine pleasure, like she's scored a freebie, so I say, "You're welcome," and mean it—which makes me think that it's been a long time since I've said, "You're welcome," and the person has genuinely been welcome.

We sit outside the coffee shop in the sort of heat that makes you feel like you're living inside somebody's mouth. I don't expect Macey to ask me anything about myself but she asks what I'm working on. I tell her that I don't really have anything right now.

"Bullshit," Macey says. "I'm not saying you have to sound smart, just answer the question."

So I tell her that I'm working on thinking about islands.

"Like. Hawaii?"

Sure, I say, or like . . . that TV show *Lost*. Like: trapped and no way out. Like: these weird moments in our lives when we look around and realize that we are in a place without a bridge or a ferry or anything. Then I explain that this is, clearly, a metaphor.

Macey says, without missing a beat, "That chubby little dude must be a crazy good lay for you to put up with so much bullshit."

"Camilo?" I ask, amazed.

"Isn't he?"

"Not really," I admit.

"Then what is it? Nipples taste like beer?"

"Jesus," I say, but I'm laughing. She keeps looking at me, waiting for me to answer. I want to say that I don't know enough about art. I want to say that I'm not very evolved yet. I want to say that I get jealous and angry, whereas Camilo and his friends are somehow managing to leave these feelings behind in their pursuit of transcendent art-driven Zen socialism. I want to say that if we are ever to improve as humans, we must recognize all of the ways in which we are inadequate, and then put in the work to become more adequate. I want to say that the problem with a capitalist world is the devaluation of community, and that when you find a community dedicated to being the best *humans* they can be, the best *artists* they can be—well. You, who are so failed and flawed, will of course not understand why and how they do what they do. Not at first. But after you try long enough, you too might reach a place of peace and happiness and liberation.

I want to say all of these things, but every time I try to shape the sentences, I hear them all in Camilo's voice. So in the end, I don't say anything. And somehow, that says enough.

"Okay," Macey says, and pats my leg. It's such a weird old-person gesture from such a hot and brassy Canadian, that I find it comforting. "It's okay."

"I don't feel okay," I say. This is something I know how to say, in my own voice. "I don't feel okay most of the time."

"Yeah," Macey says.

We sit in silence. We drink our iced coffees. Macey's sweat-and-sugar smell has become a pungent musk that I don't find displeasing. It occurs to me that I don't feel the desire to be anywhere other than here. This must be what peace feels like.

"You know," Macey says into the silence, "if you test the DNA of island dwellers, like on real isolated ones, they're all related to each other?"

"Is that true?"

"Yeah," says Macey. "Because who else is there to make *life* with? You just have to keep using each other. I mean you're all on an *island*. You know?"

"I guess so," I say, mulling the idea over.

And then Macey tells me a story.

Before Barnard (and Tinder, and Gina), Macey traveled around the world on a ship. The captain was also Canadian. He was her best friend from high school, had a trust fund but wasn't a dick about it, and had been planning the trip ever since they were freshmen. The crew was made up of Macey, her ex-girlfriend (who Macey still occasionally slept with), and a guy named Pierre who knew a lot about boats. Macey said the trip mostly went well, all things considered. They traveled a lot and they saw a lot, and they all got along. No huge fights, no huge storms.

"But then one time things go wrong," Macey says. I'm leaning forward by now. I'm listening to the story while also noticing how sweat gleams faintly on her upper lip, and I have a tiny animal instinct at the back of my brain to lick it off.

"This storm sweeps us off course and fucks up our boat. And we need some repairs, I won't bore you with the details, but we're like . . . in deep shit. Middle of nowhere. I mean *nowhere*. We're drifting and sweating and trying to figure out what the fuck to do, and we're taking on water, and then Pierre looks at these old maps and figures out that we're near this island that's half-owned by America. No idea what the deal is with the other half, but we set a course there."

Macey takes a sip of her iced coffee and takes me in. She's pleased with the concentrated focus of my attention, so she continues.

"We end up in eyesight of the island, and we radio, and they radio back and send a little boat out for us. And the second it pulls alongside, we see that—the guy on the boat? There's something wrong with him. I don't know. You can't quite . . . but there's just a little bit something wrong. His eyes and his . . . teeth? But he's friendly enough, we follow him to dock—and it's like . . . there are so many flies. And it's hot. And all of the structures are a little bit broken, even in small ways, the dock has bits of wood hanging off it, every door seems to have its door handles falling off. They tell us that they can fix the boat but we'll need to stay there overnight, and then the dude who came out for us says he knows a family that would let us stay with them, if we give them money for food.

"The second we walk into their house, we know there's something wrong with them too. It's like this sort of seeping wrongness that's got itself into every crack. Their eyes don't quite focus. The way they move is a little . . . bow-legged? It's like we've walked into a different universe where there are different laws about the way bodies should be put together. There are three kids, and they all have these super-thick-lensed glasses, and their eyes don't focus either. They all move in the same sideways scuttle. The three kids don't speak. I mean, we never hear them speak. One of them at one point runs into the doorframe? She doesn't even squeak. Just a little whoosh of breath. It's uncanny.

"The wife is gigantic—big shoulders, big arms. Her husband is much skinnier. The wife is clearly not happy to see us, and she and her husband argue about it in the other room—we can't make out words. And then the wife comes back and she's clearly lost the argument and she makes this Okay Fine sort of noise, and she goes and takes a slab of meat off a shelf."

Macey pauses here and lights up a cigarette. She offers it to me. I don't really smoke, but I want to put my mouth where Macey has put her mouth. So we pass the cigarette back and forth.

"The woman starts hacking the meat into chunks with a knife. But this meat is crawling. Flies have been running over it, and giving birth to whole new generations of flies that are running over it. This meat is rancid as fuck. And we are just . . . *wide*-eyed, we don't know what to say. Because we're so fucking hungry. And I'm thinking: *When she cooks it, will that kill all the fly eggs? Maybe she can just fry the fuck out of this shit like a strip steak.*

"She finishes chopping the meat. And she sort of spoons it onto tin plates. And she puts those plates right in front of us. Dinner! And then her husband comes in. He takes a plate and he nods to us to join him and we all sit down together, and he starts eating. And we look at each other. We don't want to be rude. We don't want to be these rude horrible people who come in on a broken boat and judge. But also . . .

"My friend and I, the captain, we look at each other in the eyes like: *Are we gonna do this?* And then my ex-girlfriend, real soft, she goes: 'I'm gonna be sick.' And we're like: 'Don't, don't.' And she's like, 'Guys, I'm so sorry.' But she's pale as a sheet. She's not being dramatic. She's gagging. So the captain speaks up and he says: 'I am *so* sorry, we thank you *so* much for your hospitality, but actually none of us can eat meat. We're all Buddhists.' The man and his wife don't know what Buddhists are. 'It's a religion of people who can't eat meat,' says my friend. This causes a commotion, because the wife just wasted all this great meat that she was saving that was gonna last them all week, and what are they supposed to do now! My friend the captain says: 'We will pay you extra for this food. We can't eat it, but we will pay you for it.' And then he says that we're all going to go check on our ship.

"We go down to the dock and they tell us it's still gonna take a while. And then we go look for a restaurant, but we can't seem to find one. We walk and walk and it's all just falling-down structures and tires by the side of the road, and shrubs. It's the saddest thing in the world. We're freaking out. And *then*. All of a sudden. We see it at the same time. We collectively gasp. The yellow arches of a McDonald's, rising up like a mirage.

"We start sprinting, I am not kidding, we *sprint* to the McDonald's. And it's real! It's open! We walk in! It's almost empty, and it's small, and there is one sad person behind the counter with the same eyes and teeth and sideways—but we don't care! We order burgers! We order fries! We order milkshakes! And those things come! We go to this small table and we're shoving food into our faces, we're making these little food-sounds, these disgusting grunts and groans, we're grotesque, we don't care . . . and then we hear this girl go, 'Oh my God.'

"We look up. There's a girl standing in front of us who looks like us. She's dressed like us. Her eyes and her teeth are in the right place. She's staring at our eyes and our teeth. She goes, 'Who *are* you?' And we tell her we're Canadians. We say, 'Who are *you*?' and she tells us she's British, she's a grad student, she's come out to this island to do her graduate studies. It's really really hard to get to this island, so she had to plan to come here a whole year in advance, she had to get booking on this one ship that leaves from New Zealand and goes to a place where you can take a ship to another place where there's a ship that comes here. Every six months, this one ship comes here. And two months ago, that ship came here, and she was on it. So she's been here for two months, and she has four more left.

"We ask her what she's studying, and she tells us that she studies genetics, and as far as genetics go, there are things she is seeing here that she has never seen anywhere else. Because, you see, the entire island is comprised of people who are related to each other in baffling genetic configurations. This is one of the few places that has been unpolluted by the outside world—people don't visit, people certainly don't move here, and people don't leave either. It's like the mecca for inbreeding."

I'm sitting so still that I'm barely breathing, except when Macey passes me the cigarette and I inhale-exhale and hand it back. When Macey pauses, I ask: "So what happened?"

"Well," says Macey, "she asks how we got there. We tell her that we came on our own ship and it's getting fixed. And then she just breaks down. This chick starts sobbing. She says *please please please* take her with us. Don't leave her here. She can't do it anymore. She needs to go home. She says she has never felt so alone in her life. She says the island is making her crazy. I've never seen anybody just come apart like that. We try to calm her down, we give her part of our hamburgers, she won't stop crying. She says she's eaten at

McDonald's three times a day for two months. She says if she sees another French fry she'll slit her wrists."

Macey finishes the cigarette. She stubs it out. She checks the time.

"Oh shit," she says. "I gotta bounce."

"Wait!" I say, a little stunned. "Where are you going?"

"Date," she says. "Tinder."

"Oh." I'd forgotten there was another world out there with Tinder, and other people, and Camilo. "But—what happened?"

"Oh," Macey says, as if it should be obvious. "We got our boat fixed and we left."

"But what about the British girl?"

"It was a boat built for four, not five."

"You *left* her?" I want to sound cool, but I'm horrified.

Macey's brow furrows, just a little. "We didn't have room," she tells me, like it's simple math. "Anyway, she had a boat coming in four months."

"In *four months*." I don't want to sound accusatory, but I do.

"Listen," says Macey. "Don't go to a fucking island if you don't wanna be on a fucking island. You know?"

She stands. She's sweaty and salty and an asshole and unspeakably beautiful. "Thanks for the iced coffee," she says.

"Thanks for rescuing me," I say.

She grins then. "I woulda made room for you," she says. "On that fucking boat." She bends down like she's gonna kiss me, but instead she just wipes the sweat off my face with the back of her hand. Then she walks down the block, hips swinging. I stare after her. I am a teenage boy. I am awkward and lustful. I have been touched by a god.

The whole rest of the day Camilo leaves me three voicemails and ten text messages and I don't reply. I just sit on the bench, where Macey left me, and I watch the air get thicker and hotter and then thinner and cooler, as the sun starts to go down. I drink two more iced coffees. I go inside to pee five times. I think about Macey and her tiny jaws working the gum, and her shipwreck story.

I think about the husband, the wife, their three children. All the eyes and all the teeth. I think that no wonder they don't want outsiders coming in, who look different and want cold meat instead of room-temperature meat, or no meat at all. I think that you love and fuck and create life with the people who are in front of you, regardless of who they are, regardless of whether or not they're the best choices, because that's sort of an evolutionary imperative. I think there are some islands people just have no business going to visit. I think about the British girl eating McDonald's three times a day. I think that sometimes you can't wait four months for a boat.

Soon after, I break up with Camilo and I move to a tiny apartment in Queens. He cries, because he's in touch with his feelings and because he rejects society's mandate that men can't grieve. He explains this in one of the many voicemails that he leaves for months after. The voicemails culminate in the morning I find a giant planter full of dirt on my new doorstep—a visual metaphor, I imagine, for how I've buried his heart. (Later, he emails to tell me that it was a visual metaphor for the rich soil of art and communication in which our relationship, had I not given up, would have flourished.)

Late at night, I lie in my bed alone. I extend my limbs and take up space I didn't even know I could take up. I don't think about art. I lie very still and in the silence I think I hear something like the ocean. It could be traffic on the BQE. It could be faraway planes, taking off and landing at LaGuardia. But I close my eyes and I imagine the sound of the waves, curling around me, bearing me further and further from shore, washing me out to sea where things are different and nothing that's coming is anything I've ever seen before.

PRETORIA

I was almost asleep when Iseya asked, "If I married you, would you stay?"

In my half-dream, I was back in Pretoria. It was summer there and the South African sun was beating down on my skin, hot and yellow, not like the thin white sun of Japan. I was turning in slow circles, smelling the wind from each direction like a dog—and there it was, far away, the salt and mercury of the ocean.

And then Iseya's voice, slipping into my dream.

I opened my eyes to the dark of the room. Outside the apartment it would be a humid Tokyo night, the sort of thick heat that had its own word: mushi-atsui. I could see that his eyes were closed, and I'd just decided that I must have dreamed his question when he asked it again, still in Japanese.

Iscya's English is better than my Japanese; he did a home stay in Australia as a kid, studied English literature at his Japanese university, and dated two neurotic American girls and one sociopathic Brit before he met me. I moved here three years ago and learned my Japanese the hard way, pointing at pictures and stuttering nouns. Iseya speaks English to me when he wants to talk about something without the time delay required for me to conjugate Japanese verbs

in my head. But always, without fail, Iseya asks his difficult questions in Japanese. I think maybe he needs the time delay then. Two
and a half years ago he asked, in Japanese, "Will you go out with
me?" Last year, in Japanese: "Will you move in with me?" And now:
"If I married you, would you stay?"

I reached out and touched the hard curve of his arm. Ran my
fingertips up it to the shoulder, then across to the jut of his collarbone, to his chest. He has a tattoo there, a small one just above his
heart, of an anchor. You'd never know it if you saw him on the street
dressed for work. In the dark, even with his question hanging between us, Iseya smiled. He always smiles when I touch him. I dated
a man for almost five years, back in Pretoria, and I can count on one
hand the number of times he was happy to see me.

"Are you asking me to marry you?" I asked in English. "Or are
you just asking me to stay?"

I flattened my hand across the anchor, over his heart. Iseya stayed
still, eyes closed.

" 'Just'?" he echoed, almost teasing. "Is that 'just'?"

I was quiet. I didn't want to talk about this now. Not with the
dream so close, salt in my mouth and the skin-memory of African
sun. The dreams are fewer now than when I moved here, but when
they come they still devour everything.

He opened his eyes, then. Something in my silence. He looked at
me through the darkness, then touched my cheek. "Think about it."

"I'll think about it," I said.

"You called the moving company," Pieter said.

"To get quotes. To get rates."

"Does Iseya know you called them?"

I sighed. "It was just for information. I haven't decided anything."

"So . . . he doesn't know." Pieter took another sip of his beer, running his long fingers up and down the glass where the condensation had gathered. "I don't know what's so hard," he said. "I can't

wait to get out of here. Got my ticket home last week, never felt better."

I'd thought I wanted to talk about this, but I was finding that I didn't. "So did you work things out with Hitomi?" I asked.

Instead of answering, Pieter winced and took a long drink.

I'd met Hitomi a few times—a pretty college girl who looked at Pieter as if he was her whole world. She'd confessed to me once, drunk, that she knew Pieter fucked other girls but that she was going to marry him. "He always comes back to me," she'd said. "Someday I'll be enough."

I'd given Pieter shit for that. "She thinks you're Prince Charming. How can you do that to her?"

"Listen," Pieter had said, as if explaining simple math to a child. "This is Japan, everybody fucks around. If you do not discuss, it is not happening. Hitomi is a great girl, but tonight she's drunk, and she knows the things she doesn't know. Tomorrow she'll be sober, and she won't know them again."

I'd looked at Pieter, the half-smile on his face, sharp jaw and long nose and sea-gray eyes, and I'd thought: Japanese girls love these guys. They love them and get betrayed by them again and again. And these boys, who could never get away with this shit in their own countries, get away with it here because their skin and hair and eyes are different, and being different has made them gods.

"You're a prick," I'd told Pieter. "If I were Hitomi I'd have left you months ago."

"You'd never be Hitomi," Pieter had said. "And we would never date."

I was brought back by the solid impact of an empty beer mug on the wood table. Pieter had drained it to the bottom, and he was signaling for another.

"That bad," I said, impressed.

"She's pregnant." Pieter took a drink from mine next.

"Did you break up with her before or after you found out?"

"Before, obviously," Pieter said, suddenly irritated. "I'm not a total asshole."

"Is she lying, then?"

"No. She's not smart enough."

"Are you back together?"

"No."

"Is she getting an abortion?"

"No."

"What are you gonna do?"

Hunched over the table, his hair bright under the lights and his eyes sharp, Pieter reminded me of the birds at the Ueno Zoo—too much wing and not enough space. A realization struck me. "You're still going back."

He nodded.

"You're just leaving her here?"

"I'll figure something out when I'm home."

"When you're home she'll be half a world away," I said. "How are you going to figure anything out from there? By Skype?"

"I don't know!" he said, loud enough for the bartender to glance at us. "How the fuck do I know?" Then quieter: "I'm going mad here. Think about it, you love Iseya and even you can't stay."

"I didn't say that!" I objected, feeling unfairly trapped. "I haven't decided that!"

Pieter laughed, but it had an edge to it. "Americans can stay here, Daniela. Brits can stay here. But for us, after home, everywhere else is too soft and clean. You start getting soft and clean too and you can't live with that."

I stared at Pieter, amazed. I'd never heard him talk like this about anything. He drifted his way through Japan, teaching English by day, partying by night as we all did. He was always leaning against some wall, always lighting somebody's cigarette, his face arranged with a twist of a smile.

Pieter saw me staring at him, but he didn't look away.

"You know it just as well as I do," he said. "And your boy does too."

PIETER AND I WEREN'T FRIENDS the way other people are friends. We were just South Africans. Even though he was from the Afrikaner side of things, and I was prep-school English, we had the same dirt under our fingernails, the same dust and salt in our blood. We'd both bought similar drugs in Johannesburg and driven, although at different times and without knowing each other, to Cape Town to party. We'd gone to the same university in Pretoria—but two years apart, and our paths had never intersected. Here in Japan, whether or not we liked each other was immaterial: we were, in some bizarre way, family.

Iseya didn't like Pieter, although he'd never said so. He'd met Pieter on any number of occasions—at Friday-night gatherings in the apartment building everyone called the Gaijin Ghetto, at bars in Shinjuku or Shibuya. He'd been polite each time, speaking in English so that Pieter wouldn't feel left out, asking Pieter how his job was. But the warmth that had attracted me from the first, the glow that seemed to emanate from Iseya like heat, was noticeably absent.

I asked Iseya about it, just once, when we were alone at his apartment.

"Why don't you like Pieter?"

"I don't dislike him," Iseya said with diplomacy.

I ignored that. "I know you aren't jealous of him. So what is it? You just think he's an asshole? Or what?"

Iseya had been washing the dishes while I dried them. Now he was quiet. He hated moments in which we might clash. I could count the number of fights we'd had on one hand, and each one of them had been ended by Iseya's refusal to fight anymore, Iseya leaving the apartment and returning later when I was calm.

At last Iseya asked, carefully, "Why do you like him?"

I hadn't expected that. "Come on. I asked you first."

"You answer, and then I will."

"Fine." I snapped the dish towel at Iseya's leg but deliberately missed. "He's funny. He makes me laugh. He doesn't say no. The Americans are always, 'I'm tired, it costs too much, I'll miss the last train,' but Pieter's just . . . ready for whatever." I considered. "And he's from the same place as me. He knows the things about me that I know about him. Yeah? Your turn."

Iseya nodded, not dismissing what I'd said, but acknowledging it. "You didn't say he's nice," he observed.

"What?"

"Nice. You didn't say that. Generous, kind. You didn't say those things."

"No," I said, a little uneasily. "I guess not."

"And that is why I do not like him," Iseya had said, and went back to washing dishes.

I HAD COME TO JAPAN assuming that I would leave. But the money was incredible. One month in the Cape Town food factory where I worked after university didn't earn half as much as a single week here. And Japan was clean. Pieter had been right about that. It was clean and safe, and as I walked back to the apartment at night, I never forgot that.

I started buying and wearing short skirts, the ones I could never get away with back home. Only Pieter had understood the gesture. Some skinny Brit had seen me in my first short skirt and said, "Sexy." Pieter had run his eyes up and down my legs and said, "Enjoy." I'd tried to explain to Iseya later: "If I wore this skirt at home, I'd get raped. And what's more, everyone would tell me I'd been asking for it." Iseya had nodded, but he hadn't understood. Not really. But Pieter had followed the same elections I had, and when Zuma was elected president despite being embroiled in a rape trial, Pieter had been the one who spent a night getting mournfully drunk with me in an izakaya.

Iseya would often scold me for not locking the apartment door, or for walking alone at three or four in the morning. "Japan is not so safe as you think," he'd say. But I would think of my first apartment in Jo-burg, the one I had locked and double-locked and triple-locked, that had been broken into on six separate occasions. I would think of my friends' mothers getting mugged in their own backyards, the one who got gang-raped at a bus stop. I would think of the beautiful war zone that was my country, and I'd pat Iseya's arm and say the phrase he most hated to hear from me: "Don't worry about it."

My parents asked me all the time, at first, when I was coming back. But in my second year they came to visit, flying halfway around the world, jet-lagged and preparing to be grumpy. And Japan had seduced them. Utterly. Shining sidewalks, glass and neon, spotless train stations, smiling attendants. Things that never happened to me when I was alone happened for my parents. I took them to shrines where old women offered us sweets. I took them to parks where children invited us into their soccer games. I took them to museums, and shy pretty college boys materialized, offering to translate various plaques for us. By the time I took my parents to Narita Airport to catch their flight home, they were wide-eyed with wistful awe.

"There are a lot of opportunities here," was all my father said. "Don't waste them." But my mother, before passing through customs and out of reach, gave me a hug and whispered enviously, "What a life you have!"

IN THE DAYS THAT FOLLOWED Iseya's question, I could think of nothing else, though we didn't talk about it. In the evenings when we got home from work, we made dinner together. We watched TV curled up on the couch, or played video games on Iseya's computer. On Friday we caught the shinkansen down to Osaka to visit his college friends, and spent a night wandering through the brightly lit and pumping streets of Shinsaibashi. We went to the adult section of Donki Hote, where Iseya bought me an S&M keychain with a tiny hog-tied schoolgirl dangling from it, and I bought him a thong with the Japanese character for *treasure* printed over the ball-sack. Not once did either of us raise the subject, but sometimes when we were walking he'd take my hand and squeeze it, and I knew he knew what was on my mind.

I MET PIETER FOR LUNCH on Monday, after our morning classes. I found him at the southeast exit of Shinjuku Station, since our favorite ramen restaurant was a block or so further.

Pieter looked bad. I couldn't put my finger on it exactly—he was well dressed as always and clean-shaven. But as we descended the long staircase toward the street, I realized what it was.

"You aren't talking shit," I said.

Pieter glanced at me. "Sorry?"

"You haven't said anything shitty yet. Nothing completely fucked up."

"We only met up five minutes ago."

"Yeah, that's sixty times five, that's three hundred shitty things you could have said."

Pieter considered my math. "Maybe today's a slow day. Your lucky day."

I looked at him more carefully. "You haven't slept."

"No."

"Drinking?"

Pieter made a buzzer sound. "Wrong."

"All right," I said, as we cut down an alley. "This is the part where either you tell me, or I ask."

I expected Pieter to make me ask so that he could be cajoled into the telling. But instead he replied, as casually as if I'd inquired about his morning class, "Hitomi tried to kill herself." I stopped in my tracks but Pieter kept walking, so I jolted into gear again. "Yesterday. In the morning."

"Is she okay?"

He shot me an irritated look. "No, obviously she isn't okay. Obviously she is completely unhinged."

"But she's alive," I said.

"Yes."

"Where is she?"

"Her parents' house."

"You told her parents?"

"I found her hanging in the fucking bathroom, Daniela, of course I told her parents. I can't miss more work, and I couldn't just tell her not to do it again and leave her alone, could I."

"How'd you find her in time?"

"She kicked a glass off the counter when she was jerking around on the rope," Pieter said with disgust. "Shattered and woke me up. Can't even fucking hang herself properly. And this is the girl they want me to marry."

"Marry?"

"She told her dad that she's preggers." Pieter made a face, rubbed a hand across his throat. "Thought the old guy was gonna kill me. Choking the shit out of me against the wall, the dude is an ageless ninja. Been drinking his green tea, I guess."

The ramen place was full with the lunch-hour crowd, and the rich smell of beef broth suddenly made my stomach uneasy. Pieter didn't seem in a rush to enter, either. He lit a cigarette and leaned against the lamppost, blocking the sidewalk.

"Are you going to marry her?" I asked. I couldn't leave it alone, but Pieter didn't seem to care. He looked relieved to be talking about it.

"I don't know," he said, dragging deep. "I mean she's a kid. Yeah? Nineteen. She can't speak English, Daniela. She still lives with her parents when she's not with me, she has *homework*, she watches anime on Sunday mornings. We can't talk about things, what can we talk about? We don't talk, we fuck. That's not marriage material."

"But it's your baby," I said, not accusing, just pointing out a fact. "It might look like you. You could dress it up. Name it."

"Yeah," Pieter said, surprising me again. "I think about that, too."

A silence, as he smoked. The crowds continued in a steady flow, people frowning from time to time as they stepped off the sidewalk to avoid colliding with us.

"She really tried to kill herself, huh."

"I'm telling you, Daniela, these girls here, they're completely crazy. Nobody does this shit back home."

"No," I said, "somebody would shoot you before you even had the chance to kill yourself."

Pieter grinned, despite himself, and I smiled, relieved to see him smile.

"What would you do," he said. "You're me. Got a ticket to South Africa and a body hanging in the bathroom. What's your plan?"

I tried to imagine being Pieter, tried to call up Hitomi's face—the wide hopeful eyes, the smooth baby cheeks, the little hats she liked to wear. Instead, I saw Iseya with his sleeves rolled up, hanging wet laundry on the balcony to dry. Iseya waiting for me on the train platform, hands shoved in his pockets. Iseya singing me the Japanese songs he'd learned as a kid: "Momotaro-san," "Kagome," "Toryanse." Iseya fresh out of the shower, the long lean planes of his body glistening and slippery with water. Iseya, having the guts to love a foreigner, having the patience to love her in a language that isn't his first.

"I don't know," I said at last. "I have no idea, how could I."

I expected Pieter to say something mocking, or something harsh, but he didn't.

"I know," he said quietly. "Me neither."

PIETER TOOK THE REST OF the day off from work. He didn't seem to care if they fired him or not—"What're they going to do," he said with weary humor, "deport me?" I left him by the south exit, next to Tower Records, and went back to teach my afternoon class. But my mind wasn't on it, and when the kids took their break, I stepped out into the hall and called Iseya.

"Would you move to South Africa?" I asked when he picked up.

A silence. I could hear background noise from the street through the phone. Iseya was outside, walking somewhere.

"South Africa," he repeated, slowly. "Where?"

"Pretoria," I said, as if I'd thought about it. I hadn't though, not until then. I'd imagined going back myself countless times, but never bringing Iseya with me.

"To visit?" he asked.

"To live," I said. "Would you move there to live, if I asked you?"

Again that silence. Cars swishing past.

"Where are you?" I asked.

"Right now?"

"Yes, Iseya." I was suddenly irritated. "Right now, where are you?"

"Walking to the conbini," he said. "Do you want a street address?"

Now he was irritated too. I felt that he didn't have the right to be angry with me for posing a question he'd posed weeks ago.

"Would we marry?" he asked at last.

"Would it matter?"

"Yes," he said, "to me it would matter."

I glanced back into the classroom behind me. Kids sipping tea out of their thermoses, like it wasn't a hundred fucking degrees outside. Two minutes left, by the clock on the wall.

"If we married, then," I said ungraciously.

"Do you really want me to go with you?" Iseya asked.

"Why else would I be asking you?"

"You're not asking me, Daniela. You're asking what-if."

And he was right. And I opened my mouth to ask him, to say, "Move to Pretoria with me." To say, "Marry me." And the words stuck in my throat. I physically could not say them. I listened to the cars passing him on his side, and he listened to the hum of the air-con units on mine. My heart was beating so quickly I felt dizzy, and it didn't make any sense to me, I couldn't imagine why.

Finally I said, and my voice was small and ashamed, "Can we talk about it tonight when I come home?"

"Yes," Iseya said, and I wished suddenly that I could see the expression on his face because I couldn't read his tone at all. "If you want to."

PIETER WAS WAITING FOR ME at the south exit, where I'd left him. I came out of Shinjuku Station into a cool wet world, and was amazed that somewhere between catching the train and arriving here, it had started to rain. He was sitting on the steps, head bowed, but when I stopped in front of him he looked up. I was startled by the clear water-color of his eyes and the way the rain made his cheek-bones shine. For a split second I wondered if I had been mistaken, if this was some other foreign man waiting for some other foreign woman. And then he quirked his mouth in that uneven half-smile and said, "Fancy meeting you here," and it was Pieter.

"Have a good day?" I asked. "Go shopping with the Harajuku girls?"

He stood, shaking water out of his hair. "You don't wanna talk about that," he said easily. "Something happened, or you'd be on your way home to Iseya instead of calling me. Yeah?"

I froze, momentarily paralyzed by his directness. Then I blurted, "I can't ask Iseya to move to Pretoria."

To his credit, Pieter didn't laugh. He tilted his head to one side, considering what I'd just said, water dripping from his jaw onto his saturated shirt.

"Why not," he said at last.

"He wouldn't last a day there. He has no idea what it's like. He's got a safe little world here, everything's clean-clean and nice-nice.

He'd be treated like shit back there, you know he would. Here he's got a good job, people bow to him, they use all their politest verb forms—there they'd just see him as a Chinaman on the corner. That's what they'd call him, how they'd talk to him. They wouldn't respect him, Pieter. No one would respect him."

I hadn't expected to say any of that and I stopped abruptly, feeling that strange dizziness closing in. But Pieter didn't look taken aback.

"Yeah," he said, like all of that was obvious. "But why can't you ask him?"

I shook my head. And so Pieter answered for me, without any accusation. Just stating facts as cold and clear as the downpour.

"Because he'll be a burden to you. You'd have to care for him, guard him. He wouldn't know danger signs or social cues unless you pointed them out, sign by sign. Day by day. Like raising a child. You would be responsible. For him. Always."

"He did that for me," I said, sick to my stomach. "Here, in his country, he does that for me."

Pieter waited. The rain picked up. It felt like we were standing under a waterfall in a place very far away. And so, from the safety of that remove, I answered his unspoken question as honestly as I could.

"I don't lock the doors at night here. I don't look over my shoulder. I don't understand what's being said all the time so I'm politer. I bow! That's who I am here with Iseya. But when I go home . . ." I took a deep breath, searching for the right words. "Sometimes I'm afraid I'll forget how to be who I am, and I'll just keep being the person he loves. And that person is too weak to survive where I come from. The longer I'm with him, the weaker I'll become."

"Just say it," Pieter said.

And so I said it. "I don't want him to come."

WHEN I THINK BACK, THAT was the moment in which I betrayed Iseya. Not in what came after. I know it's bizarre—I could have turned around right then, returned to our apartment. Iseya would have fetched a towel from the bathroom, he would have dried my hair. I would still have been the closest person in the world to him, and the barrier between us would still be yet to come.

But when I remember it, the world divides into two parts: everything up until that moment, standing in the rain with Pieter, and then everything after. And no matter how hard I try, no matter how many alternate endings I envision for myself, it always seems to me as if the second part was derived inexorably from the first. After an admission of that magnitude, nothing could have been different from how it was.

Pieter and I didn't talk about it. It was something we decided, somewhere between the third bar and the fourth one, but we didn't discuss it with words. I don't remember what we talked about. I remember the sharp wet slope of Pieter's throat tilted back, amber-colored beer falling lower and lower in his mug until only foam remained. I remember the bittersweet taste in my mouth: Sapporo, Kirin, Asahi. The small ceramic dishes of bar food: slices of octopus, cucumber, shreds of raw fish dressed with green onion and soy sauce. The food changed from bar to bar, but those little white ceramic dishes didn't. In the fourth bar we sat in a corner, and I realized that it was dark outside, that it had been dark for some time, and I wondered if the rain had stopped. Pieter paid the tab, waving away my bills, and I knew he'd decided then. We'd paid halves on the other tabs. But this one Pieter paid, and later—after wandering in circles through backstreets, the rain and the alcohol and the neon blurring the world into a place of strange and beautiful colors— later, he paid for the love hotel as well.

It HAD BEEN TWO YEARS and eight months since I'd slept with someone other than Iseya. I remember being startled by how rough Pieter was, how demanding; Iseya was gentle, always attentive. I was amazed too by Pieter's hair under my fingers, how light it was, the textured patches of hair on his chest. Iseya's skin was smooth like wet stone; I had always liked running my cheek over his bare chest, feeling both the heat of his heartbeat and the slipperiness of his skin.

The time that we spent in the love hotel is blurred when I remember it, just as our walk there was. Sometimes the memories surface as if from a strange dream, and then it seems to me as if both Pieter and Iseya were in that room together. I think I can remember the low timbre of their voices, the side of Iseya's face. But when I woke up, a few hours later, it was Pieter and only Pieter who was asleep on his side of the bed, in an easy naked sprawl that was wholly, essentially, South African.

He didn't wake up when I slid out of bed, nor as I dressed. It occurred to me once or twice that he might be faking, lying very still with his eyes shut, listening to me move around the darkened room. But I don't think he was. Iseya had been correct in his assessment of Pieter—neither nice nor kind nor generous—and it would have been uncharacteristically generous to feign sleep and let me leave. I closed the door quietly behind me, walking down the hall in bare feet, pausing only in the empty lobby to slip my shoes back on and walk out into the street.

I didn't know what time it was. The rain had stopped, but perhaps only just—the sidewalks still glistened. I wanted to take my cell out of my pocket and look at the time, but when I searched for it, it wasn't there. It must have fallen out in the love hotel, and I couldn't go back. I didn't know where I was, but it was somehow comforting to walk, carried along by my own momentum through the narrow streets.

I walked until my shoes were soaked through, stopping occasionally to puzzle over street signs, but each time that hollowness roared up in my head and a wave of nausea started in my stomach. I found I was speaking to myself out loud, in a hushed whisper, and I listened to my voice with a stranger's curiosity. "It's okay," I was crooning, "everything's okay." It took me some time to realize that I was speaking in Japanese.

I stumbled on Shinjuku Station by accident. I looked up and there it was, a neon oasis, a humming throb of life. The southeast exit lay above me, up that lengthy flight of stairs, just as Pieter and I had left it hours ago. Japanese kids were playing soccer in the plaza, and I realized that it must be late, because otherwise a policeman would have told them to stop. Host boys draped themselves over the railings of the stairs, advertising their various clubs, the white collars of their starched shirts soaring fiercely up. One of them was foreign, his hair long and tangled around his shoulders. He didn't seem to be on duty. He was walking quickly through the plaza, scanning the faces he passed, looking for someone.

Nausea hit me again suddenly and without mercy. I stumbled to my knees and was sick into the gutter. I crouched there until the flowing water had washed the vomit away, then stood and wove my way unsteadily through the plaza. The escalator had stopped running, and I took the stairs slowly and carefully, both hands on the railing, until I reached the top and discovered that the trains had stopped running as well. In that moment, Iseya suddenly seemed unreachably far—beyond trains, beyond language, beyond apologies. I felt my knees give, and, crouching outside the south exit, my back against a stone column, I cried.

"Hey. Are you okay?"

The American-accented English jolted me into looking up. The foreign host boy was standing above me, hands in the pockets of his dark jeans. I stared at him blankly, and he repeated the question: "Are you all right?"

"No," I said. It didn't occur to me to lie.

"Are you hurt?"

"The trains aren't running."

He looked at me quizzically. Everybody knew the trains stopped at midnight, I'd known it too. Right then I just couldn't seem to know the things that I knew. "Do you want me to call you a cab?"

I kept staring at him, and all I could think was that Iseya doesn't like host boys, he thinks that what they do is cheap, that you shouldn't take a gift like beauty and use it to get money from lonely people. And I wanted to say to Iseya: *But what about the people who are lonely, isn't it their fault as well?*

"A cab," the host boy repeated gently. "Where do you want to go?"

"Pretoria," I said, and put my head in my hands.

"Where's that?"

I heard myself answer as if in a dream, instructing this poor American kid who'd had the misfortune to stop and be kind to me. "South Africa. It's in South Africa."

The host boy crouched down on the ground next to me, careful not to get his jeans wet. I could hear him from beyond the darkness of my cupped hands, could feel the heat of his closeness. A silence, and then, tentatively, awkwardly, his hand patted the top of my head.

"That's very far for a taxi," he said, apologetically. "You'd never get there in time."

He got me a pen and a sheet of paper, after I stopped crying. The pen was his, but he didn't have paper, and had to go ask one of the Japanese host boys lingering in the plaza. He asked me my name, as if it would tell him anything about why I was sitting on the ground. He told me his was Ancash, then gave me crumpled bills for cab fare and left me with my back against the column. The letter I wrote to Iseya then is not one I ever gave him. I wrote it not because I intended to show him, but because it was what he deserved to hear. I don't know where it is now—I lost it later, perhaps deliberately. But one line stays with me: *The things that make me love you aren't things I love in myself.* None of the rest of it was so honest.

When I finished, I sat for a long time. Nobody spoke to me, so I didn't have to find a language to reply in. I tried not to think of my phone, left in the love hotel, or of Iseya trying to reach me—how many frantic messages he would have left, at what point he would have switched from English to Japanese, then back to English. As if the right combination of words could conjure me. As if there was a language that could bring us together.

Time stopped, and then suddenly it restarted. The sky grew light and the sidewalks stirred, the first crowds, the first trains, a first morning as if there had been no previous morning to ever arrive and find us all so raw and new. I picked myself up. I didn't know what I would say when I got there, but I put my face to that anemic, early sun and began the slow walk back.

A GREAT HISTORY OF AMERICAN MISTAKES

The thing about Topher was that he was the kind of guy who had never been anywhere. Everything I did was new to him. Everywhere I had been (Rhode Island! "Is it really an island?") was exotic, by virtue of the fact that he'd never seen it with his own eyes. He was born and bred here in Iowa, and he wore it like his baggy jeans and plaid shirts. "We're real different, you and me," he said, and the comparison was flattering, because Topher was someone you liked, but didn't want to be like. "You are gonna break that kid in two," Livvy said when Topher and I started fucking.

Unlike Topher, Livvy had seen it all. She had a mouth like a sailor and no one she knew would ever have accused her of friendliness. We got along like a house on fire, despite the fact that she disapproved of everything I did, and I thought she was a little crazy.

"He's not a kid," I said, which was my best and only line of defense. "He's twenty-two."

"And you got fifteen years on him."

"A decade," I said, increasingly defensive. "A decade is ten years."

"A decade," Livvy repeated, "is ten years."

She proceeded to point out that he was my TA, and that he had a girlfriend who was twenty, whose mother I could technically be, if I had been unfortunately impregnated at twelve. ("It happens," Livvy had said, "and if it had happened to *you*, you would be her mother.") But Livvy's main issue with our sordid affair was not actually its sordidness, the details of which were inarguable. It was that he would eventually be damaged by our affair ending, and Livvy felt this damage, even if slight to him, would be traumatic for me.

"It will warp your psyche forever," Livvy informed me. We were having hamburger night at I.C. Ugly's Saloon, as we did every Monday after I taught my evening class. "You aren't the sort of person who damages people. You're *nice*."

"I could totally damage somebody," I said, sensitive to the implied character defect.

"In thirty-two years, I bet you've never left first. I bet you've never cheated, stolen, or lied. *And* I bet you're friends with all your exes."

My silence let her know she was right. Her tone let me know that she was my opposite in each of these regards. She stole one of my sweet potato fries. Somebody put a quarter in the jukebox but nobody danced. "I'm just saying," she just-said, "you're a good person. And after you destroy him, it will be worse for you than it is for him."

OVER THE DAYS THAT FOLLOWED, I kept replaying the conversation in my head, and it bothered me more and more. I couldn't have said why. I was raised by decent, honest Protestant stock to be decent and honest. My mother was proud of me. My exes all spoke well of me. Somehow, under the penetrating spotlight of Livvy's gray eyes, this seemed less like an achievement than an indictment.

I brought it up to Seth one night when I was walking Chester, our dog. Seth had moved to Chicago right after our recent breakup, but we still conferred often about things like Chester, and car payments, and which of us was going to tell his mother that we had ended and so had her dreams of grandchildren. I'd taken to calling

Seth during the nightly dog walks, in part because his voice was comforting in the thick Iowan dark. Also in part because Topher was usually waiting on my porch, ready to take his clothes off as soon as I returned, and so I made all my phone calls while walking.

"Do you think I'm nice?" I asked.

"Of course," Seth said. He was waiting aboveground for the L, and I could hear the wind on the other end of the phone.

"Well, how come?"

"You just are. You're polite, you're considerate—"

"Do you think I could be a bitch?"

"Jesus," Seth said. "Who said that?"

"Nobody *said* that. That's what I'm asking. Do you think anybody *could* say that?"

"No," Seth said, firmly. "Sarah, is this about what happened with us? You know I love you, I'm just not *in*—"

"It's not about us," I said hastily.

"Okay." He was quiet. Chester peed. I stood still, letting him take his time. A streetlight two blocks behind me cast a dim glow through the shadows, and another one flickered three blocks ahead. Everybody always tells you how safe Iowa City is in comparison to wherever you've come from, especially if you're a woman, but the density of night here is unsettling. It occurred to me right then that, if I became a rapist, Iowa City would be a good place to start my career. I said this thought out loud to Seth. He was shocked.

"Jesus, Sarah, that's not funny."

"I'm a woman," I said.

"It doesn't matter, rape isn't funny." Seth identified as a staunch feminist. "What's wrong with you?"

"It was a joke." I wanted to sound as magnificently scornful as Livvy, when she tells people to *lighten up*, but I just sounded guilty and defensive.

"You don't sound like yourself."

"I'm sorry," I said. "It wasn't funny."

"It's okay." The tension eased in Seth's voice—I guess I sounded like myself now. "It's a stressful time for us both."

When I got back to my apartment, Topher was waiting. Even in the dim porch light, his skin was a dull gold, like cut fields after the corn. I let us in and he told me about his day. His mother had sent him a care package, it included new socks. He didn't need socks, but she never listened. I unbuttoned his shirt, and he shrugged it off eagerly, unzipped his jeans, pulled my shirt off with reverence. Undid my bra, but fumbled a bit—the hook and eye still bewildered him. We fucked gently on the couch, touching each other's faces. "You're so beautiful," he whispered. For a moment I imagined flipping him facedown. What would it be like to pound into someone without having to see their face? "I like you so much," he whispered, his breath damp on my cheek.

"I like you too," I said, politely.

THE NEXT MONDAY AT I.C. Ugly's, Livvy brought Topher up. She was telling me about how much she hated teaching history to undergraduates, whose only ability to contextualize the importance of the field was in terms of one's sexual history. "History is a series of choices," she lectured me, "but before you know it, your history has condensed into your identity. I tell them: *Know where you're from, know who you're choosing to be.* I tell them: *You can be more than your histories, if you know your histories!*"

This jarred me a little. Thinking of my entire history as a series of choices suddenly made me feel as if I had made all the wrong choices. I asked how her kids had reacted when confronted with this wisdom.

Livvy sighed. "Same way they react to everything. They stare at me with their blank little eyes and they chew on their fingernails and think about who they're fucking."

"My kids mostly write essays about their breakups," I offered.

"So . . . an equal and ongoing preoccupation with who they're *not* fucking."

"Two sides of the same coin," Livvy shrugged. But I could tell she was preparing a segue, and when it came, it was not a gentle one. "Speaking of the children, has Topher fucked anybody before you?"

"Livvy," I said sternly, "can we not call him a 'child'?" We'd gotten the $1 Frosty Mugs, and the thick layer of frost that coated our mugs was leaving rings on the table.

"Oh my God he's a virgin," Livvy said, with a sudden burst of intuition.

"For your information, he has a girlfriend."

"She's a twenty-year-old Christian from Iowa. Bet you they're waiting till marriage."

"I don't think millennials wait for anything these days."

Livvy snorted. Then: "Do you have concrete proof that he has formed the beast with two backs on any previous occasion?"

"Livvy *please*. I've never asked him. He's twenty-two and he's hard all the time, one has to assume."

"You can always tell," Livvy declared. "You know you can. Is it kind of like slow, sentimental fucking? Does he squeeze your tits like Nerf balls? Has he ever cried?"

"I don't want to discuss this," I said. Topher had cried the first three times, and I'd had to adjust his grip on my breasts until, disconcerted, he'd asked, "Am I doing this bad?" and I'd said, "Maybe just don't squeeze so hard?" and in the embarrassed silence I'd said, "That's nice, that feels good," even though nothing had changed.

"Yeah, okay," Livvy said triumphantly. In the silence, she drank from her Frosty Mug, then from mine. Livvy liked to drink from both of our drinks whenever we got the same thing, to make sure they tasted the same. ("That way you know up front if there's been any funny business.")

"Anyway," I said, "so what if he is a virgin?"

"Then you are the conduit of his worldly knowledge," Livvy said.

She'd clearly been thinking about this. "You are a cumulative series of choices that he keeps making. You are his history."

"Sexual history," I qualified.

"History is history," said Livvy.

I INVITED TOPHER OVER FOR dinner the next night. I wasn't much of a cook but I cut up and stir-fried some vegetables, and we ate in awkward silence for a few minutes until I poured us both another glass of wine and broached the subject of his sexual history.

"How's your girlfriend? Uh . . . Kelly?"

Topher eyed me warily over the glass. "Kennedy. She's good."

"How long have you guys been together?"

Topher blinked a little. I thought I saw him take a quick huff of breath. "Uh, three years?"

"Oh," I said. "Wow." Three years ago I was still living in a tiny studio in Brooklyn with the boyfriend before Seth. His name was Martin and he was an adjunct professor, and he'd cheated on me, just once, with an undergrad. (That was his phrase: "Just once!") He broke up with me because, in his words, I "couldn't let it go." But post-breakup, he spoke very highly of me. When asked, he told people that I was reasonable and that I'd let him keep the couch and also paid his rent for three months after he left, which was true, I did. I hadn't wanted any kind of confrontation—nice girls behave well, regardless of how they've been treated.

Topher set his wineglass down. "Sarah . . . I'm glad you asked me about her. I've been meaning to tell you something."

I blinked at the resolve in his tone. It made him sound strangely adult, this boy who said things like "wow" and "cool" and "dang," who squeezed my tits like he was turning a doorknob. It made him sound like he had firm adult thoughts and the need to communicate them.

"What is it?" I asked.

"I just want to say that: I have never met anybody like you. And.

Whenever I see you, I just. I feel like nobody else has ever. Kennedy and I have never. We were kids, when we started. But you made me a man, and I'll leave her for you. So."

I stared at him, alarmed. His broad ungainly shoulders, the hair on the backs of his large hands. All plaid and gold, eyes as wide and lucid as mason jars of water. I was the entirety of his history.

"I don't want you to."

"You don't?"

"No," I said. "No no. This isn't . . . We're just. You know? We're just."

"Oh," Topher said. Disappointment wrote itself across his eyes like a color. "Oh."

I wanted to comfort him, I poured him more wine. Topher took a hasty gulp, without taking his eyes off me. "I'm still going to leave her, though."

"Okay . . ." I thought I wanted to comfort him, but now the troubling thought occurred to me: *What would it be like to hurt him?*

"Whatever time I have with you," Topher said, stiff as an undergrad essay, "I will cherish it."

A slight nausea rose in my chest. "That's lovely," I said.

"And I know that maybe you just see me as a kid, but I have a much older soul." Topher blinked. His eyelashes were so pale they almost disappeared. They reminded me of very fine antennae. "And that soul is capable of great love, and that is just what I have wanted to tell you for some time now."

Livvy and I went to a poetry reading once at Prairie Lights, where we ran into her ex-girlfriend. This was the one who moved out in the middle of the night with Livvy's cat in tow, and then left her vaguely threatening voicemails for months. Staring at her ex over a small sea of poets, Livvy had said, in her Poetry-Reading Voice, "The Car of Our Evening Is Crashing over the Cliff of This Encounter."

I stared at Topher. The car of our evening did a swan dive.

"Actually I think I love you," said Topher.

The car of our evening descended onto the rocks.

Through the sound of everything silently shattering, I said: "Thank you."

LIVVY CAME OVER A FEW nights later, with news and a jar of Nutella. As she ate Nutella out of the jar with a spoon, she informed me that I hadn't seen her for two days because she'd been sleeping with a gym teacher. The gym teacher was a tall and sandy blonde, in her late forties, "translucent in that Scandinavian way," and here Livvy took a deep breath, which alerted me to the fact that the best was yet to come. "At first she seemed sort of docile and beaten down by life, so I agreed to go on a date as a favor to her."

"OkCupid?" I asked.

Livvy grinned. "Craigslist."

"Oh Livvy, you didn't!"

"Oh yes I did. I thought it might be sordid. But then she was very . . . well, docile . . . and translucent . . . so I gave up on all that. We just had a few beers and talked about the weather. So then she invited me back to her place, and I assumed there was going to be a lot of soft kissing and hair-touching, which frankly I don't have a lot of space for these days, and *then*." Livvy sucked a triumphant gob of Nutella off her spoon. "She threw me around."

"She threw you around . . ."

"The bedroom. She threw me around the bedroom. She was like, Hulk Hogan in the bedroom. She was a freak."

"Oh," I said. "That's great?"

"And here's the thing. You know I'm the alpha. Like, I'm always the alpha." Livvy looked at me severely over the jar, and I said yes, I knew that, even though I hadn't. "Well, when she started throwing me around, I was like, *What the fuck is this?* So I sort of pushed back. And then she slapped me in the face." Livvy grinned, lifting her fingers to her face, feeling for the echo. "Nobody's ever hit me before! My parents didn't even believe in spanking!"

"Did you leave?"

"Hell no I didn't leave. I got back on that bed and she slapped me around and it made me fucking crazy." Livvy shook her head at me. "There's a lot we don't know about ourselves, Sarah. There's just a lot we don't know."

"Topher told me he loved me," I said.

"Did you say it back?"

"I said thank you."

"That's the most fucked-up thing I've ever heard," said the girl who got a gym teacher from Craigslist to slap her around. "You've gotta cut this off."

"I know," I said.

"Like *now*, Sarah. Just be nice, you're always nice. *Nicely* let him down."

"I know," I said. I was always nice. All of my exes liked me, and I was nice.

TOPHER CAME OVER WITHIN FIFTEEN minutes of my text. He didn't even try to pretend he'd been busy. I hadn't thought the plan through, beyond the decision to break it off. I poured us both wine. Topher had once let slip that, until me, his history of drinking had been the kind of potent, low-grade alcohol that flows through undergrad parties. Sometimes the difference in our ages was inescapable and depressing.

Topher drank his wine like grape juice and darted his eyes at me. I asked him about his day. I didn't listen to the answer. I worked a sentence fragment around my head. "For your own best interests." Too formal. "We can still be friends." Too lame—and I didn't want to be his friend, we weren't really friends now. "Really appreciated your time and efforts"—that was so businesslike as to be cruel. The cruelty of it sent a little involuntary tingle of excitement up my spine.

I thought of Seth breaking up with me. *I love you but I'm not in love with you.* I thought of Martin. He'd broken up with me like this: *I just feel . . .*—and I'd sat in front of him encouragingly, my body language saying *Go on,* my smile saying *You are safe here.* Martin had gone on to tell me that he didn't feel like I trusted him anymore in the aftermath of the undergraduate, and feeling untrusted was restricting his emotional growth. I had told him that I wanted the best for his emotional growth. He'd left and I'd experienced a sudden flush of freedom—*Now I can sleep with the windows open! Now I can drink from the carton!* But straight on the heels of that freedom had come a crushing sense of failure. I hadn't been happy with him, but I also hadn't wanted to fail at being good for somebody's personal growth.

Maybe Livvy was wrong. Maybe it would be good for me to shatter somebody.

"I've been thinking," I began.

"Me too," Topher said, and then we stopped and looked at each other. "Go on," he said.

"No you go on."

He took a breath. "Well. I thought about what you said."

"Yes?"

"I'm not going to ask you for anything except what you want to give." Topher took another breath. "I'm not going to leave Kennedy. And uh . . ." He searched for the rest of the phrase. He must have memorized it. "Uh . . . and I think that what is between myself and Kennedy, uh, and what is between you and me, these are very different things and they mean very different . . . uh . . ." The machine faltered. "But if you ever changed your mind and you *wanted* me to leave Kennedy . . ." Topher stared at me across the expanse of table, helpless as an animal.

"Topher," I said.

"Yeah?"

"Take your shirt off."

Astonishment flashed over his face, and then he stood and pulled his shirt off over his head, one-armed, the way boys of that age do.

"Topher?"

"Yeah," he said again, but this time there was a rising anticipation in his voice.

"Walk backward into the bedroom."

"What are we—?"

"Now. And undo your belt."

His mouth twitched then shut. He undid his belt. One-handed, tall and tippy like a colt, angling backward toward the bedroom on his long inelegant legs, and me, standing now, but not following. Listening to the coldness of my voice.

"Take your pants off. And close your eyes. If you open them once, we're done."

"Sarah . . . ?"

"Shut your mouth."

He did. When he was lying on the bed, eyes clenched shut, narrow boy-chest rising and falling—I stood and walked toward him. Pulled my underwear off, left the rest of it—skirt, oversize knit sweater, socks. At the first slap, his eyes sprung open, wide blue, wild. Shock erased either anger or fear—the pure enormity of a shock that wrote itself across and through his entire body. I slapped him again, hard enough that my palm stung. I imagined Livvy's gym teacher spiking a volleyball across the net. The third time I slapped Topher, he bolted off the bed. Stood facing me, cock hard, legs shaky. He didn't know what country this was anymore. He didn't know the language. Neither did I, but I'd brought us here. Into the silence I said, "Lie down." And I don't know which of us was more taken aback when he did.

I rode him until I came, and he came just after me, in a full-bodied lunge. After he came, he wanted to talk.

"Go home," I said.

"But can we . . . ?"

"Go home."

And after a moment, puzzled, he did.

———

I RESOLVED TO BE A bad person only with Topher. Otherwise, I would remain good. This was the way in which I could justify both Topher's presence in my life, and also my history of unobjectionable blandness. And, for a week, it seemed to work. Topher texted me, and my replies were brusque. He came over, and I didn't worry about his feelings. He took his clothes off, and I fucked him selfishly, rearranging his hands when he got it all wrong, pushing him around like a rag doll. When he said that he liked me, I just gave him directions: faster, harder, not so hard. After he left, I could be found grading papers, leaving encouraging notes in the margins for my students, and paying my bills on time. It was, for the short time that it lasted in this way, exhilarating.

But then it all started to slip.

The badness started surging through me, even when Topher wasn't there. It welled up like blood from a cut. It leaked. It could not be contained. One morning I found a piece of neighbor's mail in my mailbox, and instead of leaving it for her, I threw it out. The next day, I dropped a piece of trash on the ground, and didn't pick it up. And that weekend, standing in line at the co-op, I slipped a pack of vegan Simply Gum into my pocket. I stood there, suddenly paralyzed, amazed at myself, while the cashier rang up my groceries. The gum in my pocket felt like a hand grenade. I couldn't move or it would detonate. "Have a nice day," the cashier said. I opened my mouth to chirp "You too!" but no words emerged. I grabbed my paper bag and walked out, having said nothing at all, feeling the cashier's puzzled gaze briefly flick after me.

"YOU LOOK DIFFERENT," LIVVY SAID. I.C. Ugly's, Monday night. In the dimness of the saloon she squinted sharply at me over her beer.

"No I don't," I lied.

"Yes you do." She had a bad spring cold, and it made her sound like Brigitte Bardot. "You break up with Topher, or get a MacArthur?"

"We're not dating, and no."

Livvy kept her stare trained on me for another few seconds, and then moved on. She had her own news: she thought she might be in love with the gym teacher. They were thinking about moving in together.

"Moving *in*? You just met her!"

"My lease is up soon." Livvy shrugged.

"In like, three months!"

"Yeah but I could Airbnb my place for three months, make some cash. Amy's place is nicer. I'm over there all the time anyway." Livvy grinned, unzipping her hoodie partway: "I'm wearing her T-shirt right now. This was from high school, can you believe she still fits into the T-shirts she wore in *high* school?"

When we paid the bill, I didn't tip. Walking home in the dark, I couldn't tell if I'd forgotten, or just decided not to.

TOPHER MOVED AROUND MY APARTMENT like a dancer or a fish, never still, his eyes always on me. I poured wine into jam jars because I hadn't washed the long-stemmed wineglasses. I'd started eating off paper plates. Yesterday I'd thrown out a ceramic bowl after eating pasta from it—just tossed it into the dumpster behind the house and listened to it shatter. In the aftermath, I felt both guilty and elated. Topher was talking about his day, his term paper, his bike. He talked as he moved, nervous, restless, hungry. His mother (more socks), his grades (low Bs). He started to talk about his summer plans.

"Stop talking," I said. "I don't care." In the sudden silence, I realized I'd wanted to say that to him for months. "Strip."

He did, immediately. He'd been waiting for this.

"Get down on your hands and knees."

This was new. He hesitated.

"You heard me."

He got down on his hands and knees. I stood, looking at him. The eager box of his body, the tight anticipation in his shoulders.

"Crawl to the bed." Now I sounded like a guy in a bad porno. *Crawl to the bed.* I sounded like a guy in cargo shorts with a mustache and a wifebeater and a giant erection. He crawled toward the bed awkwardly, trying not to rug-burn his knees. His left sock had a hole in the heel.

"You want this?"

"Yeah," Topher said.

"Say no."

He hesitated.

"Say no. Tell me you don't want this."

"I don't want this . . . ?"

"I don't believe you."

"I don't want this."

"Tell me no. Tell me to stop."

"No," Topher said obediently, his voice falling short of a question. His liberal arts degree was confusing him. Seth would think this was very upsetting, "an eroticization and fetishization of rape culture," he would say. But Topher was twenty-two, he wouldn't know what most of those words meant, he just knew that his nerves were jangling like church bells and his cock was stiff as a mast and nobody he knew would approve of this behavior. "No, stop, no. No, stop, no!"

He chanted this under his breath like a nihilist mantra, and when he came, he breathed *No* like a *Yes*, and I felt filthy. He asked if we could talk about our relationship. I told him to wash the dishes if he wanted to stay, but he had to leave when they were clean. So for the next half hour he stood by the sink, naked, his large eyes following me like a chastened Mona Lisa or a Labrador, and he washed jam jars very slowly.

———

As I LEANED AGAINST THE strut of the footbridge, watching Chester piss on things, half-listening to Seth tell me about how he'd started doing hot yoga, that new uncontainable badness moved in me. When Seth paused for air, I heard myself say, "Chester's dead."

"What?" Seth sounded smacked flat. Like the air had left his chest in a whoosh, and this was the voice that came after that.

"Yeah," I said, watching Chester lower his tiny hindquarters and prepare to take a shit that I had already determined not to collect in a bag and dispose of responsibly. "Yeah, I was calling to tell you that Chester died."

"You—? When—?" Seth was flailing. "You just—we've been talking for five minutes, you should have told me right away!"

"I was trying to," I said, my voice as flat and cool as a steel tray. "You weren't listening. You were talking about your chakras."

In the silence, I listened to Seth's world unravel.

"I don't understand," said Seth.

"I don't know what there is to understand," I said. "He got hit by a truck. We were walking, and he just got hit by a truck. Squashed."

"Squashed?" Seth was shaky. "Did he suffer?"

"I don't know," I said. "If *you* were decapitated, would *you* suffer?"

Chester finished his shit and as he looked at me, I want to think we felt the same surge of triumph.

LIVVY AND THE GYM TEACHER were having their three-week-o-versary, and she wanted to get the gym teacher a gift. She made me go with her to White Rabbit, and we wandered through the tiny store, picking up knickknacks and putting them back down. When I asked Livvy to explain the concept of a three-week-o-versary, she looked at me as if I was crazy and said, "We've been together for three weeks. We're celebrating that." But what I actually wanted Livvy to explain was how she had become the sort of person who put words like *three* and *week* together with a nonexistent suffix like *o-versary*. Then again, she would have wanted to know how I could become the sort of person who made a twenty-two-year-old wash jam jars after I'd fucked him, and I didn't have an answer for that. So we lapsed into a silence punctuated by an occasional "How about this?" and then Livvy would flip over a price tag and shake her head. "Something cheap but not *that* cheap," she'd say. Or: "Do you think I'm Melinda Gates?"

She ended up getting a porcelain rabbit that, if you looked at its ears from another angle, resembled a lady's face. "It's a trompe l'oeil," Livvy said with satisfaction. "It's never what it seems. Like Amy." And then: "Should I explain the metaphor to her? Or is that less romantic?"

"She's a gym teacher," I said. "Don't bother."

I'd meant it as a joke, but Livvy stopped on the sidewalk. "That's mean," she said, sounding surprised and also upset. "That's really mean, Sarah."

"I was kidding," I said. I hadn't imagined she could actually be stung. "It was a joke."

"It was mean," she said, starting to walk again.

"I'm sorry." I didn't sound sorry. I tried harder, "I'm sorry, Liv."

"Something's up with you," she said, unlocking her bike from the bike rack. My bike was locked to the rail of a bench, right below the PLEASE DO NOT LOCK BIKES HERE sign. "If you're getting your period, hurry up and bleed already, because you're becoming a real bitch."

I ATE A LOT OF takeout that week, and I couldn't seem to get out of bed. When I finally did, I looked at myself in the bathroom mirror and discovered I was unable to dredge up a smile. Not a polite one or a friendly one or an appeasing one, not any kind at all. I just looked blank and sunken and a little scared. I decided to cancel class too late to send the students a mass email, so Topher had to leave a note on the classroom door. The department head emailed to tell me that she hoped I felt better but wished I'd contacted everyone earlier, and I found it hard to sound like I even wanted her to believe

me when I typed back, "But I didn't have food poisoning earlier."
Topher, on the other hand, was concerned for me.

"Do you want me to bring you chicken soup?" he asked, when I
picked up the phone on his fourth call. "Or tea, or I don't know,
Advil, do you need Advil?"

"I'm not hungover," I said irritably. "I'm sick."

A moment and then he asked if I needed Jell-O. No, I said, absolutely not.

When he arrived at my apartment twenty minutes later, breathless from the bike ride and with a box of powdered Jell-O, I let him
in. I'd considered keeping the door locked, pretending to be dead.
I'd considered putting on jeans instead of my sad sweatpants. I'd
considered answering the door naked. In the end, I just opened it
and let him through, pulling away when he tried to kiss me.

He took in the drawn curtains and the unwashed takeout con-
tainers in the sink. "You *are* sick," he said, a little amazed, and I
wasn't sure if I was annoyed that he hadn't believed me before, or
that he did now.

We sat at my kitchen table. I made Jell-O on the stove because I
didn't have anything better to do. He watched me and whenever I
caught him staring at me, I looked away. I found myself asking if he
was hungry, if he wanted a sandwich or some coffee. I was so exhausted that it felt like less of an effort to be a good host. Topher
seemed disconcerted. He said no thanks, then searched me with his
eyes.

I made coffee anyway, poured myself a cup, and was looking for a
clean mug for him when he said my name. The urgency of it made
me turn around, and I saw he'd stripped off his shirt, his jeans were
undone, and he was awkwardly on his knees.

"What are you doing?" I said.

"Don't punish me," Topher said.

I blinked at him. "Please . . . get up."

"Don't hurt me," Topher said, in his voice that said *Hurt me.*
"Don't touch me." And his voice said *Touch me.*

"Topher." I could feel that great exhaustion welling up in the middle of my chest, making it hard to breathe around. "Come on."

"I don't want this," he said, standing to pull a leg through his jeans. He off-balanced, had to catch the back of the chair. "Please don't make me do this." He pulled the other leg off and sank back onto his haunches. His tighty-whities were beige.

"Topher." Oxygen wasn't finding its way around my body. I squinted at him through a fuzziness. "I can't right now."

"*I* can't," Topher said, bewildered. These weren't my lines, they were his, and now he was confused. "*I* can't, *and* I don't want to." He started backing toward the bedroom, still hands and knees. This time he was getting rug burns, but he didn't seem to care.

"Stop," I said, at the same time he said "Stop." We blinked at each other.

"Do it," he said, frustration clear in his voice. "Why won't you just do this?"

"I can't," I said again. I'd meant fucking him, making him wash something and then kicking him out, but as I said it, the umbrella of it all got bigger. Suddenly I meant making choices like putting on real pants and taking the trash out and teaching class and telling Seth that Chester was alive, and waking up in the morning and being a human, any kind of human, good or bad or a bewildering mix. It all just seemed impossible.

"But you like this," Topher said, from the floor. He was irritated. He'd come biking all the way over here, neglected his girlfriend for months. And now all I was offering him was coffee and a sandwich? "This is like, your thing."

"I need you to go," I said. "Please."

"You're crazy," Topher said, yanking his jeans back on so hard he almost fell over. "You're just unbalanced." He let the door slam behind him. I didn't feel satisfied, and I didn't feel mean in a secret bright way that made me excited. I just felt like I couldn't breathe. I sat on the floor for a long time, until several hours later when Chester started walking between me and the front door, whining.

He needed to pee. Eventually he peed on the carpet, his eyes rolling guiltily, and I watched him do it and I cried.

LIVVY CAME OVER LATER THAT night. She'd been having a date night with the gym teacher, but my voicemail must have alarmed her. The door was unlocked and when she walked in, she found me curled up on the futon with the whole room smelling like dog pee. "This is some next-level mental breakdown shit," Livvy said, but she said it gently, opening all the windows to the spring night. A chill in the air, but the smell of things just beneath the first layer of soil, starting to grow.

"What were you guys doing, anyway?" I asked, watching her from the futon the way Chester was watching me—wary and fragile.

"Well, we were eating ice cream out of the carton," Livvy said, coming to sit on the edge of the futon. "We were sharing a spoon, and making out, and we were going to watch *Dance Moms* reruns, and we were going to have a really normal and lovely couples night, actually. You look like shit, your hair is disgusting, when was the last time you showered?"

"Was she going to throw you around the bedroom?" I asked, from underneath my pile of unwashed hair. "Was she going to slap you around and call you names?"

"We only do that sometimes," Livvy said, as if that should be obvious. "We *love* each other, Sarah."

"You just *met* each other," I said, like a small small angry turtle. Getting smaller with every second. "You actually just *met*."

"I just met *you* when we first met," Livvy said, "and I knew I liked *you* right away."

"You did?"

"Yeah. I wouldn't be here if I didn't like you. Not on my date night, anyway."

"Am I a bad person or a good person?" asked the tiny sad turtle.

"Jesus," Livvy said. "That's not even a thing. Why are you worried about that? Those aren't even real things."

"Good and bad are real things," said the turtle. "You said so. You said I was a good person and you meant I had a history of weakness."

Livvy sighed. "You listen to me? You should never listen to me."

"You said I wasn't the sort of person who could hurt somebody," I persisted, "you said I was friends with all my exes."

Livvy reached over and pulled my hood down over my eyes, shaking me from side to side gently. "Sometimes you're one thing and then later you're a different one. People are inconsistent."

"But then how do we know what we really are?" I asked into the hood.

"Well," said Livvy, "most of us just fake it. And sometimes we like being surprised by ourselves. And sometimes we don't."

"I stole from the co-op and I've been leaving my bike where I shouldn't and I told Seth that Chester got run over and decapitated by a truck."

Livvy sighed and then she shook her head. "Go take a shower," she said. "Once you're clean I'm going back to Amy's place to get laid."

"Didn't you hear me?"

"I heard you," Livvy said, "I'm just choosing not to engage with that information. Now go take a shower. You'll feel better."

AFTER LIVVY LEFT, I SAT on the front porch in my underwear, my hair still wet, and smoked one of her cigarettes. It made the inside of my mouth taste like a different person's mouth, like Livvy's mouth maybe. I imagined being Livvy. I imagined being a gym teacher, who could slap someone and love her at the same time. I imagined being Chester, with one leg lifted and my nose buried in the damp grass. I imagined the people who had constituted the entirety of my history, who had been the conduits for my worldly knowledge. Smoking on the porch, with a breeze bringing goose-bumps up my bare legs, I reimagined my origin story: an empty planet, un-colonized, trees haven't yet been logged and dragged, rivers run rich with fish, the soil is loam instead of concrete. No boats have touched their noses to my shore. All who are to come have not yet arrived. I took a deep breath. Pure air. This is the place from which our bones move forward, I said to Chester, as he chewed on a twig. This is the place from which we start.

MARIA OF THE GRAPES

When I first met Ancash, he was bleeding. He was sitting on the front steps of Praveen's apartment building in downtown Tokyo, blood trickling down his chin and splashed on the ribs of his white T-shirt. He didn't seem at all concerned. As I passed him, he nodded and said hey and I said hey back and continued up the stairs; I'd come to visit Praveen, anyway.

Praveen answered the door, a cup of coffee in one hand and bunched remnants of a lesson plan in the other. "Eikaiwa is shit!" he announced, in his Delhi-accented English.

"Since you're the one teaching it, that's a problem," I said, accepting the offered cup of coffee. "There's somebody bleeding on your steps."

"It is the Mexican," Praveen said, with disdain. "He is always in trouble."

"Should we see if he's okay or something? Give him a Band-Aid?"

Praveen surprised me. "No," he said firmly. "I have no Band-Aid for him." Educated by missionaries, Praveen was deeply ingrained with the strictest principles of Christian charity, and I was shocked.

"You don't *like* him," I exclaimed. "Praveen, you'll make Jesus sad."

"He is not good boy," Praveen said. Remembering my penchant for not-good boys, he fixed me with a stern eye. "You stay far away, Maria. He is crazy Mexican and gay."

"Jesus *weeps*," I said, thrilled. "How do you know he's gay?"

"We talk about something else," Praveen said. "Today, I teach past tense, but my lesson plan is shit! How do I do?"

"*What* do you do," I corrected. "How do I know? I teach English to elementary school kids, we're still stuck on colors."

Praveen brooded over the crumpled pages, spreading them out on the countertop. I walked over to the window and glanced down, but the steps were blocked by the edge of somebody's balcony. Praveen saw me looking.

"Maria," he warned. "Yesterday you say to me, 'Praveen, I turn over new life. Less trouble!' you say."

"That was yesterday," I said, angling my head for a clearer view. "And I was drunk. So does he teach English too? This gay Mexican?"

"No," Praveen said, and the disapproval in his voice was plain. "He does nothing."

"He obviously does *something*," I objected, "he was bleeding." But Praveen was scowling. As close as we were, there was always a point in our conversations where I had to start watching my mouth, and I could tell that I'd reached it.

"Right," I said, turning away from the window. "The past tense."

When I left Praveen's apartment later, Ancash was gone. But there was a smear of drying blood on the asphalt where he'd been sitting.

ANCASH INTRODUCED HIMSELF TO ME a few days later. I was waiting outside for Praveen, who was late, and Ancash came out of the building in the same jeans and white T-shirt he'd been wearing before. I couldn't help my eyes going to the noticeable stains. When he saw me, he held the door, standing right next to the sign that announced, first in creative English and then in presumably better Japanese: DO NOT HOLDING DOOR FOR STRANGER PLEASE.

"Thanks," I said.

"No prob," Ancash replied. His accent was more America than Mexico, and I grinned. Oh Praveen. I could just imagine him peering out of his window at Ancash like an angry old man, disapproving from a distance.

"And yet," I gestured to the sign. "Do not holding door. For stranger, even."

Ancash looked straight at me and the corner of his mouth flickered. "I'll take my chances," he said, and thrust out a hand. "Ancash."

"Maria." I shook it. "What kind of a name is that?"

Ancash smiled. "Quechua. And yours?"

"My mother had an Italian lover around the same time I was conceived. A last desperate cry for freedom." I eyed him. "So you live here?"

"I do. And you, clearly, don't."

"Clearly," I said, "I'm just here to rape and pillage."

"Then I won't get in your way."

I gave him my nightclub smile, my street-corner smile, the one that makes Praveen recite the Lord's Prayer over my head in a cross between an exorcism and a desperate appeal to God. "I don't mind if you're in my way," I said.

Ancash looked straight at me, and smiled a bright smile that never changed his eyes.

"Arrivederci," he said. He released the door and started up the street.

SOMETHING PRAVEEN WOULD ALWAYS SAY to me: "What you are *think*ing!" It didn't matter how many times I corrected him. The words somehow miraculously rearranged themselves again and by the next occasion in which he had to ask me, it always came out the same way again: "What you are *think*ing!"

When I told him I was leaving Tokyo to go home to New York and face the music, he had been supportive. "This is very good," he'd told me. "Family is of utmost important! And you for so many years do not call, do not write."

"They for so many years do not call or write to me, either," I'd said, annoyed, but Praveen shook his head at my childishness.

"You are daughter," he'd lectured me. "It is your duty. But I am proud, now you go back and change over new leaf!"

When I'd showed up back in Tokyo days later, carrying a duffel bag, Praveen had shaken his head at me. "What you are *think*ing!" he'd demanded. "Go home right now!" But I'd slept on his couch that night and for the next few days, finally getting a little sublet and clientele from an Australian woman living near Akabane. She'd been teaching English to Japanese businessmen when her fiancé proposed to her; she told me that now she was going home to Australia to get married.

"Japan is just a phase," she'd said, after the tour of an apartment so small that the tour consisted of standing in the open doorway and glancing around. "All of us foreign devils, we know it, we're drifting. It's bloody easy to stay and drift, am I wrong?" She gave me a conspiratorial look, which I immediately disliked her for. "Well, someday something happens and you realize you've been drifting too long. Got to go home and get serious about my life. You're welcome to the furniture for an extra go-sen."

Less than fifty bucks for a fully furnished room the size of a closet.

"Done," I said. We shook hands.

"It'll happen to you someday," the woman said. "When you're older, maybe. It's exciting now, but you'll look back and it'll seem like a bad dream."

I shrugged. "I bet it beats waking up."

She escorted me out of her apartment pretty quickly after that. I took over several days later. Her Japanese businessmen should have been an easy gig, but all of them spoke English with Australian accents so thick, I couldn't understand them.

I never heard from that woman again, although from time to time I'd briefly think I'd caught a glimpse of her on some Tokyo street corner. There's tourists and there's lifers. Once you're a lifer, no matter what kind of a fantastic long-term plan you think you're going home to, it won't work. You'll only end up back here, duffel bag in hand.

As for me, I admitted to Praveen that I'd gotten as far as the departures gate in Narita before I decided I couldn't do it. I slept in the airport for two whole nights, then turned around and came back. I never even set foot in America.

"Oh *no*," he'd moaned. "Maria, you fucked up!"

I didn't mention to Praveen when I stayed the night at Ancash's place. He didn't need to know, and I didn't want to tell him.

"MARIA OF THE OLIVE EYES." That was Ancash's greeting when he opened the door. Maybe a flicker of surprise, but no more.

"Excuse me?" I asked.

"There's a painting called that," Ancash said, stepping back to let me in. "In Italian: *Maria di Occhi Oliva.*"

His apartment was as Spartan as Praveen's was messy. Only one light on, by the window, a futon already unrolled on the tiny square of floor. A book facedown and open—he'd been reading. Clothes folded on top of a wooden crate: tight T-shirts, torn jeans. Two white button-down shirts hung off the edge of the bare curtain rod. A hot plate balanced on the sink in a corner of the room. I took it all in, then turned back to Ancash.

He was watching me, unfazed. "My humble abode."

"It's not bad."

"How'd you find me?"

"Looked at the mailboxes. There aren't a lot of other people living here with your name." I'd wanted him to ask me why I was there, but then suddenly I didn't. So I kept talking: "It's bigger than my place, anyway. I mean, my old place was a palace, but I lost it."

Ancash lifted an eyebrow. "How'd that happen?"

"Thought I was turning over a new leaf. Guess not, huh." I mimicked Praveen: "'Maria, you will ruin your life and what will you do then!'"

Ancash smiled. "Are you here to ruin your life, or am I the 'what then'?"

I found myself grinning back at him. "You think you could ruin my life?"

"Only if you asked me real nice."

"You're not just pretty and dumb," I realized out loud, delighted. "What are you, some rich kid runaway?"

"Is that the story of Maria?" Ancash inquired courteously.

"I've never been rich," I informed him. "My mother tried it, and it fucked her up for good. What are you reading, *Brave New World*?"

Ancash picked the book up and handed it to me. *Harry Potter*. The torn and stained paperback copy seemed to have survived an apocalypse.

"That tells me nothing about you," I said, disgruntled. "Everybody reads that shit."

Ancash's smile flickered again. He opened the book. Inside, in the space above every line, he appeared to be writing his own book— a sprawl of fine red ink. It took me a minute to realize that the writing was in Japanese.

"I'm translating it," he told me. "By the time I finish, I'll be fluent in Japanese and then I can do whatever I want."

"What does that mean, *whatever you want*?"

"Language is the ultimate weapon," Ancash said, easily. "You might think people will do what you want if you threaten them. Sometimes you're right, but more often you're wrong. The truth is this: people will *do* what you want, when they *think* what you want. Simple as that."

"And when do they think what you want?" I asked, interested.

"When you tell them what to think," he said, "in their own language."

I couldn't tell if he was joking, but he had my attention either way. "And what do you want people to think?"

Ancash took the book back. "I can't tell you," he said. "I haven't decided if you're on my side yet."

"I haven't either," I told him, and this time the smile did reach his eyes. It made them sharper.

"Good," he said.

WHAT STRUCK ME ABOUT ANCASH, on that first night, was that when he talked about Tokyo his face softened and he looked the way most people look when they're talking about a lover. I remember that at one point in the evening, we were sitting by the window drinking shochu, the strong clear rice alcohol that could take paint off a car. Ancash jacked the window up and leaned out. "Look," he said, breathlessly. Leaning next to him, I saw the rabbit-warren back roads of our little ward all tangled into each other, the lights of hundreds of matchbox apartments piled on top of each other. I took a deep breath and smelled hundreds of dinners cooking at the same time.

"They're all eating now," Ancash said, with a certain reverence that off-balanced me completely. "You know that thing Japanese do, before they eat?" And he put his hands together, and so did I, and we chorused the traditional phrase "Itadakimasu," like saying grace.

"There," Ancash said decisively. He looked at his glass ruefully, then shrugged. "Our sustenance will be of a different kind," he added, and we toasted. Until that moment I don't think I'd ever thought of Tokyo as a place where families sat down together. To me, it had been exhilarating, merciless, devoid of stable and communal dinners.

Ancash had sparked my initial interest first by the indecent and provocative act of bleeding in public, then by Praveen's strong dis-approval. And, while it was true that I'd come looking for trouble, I was always looking for trouble. I could have taken or left Ancash himself, up until that moment by the window. Then, looking at the profile of his face—aloof, unpredictable, impenetrable—it was then that I wanted him. And his inquiry about Praveen gave me the opening I'd been looking for.

"So what is he," Ancash asked, innocently enough. "Fiancé? Eth-nic cousin? He seems pretty interested in your affairs."

"He's a friend," I said. We were drinking shochu straight from the bottle by then, passing it back and forth. "Why, are you worried because he's bigger than you?"

Ancash smiled. "Whatever chastity you have is safe with me," he said, taking a shot and handing it back. "I fuck boys."

I choked, then tried to mask it. The most intelligent thing I could think of to say was, "So you *are* gay."

Ancash lifted an eyebrow. "Have you been taking bets?"

"Something like that."

"Did you lose money? Or did I just make you millions?"

I took another mouthful and wiped the back of my hand over my lips. I'd given up on grace and seduction. "I think I just lost, actu-ally."

"How much?"

"Not money. I mean—I was putting the moves on you. You know? I was going to seduce you. So I think I lost."

Ancash laughed out loud. I think it was the first time I'd heard him laugh, and the sound startled me. It made him seem much younger than he looked.

"How were you going to do it?"

"Seduce you? I've been playing it by ear. I was looking for my opening. I figured showing up at your apartment was already pretty blatant—with most men that would be enough."

"Maybe you were just being neighborly."

"But I don't live here."

Ancash considered this. "How were you going to make the transition from stalking to seduction?"

"We're almost there. We're sitting in your window, we're drunk—well, *I'm* drunk—and you just asked about Praveen. So the way this should've gone is: you'd be all *Is he your boyfriend?* and I'd be all *No, are you jealous?* and you'd be all—whatever, I don't know what you'd be all, but then I'd be like *Because you don't have to be.* And then I'd kiss you."

"That's an awful line," Ancash said. "If you kissed me after a line like that, I'd wash my mouth out with soap."

I had to concede that Ancash had a point. "Okay, well then maybe it would go like this: we'd be staring out the window at Tokyo, and you'd be thinking about all the people you've loved and lost, and *I'd* be thinking about all the people I've loved and lost, and then we'd turn to each other. Slowly. In slow motion. And our eyes would lock."

"And we'd kiss?"

"I mean, I guess. That's usually how it goes."

"Would it be good?"

"It would be fantastic. *I'd* be fantastic. Would you be fantastic?"

"I'd be pretty fantastic, yeah."

"Well then, there you go." I sighed, disappointed. "You've lost too. It's your fault that we've lost an opportunity to be fantastic."

Ancash took the bottle of shochu from my hand and set it on the windowsill. Gently, deliberately, he took my face in his hands and turned it toward his. "Are you thinking about all the people you've loved and lost?"

"Yeah," I lied. I couldn't take my eyes off his mouth. There was something about it—some uneven line, something a little lopsided—that made it look like he was always smiling and frowning at the same time.

"Me too," Ancash said, and brushed his lips against mine. They were cool and smooth, softer than I'd expected. I kissed him back, reflexively, and he let me; after a moment, he deepened the kiss and

I felt the gentle slippery brush of his tongue against mine. And then he pulled back and let go of my face. I blinked at him.

"And now we've been fantastic," he said.

"You really for real sleep with men?"

"I really for real do."

"And not with women?"

"Generally not."

"Generally?"

Ancash shrugged. "Sometimes I make exceptions."

"Am I an exception?" I asked, less calculating and more genuinely curious.

"I don't know about an exception," Ancash said, "but you're certainly exceptional."

He was looking out the window so I couldn't see his expression. I was going to ask him what that meant, and then I didn't. We sat, side by side, passing the bottle back and forth. It was smooth and cool to the touch, like Ancash's mouth had been, like his skin was when I leaned my head against his bare shoulder sometime during that long strange night, and let his quiet voice lull me to sleep.

WE WERE INSEPARABLE AFTER THAT. I don't know why. Even then it didn't make much sense to me. But then again, maybe it was the only thing that did. Ancash dazzled me, he made me laugh and he didn't ask questions and he called me things that I didn't understand. *Maria delle Tigri*, sometimes. *Maria della Notte Fonda*. I would ask him what that meant, and he'd say, "That's a painting by a famous Italian painter." Or: "That's a famous opera." Or: "That was the name of Columbus's fourth ship. You know, the one that got lost." Ancash was always making me someone famous and captivating, singled out of history and held up to the light. And when I was in Ancash's world, when I was famous mysterious Maria, I felt at home in a way I couldn't remember having felt anywhere.

I THOUGHT, LATER, THAT IF I hadn't been so blinded by Ancash, I might have seen what was coming with Praveen. Maybe I could have stopped him. But maybe not. Ancash once joked that the virtuous may be the last to fall prey to vice, but they always fall the hardest; he was not thinking of Praveen, but I was.

The girl was named Irina, Praveen told me. She worked in a kyabakura. They'd met outside her club—she was leaving work, Praveen was waiting for a taxi. It was love at first sight. She was charmed by his courtesy, and he was charmed by her Ukrainian accent and demure smile. He was also charmed—instead of repelled, as I would have thought—by the English translation of her profession. It soon became clear, however, that Praveen had an image in his head of "cabaret girl" that belonged more in a blushing 1950s musical than a Tokyo club.

"Do you know what she does all night?" I asked Praveen. I was sitting on a cleared edge of his counter, eating one of the fruit cups that I'd brought him. Praveen had a cold and had canceled his classes, but he didn't look sick. He looked uncharacteristically happy.

"She does talking to people," Praveen said. "That is how cabaret clubs work in Japan, just friendly and pretty girls talk to people. She helps men practice their English."

I took another spoonful of fruit and debated in my head whether or not to disabuse Praveen of his notions. "Well, yeah," I said at last. "But you know how it works? There's a menu, right? With pictures, and you can just point and ask for the girl you want."

Praveen was already frowning. "I do not like this conversation 'menu,'" he reproved me. "You are talking about human peoples, Maria."

"That's what it *is* though," I protested. "So you order the woman, and she comes and listens to you talk and sure, you pay per hour, but most of the real money comes afterwards. She gets off work, you're waiting, there's a love hotel down the street—"

Praveen cut me off again, angrily. "She is not going to love hotel down the street!" he said, sharply. "Irina is very good girl, Maria. She works hard for her family, they are waiting in Ukraine and very depending on her. She care about family, Maria." He didn't even need to say the *not like you*. "All she does is talking to men. But she likes me, she is thinking of quit her job and finding new one and I help her looking."

I ate a lone grape to buy some silence. I hadn't met Irina yet, but I knew that Praveen and I, when we looked at her, would see very different things. Praveen would see all the innocence she was giving up, and I would see all the calculating knowledge that she was gaining. And so, that afternoon, there just didn't seem like much of a point to arguing.

"Been on a lot of dates?" I asked him.

"We see each other very often," he reported, beaming.

"Cool," I said. "Good luck, man."

I would find out later that every one of those dates had occurred within the club, and Praveen had paid an hourly rate like everybody else.

ANCASH QUIT HIS JOB BARTENDING the same day I got into my first street fight.

The two were connected, of course. The owner of the bar was a stocky Romanian who felt strongly about maintaining the chastity (and presumably the heterosexuality) of his son. His son was a blond Ganymede, who felt equally strongly in the opposite direction. Ancash ended up in the middle, willingly enough, and so when I showed up to meet him after work, he was being held by two bouncers while the owner beat the shit out of him. In that moment, I flashed back to my first encounter with Ancash, blood-smeared but calm, and it seemed to make much more sense.

What happened next is testimony to Ancash's pervasive influ-ence, or at least the extent to which I felt stupidly invincible when I was with him. I screamed at the top of my lungs and launched myself onto the back of the owner. He staggered under my sudden weight, then shook me loose long enough to backhand me. I re-attached myself, clinging to him like a furious rat, gnawing on his shoulder and getting my blood all over his shirt. It was Ancash who pulled me away, and we fled through the streets of Roppongi while the bouncers shouted obscenities after us in Romanian and English, but didn't follow.

We jumped onto a JR train without checking to see where it was going. It was packed with businessmen and club kids, and while we got some glances, nobody bothered us despite the fact that we were both bleeding. We got off a few stops later at Shinjuku Station and went into the same restroom to clean up. A man who had been washing his hands at the sink glanced at the two of us and left in a hurry. When I looked in the mirror it struck me how similar we were in that moment: flushed, mouths red, eyes glittering.

"That was crazy," I breathed, mopping blood off my face with a paper towel while Ancash examined his ribs gingerly. "I've never done that before."

Ancash flashed me a look. "You're wild," he said, and even he seemed surprised.

"Never seen a girl fight before?" His ribs were already purpling over, and you could see little starburst-ridges of color from some-one's knuckles.

Ancash shook his head and met my eyes in the mirror. "Never seen anyone fight for *me* before," he said. We were both quiet. I had no idea what he was thinking.

We ended up buying shochu from a conbini store and drinking it on the steps of Shinjuku Station. I loved the color and chaos of Shinjuku—the kids decked out on their way to some crazy club, the host boys walking in trios with their hair in dyed-gold manes, the cabaret girls in high heels and short dresses, the salarymen rushing home (or to a bar, more likely), the foreigners stunned by all the neon and the TV screens set into the sides of buildings. Tokyo had all the power of New York but was more dangerous. In New York, you were always aware that you were fighting to survive. In Tokyo, you got seduced into letting your guard down. New York was like a bomb going off, Tokyo like a laser show that left you blind.

"You should be a host boy," I said, watching one of them try to work a girl without much success. "You'd get paid instead of getting in trouble."

Ancash smiled. "Doesn't seem like a bad deal," he said. "Especially when you get to dress like that just to talk."

"It's not all talk," I said. "You have to make patrons think you'll fuck them in the end so they keep coming back. But you, Ancash, people just *look* at you and hope you'll fuck them. After ten minutes, you'd have them hooked. And if they keep coming back, your stock goes up. It's your dream job."

"Are you saying that I look easy?" Ancash pretended to be indignant, but I could tell that he was enjoying the idea.

"*Easy?* Kid, you look effortless. That's part of your charm, isn't it, everything you do looks like you don't give a damn."

"They call it *sprezzatura* in Italian," Ancash said. "*Maria di Sprezzatura*. That's a famous painting, you know."

"Is it."

"Yeah, commissioned by Louis the Fourteenth. Le Roi Soleil."

"There seem to be an awful lot of paintings of this Maria girl," I drawled, leaning back against the steps. "Who was she, anyway?"

"Isn't that the question," Ancash murmured, and the tone of his voice made me look up. His eyes were fixed on me. "You know, there are kyabakura that specialize in foreigners. You could pull it off too."

I looked at Ancash, startled. "Me? A host girl?"

"Why not? You're pretty. You're charming. Or," Ancash amended, "maybe you could be, if you were being paid."

"You have to tell people what they want to hear," I said. "I can't do that. There's a reason why I don't talk to my family anymore."

"It's just a game," Ancash shrugged, "and you're the one who runs it, which automatically makes you the winner. They come in, flirt with you, think they're falling in love with you—and it's not even you in that booth with them. It's someone you've created."

We sat in silence, watching the rush of crowds go by. Now that the adrenaline was wearing off, I was hurting pretty badly where I'd gotten hit. I wondered if Ancash was as well. For some reason I kept thinking of Praveen saying, "Maria, what you are *think*ing!" and I wanted to laugh, but then suddenly I wanted to cry. I was on an out-of-control carnival ride, and Praveen—with his calmness, his sternness, his unflappable predictability—had been the only person who could, even briefly, make the carnival ride slow down. But now Praveen had hopped on his own carnival ride and it would all just keep going and going. And I thought of Ancash sitting in the window of his apartment, his mouth cool against mine, tasting of shochu, and then I imagined him dressed in the white button-down shirts and tight jeans of a host boy, flirting with rich-looking Japanese girls, letting their need create the character he would play—and I felt something strange and hot and tight in my stomach.

Ancash nudged me with his shoulder. "Or don't."

"Don't what?"

"Don't play a game where you're the stakes. Maria, have you ever thought about going back home?"

"Yeah." I rubbed my forehead. My cheek throbbed. "No. I don't know. You should understand."

"There's a story," Ancash said suddenly, "about this Buddhist priest who's walking through a jungle when a tiger starts chasing him. He runs and runs but the tiger is really fast and just keeps gaining." He stopped, pensive. "I think tigers can run faster than seventy miles per hour, actually."

"That's cheetahs," I said, but I could feel myself getting steady again. "So what happens?"

"He gets to a cliff where wild grapes are growing, and the tiger is right behind him so he grabs on to the grapevine and starts scaling down it. And then he hears this snapping sound. He looks up and sees that the grapevine is breaking under his weight, and the tiger is leaning over the edge of the cliff snarling, and then he looks down and sees a long fall onto jagged rocks."

"What does he do?" I asked.

Ancash watched a trio of host boys sit on the station steps opposite us, smoking and eyeing the crowd. He turned to me and grinned. "He plucks a grape off the vine," he said, "and oh! how sweet it tastes."

Silence. And then I punched him in the arm. "Are you crazy?" I demanded. "That's the ending? That's stupid! It's not even an ending!"

Ancash smirked and didn't reply. Now we both watched the host boys preening under the neon wash, smooth and aloof like marionettes.

"But he falls," I objected. "I mean, right? He's gonna fall."

"The fall is inevitable," Ancash shrugged. "But the grape is unpredictably sweet." He grinned, then, that luminous smile that fell short of his eyes. *Maria delle Uve,*" he said. "Maria of the Grapes."

PRAVEEN STOPPED TEACHING NIGHT CLASSES. It wasn't that he canceled them, so much as that they simply became immaterial to him. In the beginning, there was always a specific reason. Irina called, she wanted him to stop by the club and ask for her, the manager was getting angry at her for not having enough patrons, she was afraid of what might happen if Praveen didn't come. Then Irina didn't even have to ask. Praveen would show up at the club and wait for hours while she was with other patrons. He would walk around Shinjuku, buy ramen at a corner stall, drop by a video arcade, then go back to the club and ask, hopefully, in his horrible Japanese, for Irina-san. I only went with him once, when he called me from Shinjuku and asked if I wanted to get dinner together. He seemed distracted and strung out for the whole meal, but when I deposited him at the entrance of the kyabakura, he became suddenly urgent and eager. I caught a flash of Irina's bleach-blond mane approaching and retreated before I could see more. The whole scene depressed me for days. Praveen was too good for this. He'd always been above me, looking down with a mixture of affection and disdain. Now he was on my level, and I didn't like it.

Ancash, on the other hand, was thriving. He went for an interview and was hired by a host club for men in Shinjuku Ni-Chome. He made quite a figure in sleek, white silk shirts, new dark jeans, his hair uncombed and shaggy. I knew that he would be popular, and he was. I didn't tell him, but it was less difficult for me to know that he was chatting up men, turning that bright blank smile on them, leaning in to let them catch the scent of his cologne. They would come and go, leaving money and gifts in their wake, and in the end it would be Ancash and Maria again, shoulder to shoulder: cartoon characters, action heroes, spies, rock stars—two of a kind, and perfect.

I got a job at a regular host club for reasons that are still difficult to explain. Sheer rebellion, probably. It seemed fitting to start a new life out of the worst mistake Praveen was making with his. A sort of *fuck you* to the carnival ride: those at the controls are, by default, the winners. Either way, I, too, stopped teaching English and spent my nights in a backless dress, making pidgin small talk with flushed, giddy salarymen. It struck me that my new job wasn't so different from the eikaiwa conversation classes, except that I was required to dress in a more provocative manner and that my clients—encouraged by their consumption of two-hundred-dollar bottles of champagne—conversed for the most part about the size of my breasts.

When I look back on that strange, extended time-out-of-time—

that all in all couldn't have been longer than three months—I remember it like a fever dream. Ancash and I worked while the world slept, and slept while the day slid from sun into shadows. It effectively separated us from the rest of the world—and brought us closer together, Hansel and Gretel in a mad rush, no time to stop, no time to reconsider, the future and the present superimposed onto each other. And when electric evening came around again, we went to work in the first glow, sending each other text messages on the train, quotes from *American Gigolo*, *Belle de Jour*, and other prostitution classics. Ancash once texted me just before I got off work: *Thou hadst a whore's forehead, thou refusedst to be ashamed.* It was the first time it ever crossed my mind that Ancash might, in his former life, have read the Bible.

After stumbling out into the pale swell of dawn, we would often meet at Shinjuku Station, the necessary midpoint on both of our ways home. Still drunk, exhausted, queasy, we'd buy hot coffee from the vending machines on the platform and doze off on a bench, Ancash's head in my lap, until our separate trains arrived.

Sometimes Ancash would tell me stories from his night, sometimes I would tell him stories from mine, sometimes we talked about entirely unrelated things: Praveen's problems with Irina, or my increasingly psychotic landlord, who we both thought might be a closet serial killer. Ancash never told me much more about his past than the bare details: he'd lived in Tokyo before as a teenager, he grew up on the move, he'd been attending a college in the U.S., a good one, and then he dropped out and came back here. Once he let slip that his father had some high-up international job—a diplomat, maybe—but when I pressed, he simply changed the subject.

Another time, he showed me his dog-eared copy of *Harry Potter*, more than three-quarters of it now covered with red chicken tracks. He said that he'd been bringing it to work so that some of his Japanese clients could help him translate. I imagined them charmed by his single-minded pursuit of something so earnest and innocuous. They didn't know that this was Ancash's first step toward world domination—*Language is the ultimate weapon,* he'd said. In my mind I saw the scene: a client bent closely over the book with him, inhaling his shampoo, a glance at the flash of smooth skin between neck and shoulder—a glance, a smile. More red writing scrawled in the margins. A hand on his knee. Ancash's downcast eyes, the careful stillness of his face. They would look at him and see innocence and want to be the ones to take it away. He would sell them innocence, every night, they'd take it and take it and still never get close to him at all. And then I wondered if, in the end, I was just like them. Ancash never told me if he was sleeping with any of his patrons. And for a long time, I didn't ask.

I think I loved that life, but I don't really know. I remember it like looking out the window of a shinkansen at night—everything is just a blur of lights, whipping past. And then, without warning, it ended.

I'D BEEN SLEEPING SO DEEPLY that the banging at the door was just part of my dream, at first, and then Ancash's voice filtered in, calling my name. I managed to drag my body off the futon, eyes still half-closed, reeling toward the door. Mornings were like this— waterlogged from alcohol, heavy with exhaustion. I unlocked the door and pulled it open.

"What are you doing here?"

Ancash, leaning in the doorway, looked worse than I did. He obviously hadn't slept yet. He reeked of smoke and alcohol, but he didn't seem to be drunk anymore. Which meant his head must be killing him.

"Maria of the Mornings," he said, and gave me that crooked smile.

"What's wrong?" I asked, stepping back and gesturing him inside.

"Can I crash here?"

"Of course." I stumbled to the refrigerator, pulled the door open, rooted around past cans of Sapporo and half-eaten conbini bentos until I found a bottle of green tea. I poured some for Ancash and he accepted it. I woke up all the way as I watched him drink—he held himself carefully, as if he was in pain.

"You should have gotten off work already," I said. "I waited for you at Shinjuku." But it was a question.

Ancash finished the tea and put the cup carefully on the counter. "I was with a client."

"You left the bar with a client?"

"It was a dohan," Ancash said. "We were still on the clock."

I studied him. Dohans were standard practice, especially with clients who'd proved to the host-bar managers that they could be trusted. They'd take you to dinner, maybe to a movie, maybe to karaoke. If you were good, you'd work it so that they ended up back at your club and spent their alcohol money on your alcohol.

"Where did he take you?"

Ancash shrugged, and for the first time I felt something cold in my stomach. "Ancash. Are you okay?"

"Of course I'm okay." But the impatience, the casualness, the brusqueness in his tone told me he was lying. I put a hand out to touch his arm, but he moved away. "Can I just—I need to shower."

"Yeah," I said, stepping back. "Go ahead. I'll find stuff you can wear."

While Ancash was in the shower, I found an oversize button-down that was too large on me, and a pair of black track pants. When I called his name tentatively, he didn't answer. All I could hear was the sound of running water. I walked down to the courtyard and bought two cans of vending-machine coffee, one hot, one cold, and drank them back-to-back. Then I bought one more, hot, for Ancash. When I returned upstairs, the sound of running water had stopped. I gathered the dry clothes under one arm, coffee in hand, and walked cautiously to the bathroom door, a fist raised to knock. A sound stopped me—a strange one, at first I didn't know what it was. It paralyzed me, a horrible mesmerizing sound—and then I knew. Ancash was crying.

I stood there for a long time, listening to Ancash cry. It was muffled, wrenching. The sound of something being prized loose from a tight dark place. In the end I couldn't take it. I left the clothes and the rapidly cooling coffee outside the bathroom door, and went back down into the courtyard.

WHEN I RETURNED THE SECOND time, Ancash was sitting on my futon. He looked calm and composed, but exhausted. Smaller, somehow, even though the clothes themselves were tight on him. He was drinking the coffee slowly, as if he was afraid he'd be sick. I didn't know what to say, but he spoke almost immediately.

"It isn't what you think."

"I don't know what I think," I said.

"You think someone—took advantage of me. Don't you."

"Did they?"

"You think someone took me somewhere, hurt me—made me do things—and I was afraid to say no—that I didn't know what I was doing." There was an ugly edge to his voice.

"Isn't that what happened?" I was keeping my voice very quiet. I'd never seen Ancash like this before and it scared me.

"No," he said. "No, see, that's where you're wrong. I knew exactly what I was doing."

"Okay."

"Nobody made me do anything. I left the bar with him. I did that."

"Okay."

"This is who I am. I'm choosing this, Maria."

I sat down on the futon next to him, still not touching him. "I know that."

"This is my game," Ancash said, quiet. The harsh edge in his voice was gone. "These are my rules. I'm winning."

He was silent for a while. In the end, I had to ask. "Have you . . . before this . . . ?"

Ancash flickered a glance at me, but he understood. And after a moment, almost reluctantly, he nodded.

"Your dad has money," I said, "if you needed money . . ." Ancash turned away, and I knew I should stop. I knew I couldn't possibly understand all the things he'd chosen not to tell me. But I couldn't stop. "Last night . . . ?"

"Sometimes shit happens. You think it's your game and then it's not, it gets turned on you, but if you stay with it, it becomes your game again."

I spoke before I knew what I was going to say. "Don't sleep with them anymore."

I'd surprised him. "Maria—"

"Don't do it. Even when it's not like this, even if it doesn't go badly that night, or the next night—Ancash . . . It'll do things to you."

The Ancash who'd knocked on my door and wept in my shower was gone, now. The Ancash I was used to stared back at me, haggard but calm.

"It's not that," he said. "I just—I'm just tired. I'll be fine. I just get tired."

I should have dropped it, but I couldn't. "I haven't done that," I said. "I haven't had sex with *my* patrons." I had meant my tone to be reproving—perhaps with a moral edge—but it didn't come out that way. Whatever was in my voice made him look at me then, long and serious.

"If you're waiting for me," he said, at last, "don't."

I don't know if I'd known what I was saying to him until then. I hadn't stopped to consider it. But when I did, I couldn't say that he'd misunderstood me.

"What would be so wrong with it?"

Ancash closed his eyes and leaned his head against the wall. Framed against the mid-morning light, he looked like he was a hundred years old. Without opening his eyes, he said, "Maria, I will never forget you. You know that, right?"

"Ancash—"

"Even if you left Japan, even if we never saw each other again, you'd be entirely unforgettable to me."

"But what does that *mean*?" I said, frustrated.

Ancash opened his eyes. "You think you want me to touch you?" he asked, very softly. "You could have that from anyone, any night of the week, and it wouldn't mean a thing. It doesn't mean anything."

In the silence, I found myself wondering, *When did I fall in love with you? When did that happen?* I remembered then, the exact moment. *Maria delle Uve*, he'd said, laughing with all of Shinjuku flickering and alive around us: *The grape is unpredictably sweet.*

"Everything with you means something to me," I said, and the softness of my voice matched his.

Ancash was quiet for a long time, sitting beside me on the futon. I thought maybe he'd get up and leave. Or maybe he'd lie down and sleep, and we'd pretend that none of this ever happened. And then, without warning, he reached out and touched my cheek. I looked at him, surprised, but his face was absolutely still.

"Maria of the Exceptions," he said, and he leaned forward and kissed me.

THERE WAS A MOMENT IN which I could have stopped him. Later, it was that moment that I remembered first—one that, at the time, felt like it was flashing past, but in which I made a choice. I kissed him back. His mouth tasted like coffee, like salt, behind that the sharp tang of alcohol. Then something smoky, something like licorice. It occurred to me to wonder if he accepted drugs from the clients, as a number of the host girls in my bar did. I wanted to ask him, but I was afraid if he had a moment to think, this would stop.

When I replay it in my mind, there is so much chronology that escapes me. Was it Ancash or I who pushed the other down on the futon? Which one of us started undressing the other? Did Ancash try to stop? But I don't think so, I don't think he did. What comes to me clearly are specific details—the shallow cup of his collarbones, a scar running parallel to his ribs, a small blue tattoo of a koi on his chest. I'd never known he had a tattoo. The taste of his sweat against my lips, sweet-salty. The heaviness of his body against mine, nothing between us but skin, and our bones resting against each other. I remember I thought, *Let's be buried like this,* but I don't know if I said it out loud. I remember that Ancash felt real to me. The whole thing was like a dream, but it was more real than anything else in years. And I remember that when it was over and we were tangled around each other, half-asleep, I said, "Stay," and Ancash said, "Until the busy world is hushed."

It wasn't until after Ancash left, slipping out into the first glow of evening, that I remembered where those words were from— a remnant from my own rebellious Catholic-school days. It was so out of place to hear the Prayer of Solace in Ancash's mouth that I had let it slide past without recognition. But later that night, sitting in my empty apartment where the sheets smelled like him, already late for the host club and making no move to get up and dress, I found that I could recall the whole thing. And so I said it out loud, listening to the sound of my voice against the hum and rush of Tokyo, against the sound of Ancash's absence: "May Christ support us all the day long, until the shadows lengthen, and the evening comes, and the busy world is hushed, and the fever of life is over and our work is done. Then in his mercy may he give us a safe lodging, and holy rest and peace at the last."

I DIDN'T SEE ANCASH FOR weeks after that. Seeing him would have been like looking directly into the sun. I closed my eyes so I wouldn't go blind. He called me, repeatedly at first, and left voicemails. They were short, succinct: *Maria, are you okay?* Or: *Maria, where are you?* Or, toward the end, sadly: *Maria, I wish you'd talk to me.* Then his voicemails tapered off, but he kept texting me. Then even those stopped. I left work earlier or later than usual, in case he was waiting for me, but I never actually thought he was. Ancash was not the type to linger outside, as Praveen did for Irina every night.

Praveen called me one night when I was at the host club. It was during a lull, and I was sitting in the back room, smoking. I'd never smoked before, but now it seemed like just another bad habit that wouldn't kill me quick enough but might make the going sweeter. We weren't supposed to answer our phones at work, but when I saw it was Praveen, I looked around, saw that the only person nearby was the apathetic bouncer who was also smoking, and picked up.

"Praveen, what's up."

"Maria, where are you?"

"At a club," I said. I hadn't told him where I was working, and in the past two months he hadn't asked what I'd been getting myself into. "What's up?"

"I need to talk with you," Praveen said. He sounded distraught. "I need to meet you."

"What? Prav, I can't meet you right now. What's wrong?"

"I need to see you," Praveen repeated.

The urgency in his voice was so clear that I responded without thinking. "Shinjuku Station by the southwest exit," I said. "Twenty minutes." I ground my cigarette out and tossed it in the ashtray. The bouncer said in Japanese, "They'll fire you," and I said in English, "Good, I quit."

I was still wearing the gold backless dress when I walked out.

WE SAT IN A SMALL square under the flicker of a giant TV screen implanted in the side of a building. On TV, white people were skiing and laughing and drinking Asahi beer. The crowds poured past us in tides, coordinated with the train schedule, ebbing and flowing. Praveen seemed dazed. The story itself was simple.

"She ask for loan," Praveen said blankly. "I see her every day, we make a plan together that she pays off debt, she leaves the club and we marry. Her father, he writes me letter from Ukraine, he says he wants me to marry with his daughter and he will pay off loan by wire of money."

"When did she vanish?" I asked, knowing the end of the story before he got there.

"I see the letter," Praveen continued, as if he hadn't heard my question. "A man's hand lettering. Maybe I don't read Russian but she tell me what it saying. An address, Maria, her father's address. Photographs. Wouldn't you believe her?"

He looked at me then, with wide empty eyes. He wasn't even angry, he was bewildered.

"When did she vanish?" I repeated.

"All my money," Praveen said. "I save, Maria. So much, I save, I do not eat at expensive restaurants, I live cheap apartment, always saving."

We were quiet. On the screen above us, a movie preview was playing—something about five black guys on skateboards toting AK-47s.

"Three days ago," Praveen said, and it took me a second to realize that my question had just reached him, and he was answering it. "I think, maybe she have cold so she skips work. Then I think, maybe she working different hours, so she is not at home. Then her landlord, he say three days she isn't home, and I'm waiting on doorsteps, in doorways, waiting and waiting and she doesn't pick up her phone and I keep thinking, *She would not do this to me, it is not what it looks like.*" He ran his hands across his face and through his hair. We were silent.

"The money, I don't care money," Praveen said at last. He gestured, an open-handed pass over the square in front of us, the blinking, glittering buildings around us. "Her smile, Maria, it is brighter than all these lights. You want to walk into it and stay there."

I thought of Ancash, then. The way he'd looked in the mirror right after that fight, his mouth tight and his eyes luminous. The thought struck me that he'd looked the same way in my bed, and I wondered how do we bear this. We're born at the top of a cliff, the moment we leave the womb the tigers come, there's nothing before us but a vine that won't hold, and I wondered right then how we can endure any of it, this inevitable, prolonged, graceless fall.

Praveen murmured something, I didn't catch it. I took his hand. It was cold.

"She's lucky," I said. "In this crazy city, to have somebody notice she's gone. I'd pay real money for that."

I didn't think Praveen was listening to me, he seemed so far away. But after a few minutes, his fingers tightened around mine. "How is the Mexican?" he asked.

"I don't know," I said, not bothering to correct him. "Haven't seen him."

"Oh Maria," Praveen said, with a gentleness I hadn't expected from him. "Poor bad Maria."

I HELPED PRAVEEN PACK. HE didn't want to take much. Clothes, some books, nothing that wouldn't fit in a suitcase and a duffel bag. He tried to give the rest to me, especially after I bought his one-way ticket to Delhi, but I didn't know what I would do with chairs and bookshelves and potted plants, so in the end we sold it all to the next occupant, a blue-eyed German kid who'd come to Tokyo after too many years of watching anime.

"I'm so excited to haf come here!" the German told us, his eyes whisking around the apartment. "You haf no idea, maybe in a past life I am a Japanese, I feel so at home!"

"Good luck," Praveen had the grace to say.

"Welcome to the jungle," I added, with less grace.

The German thought Praveen and I were married. He wanted to know why we were leaving.

"Someday something happens and you realize you've been drifting too long," I answered before Praveen could correct him. "Got to go home and get serious if you want a life. You're welcome to all the dishes for an extra go-sen."

"How much is that?" the German asked.

"Fifty American dollars," I said. "Up front, cold cash."

I helped Praveen carry his two bags downstairs, and called him a taxi. He gave me the go-sen, even though I protested, and asked me not to come to the airport with him. "I will remember you here," he said, "in the sun." He hugged me. "Maria, be careful."

I waved until the taxi swerved around the corner and was gone. And then, in the first flush of evening, I caught the subway home.

I DON'T KNOW WHEN I decided to leave. Maybe it was the moment in which I first lost sight of Praveen waving to me from inside the taxi. Maybe it was before that, when I walked out of my job in that ridiculous gold dress. Or maybe it was before that, even—when Ancash slipped out of my bed and was gone.

Rocking with the motion of the subway, I realized that there was a gnawing feeling in my stomach as if I hadn't eaten in weeks. But back in my apartment, the smell of my dinner cooking made me sick. Praveen was the last thing to ground me to this life, and now he too was gone. I opened the windows so that I wouldn't have to smell the food I'd made, and instead I started smelling all the dinners that my neighbors around me were cooking. I imagined them all as I had that first night with Ancash—sitting down together, clusters of families all across the city, saying whatever version they had of grace. I leaned out the window, both nauseated and painfully empty, and I thought, *Where's my family? Where are they right now?*

So maybe that was when I decided to go back. After that, everything was a blur. Details, really, that passed by me. The minute I finished something, it was done and there was a new detail waiting to be taken care of. Booking a one-way ticket. The landlord. The bills. The last thing—and the hardest—I left for the end. I began to think I couldn't do it at all. And then, the evening before I was to fly out, on my last full day in Tokyo, I sat down and wrote Ancash a letter. I had to start over twice, but the third time I managed to finish.

> Ancash. It's been so long. There's so much I want to tell you, but I don't know what I would say. I'm sorry. I'm leaving Tokyo. Maybe you don't want to hear from me now. I would understand if you didn't. But if you get this today, and if you want to see me, come to Shinjuku Station, the southwest exit. I'll wait there until the last train. Maria.

The letter was brief, and I didn't reread it because I was afraid I would tear it up. I folded it in half, then in half again. I stopped by Ancash's host club, although I knew he wouldn't be there yet. I gave the letter to another host, a thin Japanese boy with a torrent of bleach-blond hair, and told him to deliver it to Ancash, that it was important. He looked at me curiously but promised that he would. As I walked away from the host club, I thought: *Peace at the last. Let this be peace at the last.* I wasn't praying, I don't believe in that. I was just asking nicely.

THE WHOLE WAY TO SHINJUKU, I considered just catching a train or a cab directly to Narita. Waiting the night in the airport for my flight so that I couldn't change my mind. Never knowing if Ancash showed up or not. But I couldn't do it. I'd already betrayed Ancash once. Twice, if you counted sleeping with him. I couldn't do it a third time.

And so I waited for him outside Shinjuku Station's southwest exit.

I don't know how much time passed. People moved steadily around, past, below. Japanese kids skateboarding. Hosts on their way to work. Then, later, salarymen leaving work in a rush of black suits, like a mob of penguins. Street musicians. Tourists. The tinny high clang of bike bells, negotiating carefully around and through the gathered masses of the crowds.

And while the city beat time all around me like a vast heart, I told myself the beginning of a story: *Once upon a time there were two runaways in a jungle*—neon tigers all around, so beautiful, every sharp tooth another TV screen, fluorescent tongues, grapes for the plucking, fat bunches of grapes for the bold, a night without darkness, a fall without end.

WHITE PEOPLE

When our marriage ended, I told Seth it was because we had too many White People conversations. He pretended not to know what that meant—"But we *are* white, Cynthia, we *happen* to be white"— but I knew he did. To drive the point home, I read aloud the last string of texts we'd exchanged: *Pea soup for dinner? / NO too wintry. / Asparagus then? / Asparagus is overplayed. / Well you stop by Chelsea Market yourself and see what you'd prefer to eat, Seth.* We're even *fighting* like white people, I said, and again Seth protested anemically that white people don't fight any differently from other people. But we both knew they do. White people fight in very low voices, in public, while smiling. My parents did it. His parents did it. And this was something I didn't want to do anymore.

When I met Elias, I knew that he was the kind of man that Seth would feel threatened by, but I wouldn't say that was what made me like him. I think we had a real connection, and if Elias happened to be Venezuelan, if he happened to have tattoos up the corded muscle of his right arm, if he happened to be a modern dancer who special-ized in a "physical and metaphysical silent dialogue about race" (his words), well those things were just points of interest over which we connected. Points of interest that Seth and I had unfortunately never shared.

"I didn't know you had any interest in *modern dance*," Seth said pointedly over what we were calling a Divorce Dinner. We were having Divorce Dinners once a week, to amicably discuss how to be amicable, and also to divvy up shared possessions—who wanted the record player, who needed the hooked rug from Morocco, who got to keep which friends. It was at one of these Divorce Dinners that Seth told me he'd started seeing a twenty-one-year-old Women's Studies major at Barnard named Macey. I ground some pepper in a light sprinkle over my hand-raised quail, and then expressed that I was very happy for him, that I had myself actually almost been a Women's Studies major, although quite possibly he didn't know that about me despite our six-year marriage, and that I had, myself, started "seeing" a twenty-seven-year-old Venezuelan modern dancer named Elias.

Seth didn't sprinkle pepper over his own hand-raised quail. He just stared across the restaurant table at me, his blue eyes narrow. And then he questioned my interest in modern dance. I expressed to him that I quite liked modern dance, that Merce Cunningham was very inspirational for me, and that I had once read the biography of a German modern dancer whose name I couldn't, in the moment, recall. Seth expressed that he thought my interest in modern dance was a crock of shit. I expressed that I thought Seth was an asshole with a tiny flaccid cock. We ate our mutual hand-raised quail silently, with ferocity, for a few minutes. Then Seth pointed out that I did not seem like myself. That kind of crass language was childish, and I was actually a very rational and mature person, with whom he could usually have rational and mature conversations, and this whole thing wasn't like me at all.

No, I said, *it isn't.* And that felt good. To be unlike myself. So then I ordered dessert.

WHEN I TOLD ELIAS THAT I was still married but in the process of extricating myself, he just said, "Oh," and kept stretching. He was developing what he called a "portfolio of gestures" for his upcoming dance-meditation at Judson Church, and I was trying to help. Watching Elias work inspired me. It made me imagine the life I could have had, if I hadn't married Seth, in which I wore paint-spattered denim and had two full tattoo-sleeves, and also muscles, and also a portfolio of my own gestures that people wanted to watch me perform.

I asked if Elias had any feelings or questions about Seth, but he just looked at me a little oddly, said "No," and kept stretching. Seth would have had a lot of questions. Seth would have wanted to measure himself against this other guy and make sure that he was better in some way. Elias's quiet confidence and lack of curiosity were almost as inspiring to me as his portfolio of gestures. And then it occurred to me: passive jealous probing wasn't in his cultural heritage. That was a white thing, and Elias was Venezuelan. I wanted to tell Elias how grateful I was to be able to learn from him, but he'd already turned his back on me.

The first set of gestures in his portfolio involved tucking one foot behind his knee and tilting, without falling. Every time he appeared about to fall, he would take a tiny hop, and rebalance himself. If you thought about this as a political metaphor, it was clearly about self-rescue, and not waiting for a higher power to step in. I started to imagine Elias as a small boy in Venezuela. We'd never discussed his past, which I assumed meant that it must have been a hard one. I imagined him barefoot, walking along a dirt road. Goats somewhere, grazing off meager grass, their small noses brushing chewed-bare earth. Elias, mouth dry, liquid brown eyes squinting into an unforgiving sun. Where was his mother? Maybe a nanny, already in the U.S., maybe working to send money back to his grandmother who was looking after all of her children. Motherless and neglected,

Elias would wander out into nature and spend hours communing with the wind and the sun, the soil beneath his bare feet. No wonder he spoke so little. No wonder he needed nothing from anyone. He'd brought himself up this way, as his only alternative to privation.

I found that my eyes were full of tears. I brushed them away, before Elias turned back around. Hop-tilt-hop. Hop-tilt-hop. He never fell, and he never turned around.

IT BECAME CLEAR TO ME as time passed that, despite our lack of discussion about it, Elias understood my multitude of conflicting feelings about Seth. Elias's lack of curiosity about all of these things was a manifestation of his understanding, and his eyes, which were very large and dark, held a lot of unspoken compassion.

"Everybody runs around chattering all day long," I remarked to Seth at our next Divorce Dinner, after he'd spent half an hour telling me about a panel on gender violence that he'd attended at Barnard. "Everybody just can't shut up. Elias practices a sort of intentional silence, which is refreshing and yet also communicative."

"Intentional silence," Seth repeated. "You mean he's a mute?"

I was very surprised that Seth would use ableist hate-language, and I expressed that.

"Listen," said Seth, "I think intentionality of any kind is admirable because this is a world in which people just sort of go around doing whatever they feel like, like breaking up their marriages just on a whim if they feel like it, so I appreciate people who have any sort of, uh, responsibility and collective intention. So I really do want to express that I feel admiration for Elias, if that's something that he practices. But I also think it's very easy to confuse *practice* with lack of ability to *execute*. So."

I was very surprised that Seth was quick to assume inability from a person of color, and I expressed that.

"You don't get to play that card," Seth said. "Dating a brown guy doesn't make you brown." And then he walked out of the restaurant. I thought about following him, but Elias would never follow anybody out of a restaurant, following is reactionary behavior, and Elias is all about living in the moment from a place of self-directed truth. So I finished my hand-raised bison burger, and then I finished Seth's, and I was eating the last of his fries when he came back in and sat down.

"You ate my dinner," said Seth.

"You left your dinner," I said. And we stared at each other across the table, warily, like two adventurers in a dark country who had come face-to-face in the shadows. We searched each other's faces for any clues as to our whereabouts.

ONCE I STARTED SLEEPING AT Elias's, I started journaling. I'd never kept a journal before, but it seemed to be a thing that creative and self-actualized people did, and these days, I felt like both. I woke up in the mornings and sat at the small wooden table in his kitchen, across which he'd arranged bleach-white seashells, and I wrote for twenty minutes without stopping. I always started with the date and the time, so that I knew exactly where I was, and then I tried to "walk inward from there," which was advice that I'd recently read in an article about people who journaled. My process of walking inward was describing how my body felt (shoulders tight, chest tight, face slightly congested), and then my heart (I used words like *big* and *spacious* and synonyms for *rebirth*), and then I talked a little bit about where Elias and I were in our relationship. We hadn't really discussed this in such terms, so I went off context clues, which I recorded in lists that I could consult later when I felt insecure.

Context clue one: we were spending most nights together. We hadn't discussed monogamy, but then: back to context clue one. And, if monogamy was implied, then other things must be implied as well, such as commitment and shared values and a shared future life. I imagined a life in which our practices were intertwined. His modern dance and my writing. I might become a writer. Context clue two: I was suddenly writing.

I imagined a life in which we lived together, maybe in Portland, and we'd wake up and he would stretch while I wrote, and later we would work in the garden and then cook together, and then take our two dogs for a walk. I imagined Elias's mother coming to visit, from Venezuela. She might be wary of me at first, and I would understand that—perhaps the only white people she knows have been her employers. But I would be so warm and so welcoming that eventually she really would feel that mi casa was su casa. And she would say to Elias, "What a woman you've found!" She would say, "She's like one of us."

The other thing I wrote about in the mornings was Seth. He hadn't officially moved out of our apartment, but he was spending most of his time sleeping with the Barnard student, which I thought was strange and a little unfortunate, to be Seth's age and sleeping over in a dorm. To me it smacked of a midlife crisis more than a love affair between equals and fellow artists. I didn't see Seth ending up in Portland. I saw him ending up in jail. It was helpful to work through these concerns in my journal, and I earmarked the passages that I thought might make their way into a first novel, someday.

When Elias came downstairs in his running shorts, groggy and focused on making coffee, I would ask him if he wanted me to read to him from my journal. But he usually just looked at me blearily, shook his hair out of his eyes, and said, "No thanks." And then he'd drink his coffee in a kind of elongated gulp and go out for a run, letting the screen door slam behind him. I always appreciated the importance he placed on individual privacy, on the value of an artist exploring her inner life in a safe and protected space, and I saw this as yet another way in which he anticipated needs that I hadn't even known I had. But all the same, I sometimes felt a twinge of desire to have my privacy intruded on. And I found this, too, indicative of something in myself that I had never fully explored, and so after

Elias left on his runs, I would end my writing practice for the day by journaling about this.

One morning, as Elias was out running and I was journaling, there was a knock at the door. I answered it, and found a girl standing there—tousled black hair, spandex, skin the color of olives. She had a mug of coffee in one hand, mail in the other. Her fingernails were gel-red and chipped. She must be an artist, maybe an Iranian poet. I was suddenly aware of the ratty bathrobe I was wearing, the same beige color as me.

"3B," she said, by way of introduction. "I think I've been getting your mail?" She thrust the mail at me, and then turned to go back up the stairs.

"Thanks," I said, and then felt the need to add, "this isn't my mail, this is for Elias."

3B turned around. "1B?" she asked, cautiously.

"Yeah, Elias lives in 1B. I'm his girlfriend, so. This mail is for him."

"Okay," said 3B. "Well." She turned to climb the stairs again. It occurred to me that she might be wondering why I was in a bathrobe, why I wasn't at work already, if Elias was dating some white trust-fund baby who didn't even *need* to work. I studied the lines of 3B's shoulders as she climbed the stairs, wondering if there was an angle of judgment in them.

"I'm a writer," I called after her.

"Huh?" She turned around on the top stair, her face scrunched into confusion.

"I said, I'm a writer. I write. In the mornings. From home?"

"Okay . . . ?"

We stared at each other. I guess she hadn't been wondering.

"Thanks," I said again. "I'll give these to my boyfriend when he gets home." I ducked back inside and closed the door. I said it again, quietly, to myself: "My boyfriend." It sounded a little juvenile. Like we were still in high school. "Mi novio," I said, choosing the Spanish, and that sounded much more sophisticated.

———

IT HADN'T BEEN MY INTENTION to read his mail, I need to say that right away. There were only three pieces, and I put them down on the counter by the orange bowl, but then I got worried that there might be something important that he wouldn't see. And it occurred to me that if there was something important, he might want me to tell him about it when he came back from his run. He might want me to say, "Elias, you have a summons for jury duty." Or if there was good news, maybe I would want to go out before he got back and get us coffee, pastries, something to celebrate. And then I could say, "Elias, there's good news!" and the pastries would be sitting spread out, flaky and buttery and sweet, on his little wood table between the bleached seashells and my journal.

The first envelope was a Time Warner bill, and the second was a tax form of some kind, and the third one was a postcard. I just flipped it over and there it was: all of this writing, spilling out, spidery and open and uncontained. In English, even. I read it without intending to read it. It was from someone named Cici, and she spoke to him the way one speaks to a recalcitrant child, so she must have been family of some kind. She told him to "call Mom," and she asked if he was looking for any kind of job, and she said that she and Frank were on a trip for Frank's job (hence the postcard), that they hoped he was "adjusting," although she didn't say to what. As soon as I read the postcard, I could see it so clearly: Cici, eldest sister, maternal stand-in. Mom is in America, cleaning people's houses. Cici is with the grandmother, wiping noses and making sandwiches. *Where's Mom?* young Elias asks, because he doesn't yet understand. Cici tells him to be strong. *Someday you'll understand*, she tells him. *Everything Mamá does, she does for us*. And later she will grow up, she will marry a man named Frank, which is a white name, which implies a level of privilege and education, both of which might feel comforting for Cici, but also ultimately alienating. Frank's childhood was middle-class, untroubled by issues of abandonment, his mother may have been over-involved (as was Seth's, and believe me, that creates issues of its own), but she was not in a foreign country mailing checks home. And so Frank does not understand why sometimes Cici stares out the window. Why sometimes her eyes are so sad, and why she writes postcards to her little brother, remonstrating him. "Leave that to your mother," says Frank. "Let the kid be a kid, he's only twenty-seven!" And Cici looks at Frank and loves him, but knows that he can never grasp the bond between her and Elias.

When Elias got home, I couldn't take my eyes off him. I watched him toe off his sneakers, ball up his socks, throw them at the laundry basket and miss, make and devour a peanut butter sandwich. I couldn't stop seeing him through the eyes of the devoted older sister who had to raise him. I wondered what he'd do, when he saw her handwriting. If a misty distance might come into his eyes. If, like Cici with Frank, he would imagine that I could never understand. *But I do*, I wanted to cry, *I do understand!*

Finally Elias asked, "What's up?" He meant: you're staring.

"You have some mail," I said, weirdly nervous. "Your neighbor upstairs dropped it off, I guess she's been getting it . . . ?"

Elias flipped through, put it back. He didn't bother to read the postcard, and his face didn't change. "Cool," he said. "I'm gonna shower."

"You got a postcard," I said, because I couldn't help myself. I wanted to say: *It's okay.* I wanted to say: *Tell me what it was like—the hard earth and the hot sun and all those baby goats, bleating and chewing.*

"Yeah," Elias said. "I know." He headed up the stairs.

"Do you want me to shower with you?" I asked, instead of all the things I wanted to say.

"It's okay," said Elias. "I'm gonna be quick." But maybe he wanted to put his face against the tile wall. Maybe he wanted, under the self-erasing rush of hot water, to remember the small boy he once was. To mourn that boy, and his lost mother.

I almost said, "You can tell me, I already know." But the bathroom door closed and the sound of the shower drowned me out.

———

I DECIDED TO WRITE ABOUT Elias. They say "write what you know," and two weeks into my new life with Elias, the knowledge that I had of him was one of detectives and conjurers, archaeologists and poets. It began as a story, my first stab at short fiction. But I also thought of it as a love letter to him, to the time and place of his lost childhood, and also to my new life, and also to the beginning of our shared artistic practices.

At first I wrote it in my voice, but then I found myself slipping into his. *The ground is baked hard underneath my feet, my sister watches me from the window of grandmother's shack.* I found myself knowing things I didn't know I knew. I'd never touched a goat, but the me-that-is-Elias, the Elias-that-is-me, we described in the first person the coarseness of goat hair under our boy-fingers, how we hugged the goat to our chest when we realized that our mother was truly gone. *America,* we whispered into the goat's curved ear, and it twitched under our breath. *America.*

I asked Elias, one night in bed, if he believed in telepathy. He looked at me, one of his long unblinking looks. I began to wonder if he was communicating something to me telepathically—*Yes I do,* perhaps—but then he said, "Like, seeing the future?"

"No, like people sharing thoughts. Speaking to each other in their thoughts."

Elias considered this. Then: "No," he said, and pulled his shirt off. He reached for me. Normally I waited for this moment, the moment where his heavily muscled brown arm encircled me, yanked me close. (Seth never yanked. Sometimes he apologized.) But this time, I asked, "You don't think that two people can share things sort of . . . beyond language? Without language?"

"Yeah," Elias said, already hard against my hip. "Fucking."

I laughed. The word always sent a jolt up my spine when he said it. Seth had never used the word for what it was, for what Elias had shown me it could be: a description, an invitation.

"No," I said, "like, for example, do you think it's possible that I could know things—about you—that maybe you didn't tell me? But like . . . you maybe *did* tell me, in your mind?"

"Things about me?" Elias's mouth was on my ribs working upward.

"Your childhood, for example." I was going to say more, but Elias's mouth covered mine. So he never said if he thought it was possible. So maybe he still did.

SETH AND I MET AT Il Buco for a Divorce Dinner. We hadn't had one in a little while, and he looked good when he walked in—in a pale blue button-down, dark jeans that must have been new, Fluevogs that were definitely new. I was wearing distressed jeans (Rag & Bone, new) and a low-cut black T-shirt (Anthropologie, new), and I'd gotten three inches cut off my hair (Alibi, SoHo). I'd hoped to get a tattoo sleeve before the Divorce Dinner, but according to Elias the only good tattoo artists live in Brooklyn, and so far it seemed that tattoo artists in Brooklyn all have waiting lists.

"You look good," Seth said, appreciatively.

"Thanks," I said, casually. I positioned my face when we cheek-kissed so that he could see how prominent my cheekbones were, now that the hair was off my face. ("Your cheekbones will be so prominent, once we get this hair off your face," said the lady at Alibi.)

We sat down. The server tried to put us at a table in the center. "We'll have the one by the window," I said, warmly but confidently. She led us to the window instead.

"I love people-watching," I said. "Sometimes I sketch them." I don't know where this came from.

"You draw now?" Seth asked. He sounded impressed and like he didn't want to sound impressed.

"As a hobby," I said, coolly. "Anyway, how are you?"

Seth told me that he was really good, that he'd started jogging. That he felt really relaxed and refreshed, that he'd started meditating—"just sort of casually, no big deal." That he went to a lecture on Judith Butler the other evening, with Barnard, and they had a great discussion about gender parity and queerness in the Lyft back to her building on the Upper West.

"I thought she lived in a dorm," I couldn't help but say.

"Oh," Seth said, "no. No no." And then he put the nail in the coffin: "The dorms are essentially a paternalistic metaphor. As a queer woman, she couldn't live in the dorms."

As Barnard's level of sophistication soared past mine, I heard myself asking faintly, "Oh . . . she's queer?"

"On the spectrum, yeah," Seth said, and then ordered a martini, stirred not shaken, hold the vermouth, up with a twist.

I ordered a Bulleit, neat. Seth lifted an eyebrow. "Elias got me into it," I said, with a self-deprecating chuckle. "Declassé, I know, but some nights, we just drink Jameson."

"Jameson," Seth repeated, the other eyebrow lifting.

"Elias grew up on the streets," I said. "A rough neighborhood in Venezuela. He doesn't have much use for"—I indicated our surroundings, Seth himself, with a wave of a languid hand—"all of *this*."

We eyed each other. A childhood on the streets versus eating some pussy. Who won? We were unclear.

"I'd love the Seared Spanish Octopus," Seth said to the waitress, when she came by.

"I was going to order the same thing," I admitted.

Seth grinned at me. I noticed all over again how blue his eyes can be. "So, do."

"I'll have the Seared Spanish Octopus too," I said to the waitress, and Seth and I smiled at each other, like we were in on a joke that only the two of us could share.

ELIAS OCCASIONALLY WANTED NIGHTS ALONE—"some space," he would say—and I didn't mind giving him his space. In fact, as I sat typing in my apartment, it felt like Elias was right there beside me. Only this Elias was a younger one, more communicative, more vulnerable, more pliable. This Elias had just arrived in Los Angeles, where his mother (I called her "Mamá" since I didn't know her name) was working three jobs. This Elias marveled at the urban jungle sprawling before him, not yet knowing that someday, say fifteen years in his future, he would live in Brooklyn and travel everywhere by bike, and meet a sophisticated older woman whose life he would transform.

Those were good nights, the writing nights. I knew that in his apartment in Brooklyn Elias must be stretching, coming up with new gestures, maybe thinking of me. Maybe coming up with a gesture somehow intended *for* me, for my specific viewing experience. Maybe lying down to sleep alone on the large futon that held my scent now too, maybe putting his face against the pillow I had come to think of as my pillow. I liked to think of all the other great artist couples who had fed each other's work with their passion. Frida and Diego. Ted and Sylvia. Marina and Ulay. Cynthia and Elias.

It was getting harder and harder not to tell Elias about what I was writing, but I wanted to be able to say, "Look what I did for you," and hand him the finished thing. A novella—published, bound, with an inscription in the front. Maybe it would say: *To Elias, whose story is all of our stories.* Or: *For Elias, my inspiration, who exemplifies the American dream.* Or: *For Elias, who is my American dream.* I liked this last one the most, because it was romantic and also political. It was the image of handing Elias a finished object that was romantic *and* political, that kept me from blurting it all out. But sometimes in his bed I'd smile to myself, in a beautiful and mysterious way, in case Elias asked, "What?" Elias never asked "What?" but it didn't matter. I understood his relationship to privacy, to secrecy, to a difficult past. I understood why he didn't ask.

And then one morning, I was writing while Elias was out on his jog, and my phone rang. Seth. This was unexpected enough to be alarming—we were four days out from our last Divorce Dinner, and already had reservations at Eleven Madison Park for next Tuesday. So I picked up the phone, stepping outside into the little garden behind the house so that if Seth asked where I was, I could say, "Oh I'm just in Elias's garden, having a coffee in my bathrobe. The hours one keeps with an artist!"

Seth didn't ask me where I was, though. He didn't ask how I was, either. He sounded very dejected and sad, and he asked me if I knew what *mansplaining* was.

"What *what* is?"

"Mansplaining," Seth said. "Have you ever . . . like *ever* heard that term?"

"No," I said, "what's it mean?" And Seth told me that he'd just had a fight with Barnard, in which she had accused him of mansplaining everything to her all the time.

"She said that I was mansplaining feminism," Seth told me. He sounded like a kicked dog. "And she said that I had mansplained her period to her. And I told her that I don't know what mansplaining is, but a conversation is when two people exchange information about a thing, and those two people don't always have the same *amounts* of information, and then she said that I was mansplaining conversations to her and then she asked me to leave."

"Oh wow," I said. I felt an unexpected pang of empathy for Seth. "And then what happened?"

"And then she told me that I have hairy wrists," Seth followed up, glumly.

"You do, sort of," I said.

Seth was startled into laughing. "Cynthia!"

"I mean you do. They're hairy. That's okay."

"Stop mansplaining my wrists to me," Seth muttered, but he sounded better.

"Where are you right now?" I asked.

"Just got off the subway, I'm right by our—your—place." Seth hesitated, and then: "I was thinking I might go there? Are you there?"

"No," I said, and surprised myself by not mentioning the garden and the bathrobe and the hours that Brooklyn artists keep. "I'm out right now, but you can go there. You still have the keys, yeah?"

"Yeah," Seth said, and he didn't even try to keep the relief out of his voice. "I have the keys." A beat, then: "Thanks, Cyn."

"No problem," I said. We both waited a beat, and then hung up at the same time. That beat was the place where we used to say "I love you."

I WENT BACK INTO THE kitchen, gathering Elias's bathrobe tighter. I'd write another chapter, wait for Elias to get back and shower, maybe shower with him. If he was going to Judson Church to practice gestures, I might go back to the Upper West. See if Seth was okay. See if he wanted to get some lunch.

"Cynthia." Elias's voice jolted me out of my thoughts. "What is this?"

Startled, I looked up. Elias was standing in the kitchen, sweat-damp, hair in his face, running shoes still on. My laptop open. Oh. My laptop.

"What the hell *is* this?"

"Oh," I said. Time slowed down and also time speeded up. I had thought of this moment in so many ways, and this was not a way I had thought of it. Language deserted me.

"Are you *writing* about me?"

I couldn't tell if Elias was mad, or glad, or if he was about to laugh, or if he was shocked. All I could tell is that he was very much feeling something, but that something was as unreadable to me as always.

"Yes," I said, searching for and finding the simplicity of truth. "It's for you. And it's about you! And it's for me but it's also for you."

"Cynthia," Elias started to say, but now the words were pouring out of me.

"I know that you've had it rough, you never talk about it, but—and I wanted to acknowledge that, to make it beautiful somehow, to sort of—I mean I can't know what Venezuela is like, but also there's a poetic truth to Venezuela that maybe I *do* know because I saw it in you. You changed my life, Elias, and I'm writing a story, a novella, but also it's a love letter, about you and to you and so that America can understand how so many people like you got here and made us a stronger, braver, more beautiful place to be."

I stopped, out of breath. There was so much more I wanted to say, but I couldn't remember what it was. Into the silence, Elias said, almost gently, "This is crazy."

"I know it might seem a little—"

"Cynthia. I'm not from Venezuela."

I blinked at him. "What?"

"I'm Jewish. I was born in Queens. I studied abroad in Venezuela for a *semester*. I don't speak Spanish."

I thought he was joking. "Elias, come on."

"No *you* come on. 'Elias'—what the fuck kind of Venezuelan name is that?" Now his voice had raised a little, he was on the balls of his toes as if sheer outrage had lifted him by the scruff. "I mean did you ever *ask* where I was from? Did you ever *ask* anything about me? I woulda fuckin' told you I was Jewish. I mean where's my *accent*? Where's my fuckin' Venezuelan *accent*? You know?"

I could barely put words together. "But you said—you said—"

"For a *semester*, my God! I drank a lot, I smoked some weed, I didn't . . . a baby *goat*, my *God*."

I looked at Elias. I saw a new man standing before me. Curly hair. Stocky build. Young Elias goes to synagogue with his father. Young Elias takes the subway. Oh Jesus. Young Elias, if he has an accent at all, has the broad smack of Queens in his voice.

"And all that shit about my sister, about my mother? What the fuck! My mom is a dentist, she never—like, where did you *get* this shit?"

The baby goat died. The Venezuelan sun sputtered out. Cici was hit by a meteorite, as was Frank. The soft sadness in Elias's liquid, lyrical eyes . . . was a mixture of outrage, laughter, and resentment.

"I'm sorry," I said, because there wasn't much else to say.

"What the fuck," Elias muttered softly. We stared at each other. Then: "You didn't ask," he said, an accusation, "you didn't *ask*."

"You don't talk," I heard myself saying. I hadn't known I felt this way until I was saying it. "You just run and sweat and make gestures and run errands and ignore me, unless we're fucking you ignore me. I didn't *ask* because I didn't think you'd *tell* me."

"What am I supposed to tell you!" Elias was on the balls of his toes again. "It's not like we're *dating*, it's not like we're like . . ."

"We're *not?*" Now my voice was spiking. This note of outrage was so pure and true that it struck Elias out of his own indignation and into silence. He stared at me wide-eyed.

"Cynthia . . . I thought you *also* . . . I thought . . ."

"What are we doing if we aren't dating?"

"Hanging out," Elias said, with the game lameness that only a twenty-seven-year-old boy can muster. "You know. Chillin'."

"Fuck you," I said. I grabbed my laptop, threw it into my bag, grabbed my coat, shoved my feet into my shoes. Razor and toothbrush in the upstairs bathroom, goodbye. I will not go up those stairs for you.

"Cynthia," Elias said, "wait." But—panties in Elias's laundry, goodbye. You were a good pair, and a new pair, but I am not digging through this boy's laundry for you. I will not wait.

"Cynthia!"

"We were *dating*," I said, with cold and forceful outrage. "You stupid, conceited *child*." I walked past him, out the door. Right before the door slammed, Elias grabbed it, shoved his head out, and shouted after me: "Chinga tu fuckin' madre, in *Venezuelan!*"

I guessed, as I marched toward the subway, that he'd picked up some Spanish on study abroad after all.

Seth was on the couch when I came in. He'd made himself an open-faced smoked herring sandwich, with a small tossed salad of baby kale, capers, and a lemon-mustard dressing. He had his feet up and was watching Jon Stewart, but he paused it when I came in.

"You're back," he said, and watched me.

"Hi," I said.

"I hope it's okay that I'm still here."

"Yeah," I said, kicking my shoes off. "It's okay."

"You want a sandwich?"

I looked at his, and was reminded that I hadn't eaten. At the same time, my stomach felt odd and upset. The way Elias had looked at me, the way he'd talked to me . . . the disdain in his voice. *You didn't ask.*

Seth's voice cut in, easy and gentle. "Or you just want some of mine?"

"I want some of yours."

I sat on the couch next to Seth. He smelled like Tom Ford and laundry soap. He smelled like herrings and capers. He smelled like Seth. He held up the sandwich and I took a bite.

"You okay?" he asked.

"Shouldn't that be my question for you?"

Seth shrugged. "It's nice being on our couch." Then: "You look . . . I don't know."

"Elias accused me of . . . well. A lot of things."

"Mansplaining?"

"Worse than that. Being wrong. And being . . . um. Impervious. I think. To his actual details."

"Im*per*vious to his *de*tails," Seth said, drawing the words out. "Well, what makes his details so goddamn important?"

I had to laugh. "Yeah," I said. "What *does* make his details so goddamn important?" And then suddenly I was really laughing, and I couldn't stop. The goat and the laundry line and the sad sister, that sad fucking sister. Versus, what, Queens and a synagogue and his mother extracting teeth, and maybe a brother, two brothers, however many brothers. Just details. That's all. What made anybody's details so important?

"Hey there," Seth said. He looked a little worried. "Take a breath. Take a bite. Okay? Relax." I took a breath and then another. I managed to stop laughing. "There," said Seth. "That's better."

"It's nice," I said, "being on our couch."

I took another bite of his sandwich.

I was suddenly starving. I was going to eat the whole thing.

THE SAFEST PLACE IN THE WORLD

Risa says, "I've *got* this." She says, "Nothing will happen." She says, "Japan is the safest country in the world so I don't know what you're so worried about."

This is after Shinichi has offered to buy her an apartment, but I don't know it yet.

This is after Shinichi explains to her: "If I buy you an apartment, I could visit you there. It would be our secret, just the two of us."

This is after Risa meets Shinichi's son on her way out of Shinichi's penthouse, and he asks his father, "Who is this?" and Shinichi says in front of her, right in front of her, "No one."

This is right before Risa asks me, "Do you know this yakuza? What they are?" And I search my mind but it's just another foreign word in a sea of foreign words, and later I will wish that of all the words I'd known this one, so that I could say, *Beware.*

But no.

Right now it is night and we're alone together on my futon, naked. Risa is propped up on her elbow, laughing, playing with my short hair, rubbing her fingers through it like you would with a dog. I'm telling her that I don't like it when she leaves the factory by herself, when she walks alone in the dark. I'm telling her that anything could happen to her, and what would she do? Who would know?

The light is soft on her collarbones, on the long easy lines of her wrist and arm, the slats of her ribs when she leans up to turn off the light. These days, I'm always staring at her. She says, "Well, *you* would know." She says, "Nothing happens here, it's too safe." She says, "Yuliya, you're *staring*," and I am, I am, I've never seen anything so beautiful. Something so beautiful might cross your path every two million years, and if it does, you'd be a fool to shut your eyes for even a second.

RISA—HER SMALL ANIMAL EARS CLOSE to her head, her sharp little lynx-teeth, the ferret-jut of her cheekbones. Whenever I remember her, she's caught in a moment of impatience. When you move so quickly, you get tired of waiting for the rest of the world to catch up.

On the days when her shift ends before mine, she leaves the factory, comes back to the gaijin boardinghouse, takes out her thin metal hair-clip, picks our lock and infiltrates our tiny apartment like a criminal. She doesn't carry keys, even though she has one just like I do. She says we should leave the door unlocked—"This is Japan," she says, "who's going to break in?" When I get back from my shift, I'll find Risa sprawled on my futon in front of the tiny whirring fan, with her shirt unbuttoned and her skin glistening with sweat. She makes fun of me, with my key safety-pinned inside my pocket, the way I walk—shoulders bent and head always down. "Relax!" she tells me, impatient. "There's no danger in Japan."

Risa. Eighteen and fierce and feral and she smells like strong Colombian tobacco, sometimes like hashish even when she denies smoking with the Turks downstairs. She was the first tenant in this small factory-owned room, arriving only a few days before me. How quickly she went from stranger to roommate to provocation to my obsession. I dream about her at angles, always turning corners away from me. In my dreams, I catch the exposed flash of sunlight on her skin—the back of her neck, the swerve of her inner arm, the curve of a breast. She knows I dream about her and she laughs at me with her crooked mouth and her bright eyes. "What's the big deal?" she says in English, bad-ass like an American rock star or cowboy in those stupid movies she's addicted to. "¿Qué tienes, mujer?"

The big deal is that I'm twenty-six. The big deal is that I'm a coward. The big deal is that I've never seen anything like her, and I never will again.

"No soy Lolita," says Risa, unconcerned. "And you—no eres hombre."

"Is it only a crime if it's a man?" I ask.

"It's only a crime if I don't want it," Risa says, and grins.

And Japan is good to her. This country is an assortment of surprises, strangenesses that catch her attention and her awe. One night she comes in from the street, breathless with excitement, her hands sharp with the scent of gunpowder. "Pero no tienen pistolas aquí," she says wide-eyed. "Sólo cohetes." But they don't have guns here, only fireworks. Japan has many gifts for Risa, but Japan's gift to me *is* Risa. And that's more than I could have thought to ask for.

RISA IS OBSESSED WITH HOW we *got* here. All of us gaijin, as they call us.

"How did you *get* here?" she'll ask in her imperfect gangster English. Complete strangers. She'll walk up to them in the street: "¿Cómo viniste aquí, vos?" And they'll tell her, just like that, like it's nothing.

She asks us both her favorite question one night: "How did we *get* here?" This is the beginning of August, she is sitting at the end of my futon, which has been for months now our futon, and I'm sitting next to her. We pass a lighted joint back and forth, Risa got it for free from Shinichi, but I don't know that yet. And she asks it again, just like that but a little different this time: "How did *we* get here?" with unsimulated awe. A country of fireworks and not handguns, it never fails to inspire awe.

I exhale thick sweet smoke and say: "On a plane. You from Me-dellín. Me from Saint Petersburg. And we'll work in this shithole until we have some money, and when we die here, more people like us will come here on planes like the one we took and they'll take our jobs and work like we worked and die like we'll die and that, lyubov, my love, mi amor, that is how we all Get Here."

Risa says I'm a fucking liar and takes the joint back. She says: "We got here because we're all on our way to something better and this is the way you take to get there."

"Yeah?" I say. "Then how come everybody hates us and the food is strange and there's nowhere to work but factories."

And Risa says: "If you left the house more you'd see it's not all like that."

"I leave the house to work," I say, and press my lips together in my mother's firm line.

Risa knows not to push it. She has a loud bossy mouth, but there are certain things she knows not to push. And at night sometimes when I have the old dreams and I wake up shaking in a cold sweat, she knows not to ask. She gets me a glass of water, sits there while I finish it. When we shower together, she doesn't touch the white lines of old scars on my skin. She doesn't touch me unless she knows I've seen her—she says my name before she shakes me awake in the mornings. "Yuliya," she says, "daijoubu, daijoubu, it's okay." As if it's normal, Japanese in her mouth.

This is how I keep track of the days we've been here: as the count rises, so do the number of Japanese words in Risa's mouth. I don't know where she learns all of them. The factory, she says. The street. Later she will say, "From Shinichi," and I will say, "Who?" and she'll say, "This guy, I'll introduce you sometime."

By the time she does, I will have learned to hate him. The weight of his name in her mouth is too heavy, too big, it leaves no space for mine.

———

THE TRUTH ABOUT ME, AT this time, is how frightened I am by everything. Risa most of all, of course, but not only.

When my shift is over, I come scurrying home, hide myself away until it's time for work again. Risa makes friends with a group of Nigerian guys who sell hats by the train station. She likes to tell me about them—she says they love Japanese baseball, they make her laugh, she wants me to meet them. I say I will, but we both know I won't. The country is too alien for me to make friends, its angles are off, I feel dizzy all the time. It's easier to stay inside.

"You're my friend," I say, and Risa scowls but she's pleased too.

"Until I get tired of you," she says. But she won't. After all, she chose me. I've seen her with coins and jewels and broken bits of things from the gutter. Doesn't matter what it is—she keeps the things she finds.

IN THE FIRST DAYS OF September, Risa turns nineteen. I ask her what she wants to do, and she says: "I want to go into Tokyo. We work and work and we never get to see Tokyo."

The idea terrifies me, it dries the spit in my mouth. "We don't have any money," I say, trying for nonchalance—and that's when she brings out a crisp roll of bills, one man, two man, three man, she counts to six man and stops but there's still more, smaller bills. "Shinichi said we should amuse ourselves," she says.

My hatred would burn whole forests to the ground.

"Then tell me what you want to do," I say, and smile. It's a terrible smile, paper plastered over a gaping hole, but Risa is counting the money again and she doesn't notice.

So: Tokyo.

It's a neon chasm. Loud and fast and clean, the cleanness of it scares me more than anything. No city should be so clean. A city without trash is a city of the dead, a city of bodies that take in nothing and generate no waste. We pass pachinko parlors and when the doors open, in a rush of air conditioning and inhuman noise, I think I've discovered hell. Risa, on the other hand, has never been more excited.

I wouldn't know how to go about spending six man in one day, more than my share of the month's rent, but Risa doesn't seem to have any difficulties. We go to Shibuya and walk through streets lined with shops, and she buys herself clothes, outrageous expensive scraps of clothing. She wants to buy me clothes but I say no. I say it's a waste. The truth is, I don't want to wear Shinichi's money next to my skin.

She lets me say no at first to baseball caps, scarves, wristbands. But then she gets tougher. "Shut the fuck up," she says, pulling jeans off a shelf and a green shirt. "Come on," and she shoves them at me. "Go put these on."

"Risa, stop." I'm embarrassed, people are watching.

"Just put these on," Risa insists. "They'll look good."

"Come on," I say, trying to push her hands away. "I don't need clothes."

"Then what do you need," Risa demands. She's angry, but more than that, she's hurt, and both of these things confuse me. "Tell me what the fuck do you need, porque yo no sé, you won't let me give you anything."

I stare at her, slack-jawed. The Japanese are all watching from the corners of the shop, but I can't take my eyes off her. I suddenly don't understand what is happening.

"I didn't know you wanted to give me anything," I say, stupidly. "Why do you want to give me things?"

Risa blinks at me and then she shakes her head. "Oh for God's sake," she says, "you're worse than a man." She turns away, then turns back: "You think I don't have anywhere else to sleep? You think that?"

"No—"

"Because I have a lot of other places I could sleep."

"I know you do, I'm sure you do."

"And I could get my own place," she says. "I could just move if I wanted to, there's places that are a lot nicer than where they put us."

"I know that," I repeat helplessly.

"No you don't know that because you've never seen anything, you've never gotten on the fucking train and gone anywhere, you just go to the factory and go home. This is the first time you've gotten on a train since you got here, do you know that? And I had to beg."

I'm just staring at her. "Risa," I say, "I don't understand what you want from me."

Risa takes a deep breath and turns away. Then she turns back to me. "Put on the jeans," she says. "Go into that little changing room and put them on. That's what I want."

So I do. It's simpler than standing there and looking at her and not knowing what to do or say, wanting so badly to do something right.

Alone in the confines of the small dressing room I lean my forehead against the mirror for a moment. I look for words but find only images: Risa curled on my futon, asleep; Risa hands on hips, annoyed; Risa walking through the Tokyo streets like a kid at Christmas. I pull on the jeans, turn in a circle before the mirror. I've lost weight. They're a little loose, but they look good.

"Are you ever coming out of there?" Risa's voice, close and impatient on the other side of the changing-room door. Before I can answer, she opens the door and slips in. She's already laughing.

"You're not supposed to be in here," I start to say, but I don't finish the sentence because Risa leans forward and kisses me. It's the first time we've ever kissed in public—or, if this isn't public, then in a place that is not our apartment. She pushes me back against the changing-room wall, so I kiss her harder. It's like a switch being thrown in my brain, and I can't think, I can't stop, and when she breaks away, she says, "I'm buying them for you," as if she's continuing a conversation we're still having.

"What?"

"The jeans, the jeans. And you won't argue with me. And then we're going to lunch and you're not going to complain about money, we're just going to eat what we want. Like rich Japanese girls."

I blink at her, lick my lips, taste the slickness of lip gloss that isn't mine. Risa stares back at me, arms folded, waiting for argument. I don't have the energy anymore. All I can think about is that suddenly this thing between us has weight and shape and substance. It has existed outside of our apartment, it has existed in a world that other people exist in too, and that makes it real and live.

"The money," I say weakly. "Risa, the money, though."

Risa reaches up quickly, fingertips brushing my lips. "Shinichi wanted us to spend it," she says, "today. For my birthday. If I ask for more, he'll give me more. It's okay."

And that makes my stomach twist because it's worse than I thought. I know girls who said that, back home, girls who asked for more and got more and eventually the men got tired of them, got tired of More.

"Risa," I say again. "Please, be careful—"

"I'm fine," she says automatically.

"But something could happen." And I don't plan to say it but then I hear myself suddenly: "Don't sleep with him, are you sleeping with him? Don't sleep with him."

Risa stares at me, and then she laughs. She steps forward fast, winds her arms around my neck so that she's pressed up against me and I'm pressed into the wall again. We stand there like that, so strange and good, the weight and shape of her. If I can hold on to her like this, everything else will recede, Japan won't touch her and Shinichi won't touch her, and Colombia, not even Colombia will touch her. Just me. Only me.

"It doesn't matter," Risa says against my neck. "He likes to give me things and I like to take them. It has nothing to do with us."

————

WHEN AT LAST I MEET Shinichi, I'm not prepared for how polite he is, or how much of the oxygen in the room he absorbs, so that there isn't enough for other people. I'm not prepared for the niceness of his black suit, for the way he walks into the expensive café—where Risa has convinced me to join her—or for the men who accompany him. Some of them stand in the doorway, some of them walk behind him, well dressed and watchful, some are men and some are still boys. One of them is a very small man, the size of an eight-year-old, and I catch the glimpse of tattoos running from the insides of his wrists up under the sleeves of his sharp suit. I turn to Risa as a thin thread spins itself tight in my chest—"Who *are* they?" I whisper, and she says, like it's normal, "It's okay, Yuliya, they just work for him." She nods toward the small man: "That one is Yuki-chan, he's nice." I look at Yuki-chan. He looks back at me, face impassive, and something prickles in my gut.

Of the things I am not prepared for, the most nauseating is the way Shinichi sits down beside Risa as if he has a right to be there. He orders her a drink, without asking what she wants, and orders me one as well. He reaches out, adjusts the fall of her hair into her eyes, adjusts the necklace she's wearing.

"I like this one," he says, in Japanese, and she says, "I know."

The rest of the conversation is over my head. I know only the most basic words at this point, and so I sit there shell-shocked. He doesn't acknowledge me for a few minutes; he just sits and drinks Risa in with his eyes, and she laughs and chatters away in a stream of broken Japanese that I didn't know she could command. And then, without warning, he turns toward me and smiles. It astonishes me briefly—the warmth of that smile, the confidence, the power. He says something to me, and Risa nudges me, so I say, in my terrible Japanese, "Hajimemashite." *Nice to meet you.* He laughs, says something to Risa, who is also grinning behind her hand. I hate her, very briefly, for laughing at me with him.

But then he leans over and kisses me first on one cheek and then the other, awkwardly but with determination. It is the first time I have ever been touched by a Japanese person. I'm stunned into paralysis.

"Gaijin no aisatsu, deshou?" he says to me, and I recognize the words *foreigner* and *greeting*. Risa is laughing openly now. I'm still shocked—by his sudden closeness, by the heat of his body—but I nod. He nods back, looking at me closely. And then he smiles and motions to one of his boys who comes over immediately. Shinichi gestures to me, and the boy bows. I nod back. The boy asks me something in Japanese that I don't understand, and when I look to Risa, nervous, Shinichi leans forward across the table.

"Desaato," he says, gesturing to the Western-style pastries under glass. "Amaimono kirai no?"

"He wants to know if you like sweet things," Risa translates.

"Risa," I say, and the tight feeling in my ribs is back. "Can we leave soon?"

Risa sighs. "Be nice," she says. "He just wants to talk to you."

"It isn't me he wants to talk to," I say.

"Be nice," Risa says again, "we're just having coffee."

Shinichi is looking back and forth between us now. He asks Risa if everything is all right, and I don't have to speak Japanese to understand that. She smiles and nods, everything is fine, Yuliya is shy. She says something to the boy, flashes her smile, and the boy goes to the glass case and returns with a plate of pastries. He places them on the table, withdraws immediately with a bow. Shinichi's got these kids on a leash, I think, they're scared of him and they're hungry for what he has, and I don't even have to know the word *yakuza* to know about that. My country has them too, powerful men attended by scared and ambitious boys. I've seen this a hundred times, it's too old and too clear to need translation.

The rest of the meeting is a blur. I don't know what's being said, but I understand better than Risa what isn't. I watch Shinichi surround her with his glances, his nods, his constant attentive service, and I watch Risa love it. Not him—I'm jealous but I'm not stupid— it's the power, of course, what nineteen-year-old doesn't love power like that. At the end, Shinichi stands up. His men all straighten. He holds out a hand, Risa takes it and stands as well. He says something, and while his boys go pay the bill, he leads Risa out toward the street. Yuki-chan precedes Shinichi by a few paces, eyes scanning the street as we step out into it. A black limousine pulls up in front of us, and Yuki-chan leans in the window, says a few words to the driver.

"Risa," I say, a warning, but she shakes her head.

"He's just going to give us a ride, it's okay."

"A ride where," I say, and she glances at me over the thin pretty curve of her shoulder, Shinichi already opening the door for her, and she says soothingly: "Home, Yuliya." And there's a promise in her smile, even as she flicks her eyes away from me and back toward Shinichi.

I get in the limousine, and watch the world slide by removed and tinted. Nobody in the outside world can look through the smoke-colored glass and see me. And right then, in that exact moment—and only for that moment—I understand what it would be like to want this and have this, and why Risa will never say no.

I DON'T WANT HER TO see him and so she compromises by not telling me when she does. She doesn't talk about him at all. She pays for things with money that she swears is from the factory. But I know that she's lying. She has so much of it, and she's sending more and more home every day. And then come the days when she says that she worked an extra shift at the factory, stayed late, slept while I was at work, that she's sick, that she's busy. We're not sleeping together anymore. She's hardly ever home when I am, and the futon is empty without her. I try to sleep in the furrow that her body has left. Her smell on the pillow is the thing that lets me know she was there at all, and then, eventually, it fades. I know that she has stopped sleeping at our apartment long before I know that she has, in fact, quit the factory job.

She doesn't tell me. Perhaps she wouldn't ever have told me, would have kept up the lie forever, but one of the other women, from Cape Verde, tells me. She says, "Your Colombian friend is lucky, hey," and I say, "Lucky, what do you mean lucky?" and she says, "If I found a rich Japanese, I wouldn't be working here either." It's only when I confront Risa, that she confirms what I had guessed: Shinichi has bought her an apartment, and he visits her there, and when she is not with me and our cockroaches and our thin walls—which is always, now—that is where she is. I'm ashamed to admit that I shout, I cry. She stays calm, and a little impatient. I try to kiss her. She doesn't stop me, which is sadder than if she had pushed me away. I want her to get angry, I want her to remember that fighting for someone is loving them, that I am still fighting for her. Instead, she tells me that I don't even need another roommate, that she'll still pay for the room.

"It'll be better for you," she says. "You'll see."

"I'll still see you," she says. "Things will be like they were."

She says, "Please stop crying, I'm just a few stops away."

But she's farther than that. And we both know it.

We have one last direct conversation about Shinichi, before a great silence falls between us. It is in Risa's new apartment, in a neighborhood where neither of us would—before Shinichi—have dreamed of living. I've come over, and she's cooked for me. The wary politeness between us is new. So too is all the space. My body is used to pressing up against hers, I'm used to putting my face against the side of her neck and breathing her in. But now we sit politely on opposite chairs, while I fill her in on the gossip from the factory. It's all an old story of too many hungry people shoved into the same small space in a country that isn't theirs. Risa listens to who got knocked up, who drank too much and beat his wife, who got beat up but said she fell—and then Risa says: "You're better than that. You shouldn't be there."

I feel it like a slap, but when I reply, my voice is quiet. "Where should I be, then? Here, like you?"

But Risa isn't trying to fight. "Yes," she says softly. "Why not? You're smart, you're pretty, Shinichi has friends—"

"I didn't leave a ruthless man to come to a new country and find more ruthless men," I say. The words fall into the air with surprising weight because, except for the nightmares, I've never made reference to what happened before this.

"Japanese men like Shinichi, they aren't like that," Risa says, still soft. "They're not running around trash heaps with guns and drugs like dirty little boys. They dress well, they're educated, they're—"

"They're doing the same fucking things," I say without heat. Japan is making me cold, I argue coldly, I grieve coldly now. "It doesn't matter if they're Colombian narcos playing war or Japanese yakuza in Armani. They're the same fucking men. They look at you and they all see the same thing."

"And what's that?" Risa asks.

"Just a body," I say. "Among other bodies."

"But that's what I see when I look at them," Risa shrugs. "I'm not going to fall in love with him." And then her face softens and she says, low, "It's still going to be you." That hurts more than any of the fights we've had. I take a deep breath to keep the cold there in my chest. I can function as long as I can stay cold. But Risa is still talking.

"He loves me," she says with certainty. "He would never hurt me. He's like a kid with me, he just wants to see me happy. And his friends, Yuliya—"

I cut her off, and my voice is so steady, I barely recognize it. "Men like this—they don't like to lose. Even things they stop wanting, they don't like to lose them. If you ever wanted to leave—there would come a point where you couldn't do it. Maybe you've already passed that point, I don't know. You've seen me." I gesture to my body, scars under clothing, and Risa flinches but doesn't look away. "I did what you're doing," I say quietly. "The game you're playing, it could go even worse for you, and nobody here to help you."

Risa and I are both silent for a long time. It's raining outside, and cars hiss by. A train, far away, and I think again of our little apartment, now mine, at the end of the JR line. Far from here, dirtier than here. At last Risa says, "I have you, right?" But it's a question.

"What?"

"You said nobody here to help me but I have you. Don't I?"

I lock my jaw against everything I want to say. *Come home with me, let's get out of here, fuck this country and fuck yours and fuck mine, let's go somewhere else together, you and me, now, now, now.*

"Yeah," I say. "You have me."

AND THE DAYS PASS INTO weeks, and weeks into months, it is November, and then December, the bright colors of the fall leaves have faded into winter drab, and then it is January and the new year. I see Risa two times a week, and then once a week, and then weeks pass in which I don't see her at all. I sleep alone. The walls are thin and uninsulated. I lie in bed holding myself, and pretend that the only thing keeping me awake is the cold.

Risa tells me in the second week of February that she's going back to Colombia for five or six days to visit. She says she misses her mother. I'm glad that she's going back—the more distance between her and her new life, the better. I go over to her apartment the evening before she leaves; Shinichi is coming over later, and so I come early. We don't talk about this, but Risa and I are careful now to make sure that Shinichi and I don't cross paths. We sit and drink tea, and I can't help but note the elegant teacups, the expensive tea.

She talks about Colombia, her little town, her mother and her two younger sisters. She asks me how my mother is doing and I say that she's well—I got a letter from her a few weeks ago, the rent is paid, there's food on the table, can I send more money. I don't remember what else we talked about. I wish I did. When it gets close to eight, Risa glances at the clock, and I know that Shinichi will be coming soon. So I tell her that I have to get home, I have an early shift tomorrow, and she seems both saddened and relieved. She walks me to the door and leans into it smiling at me.

"I'm glad you came over to say goodbye," she says, light.

"Of course," I say. "You'll be back in a week, right?"

"Right," Risa says, "in about a week."

"Well . . . let me know when you're back, okay?"

"Okay," Risa echoes, and then she steps forward into the hall and wraps her arms around me in an embrace so tight, so impulsive, that I'm overwhelmed by the memory of the two of us in a Shibuya changing room, my back against the wall, her lips on mine. But she doesn't kiss me this time. She just hugs me, hard, and then lets go.

"Risa," I start, but I've never been good at saying anything I want to say, and she cuts me off anyway.

"Be good," she says, as if I'm the one going on a journey. "Make friends okay? Make some friends." And she slips an envelope into my hand.

"I don't need friends," I say automatically. "Hey, what is this?"

And she turns, framed in her doorway with the light spilling from behind her. "Nothing," she says, "open it later, okay? On the train."

Something in her tone makes me ask: "You *will* call me when you get back, right?"

Risa smiles at me, blows me a kiss. "Claro," she says. "See you soon." And she stands there waving to me until I turn away, walk down the stairs.

I open the little envelope on the train, and I don't know what I'm hoping for. I know better than to hope for a love letter. But a note perhaps: *I miss you.* Instead I find twenty one-man bills. Twenty man. It feels like a ridiculous sum of money—almost two thousand dollars. I stare at it as the train stations rattle past, as if I don't know what it is. I miss my stop, don't realize it until we've already gone two more stations down the line. Then I tuck the envelope into my bag and hug the bag tightly the rest of the way back, either terrified that someone will stop me, or terrified of the money itself.

AND AFTER THAT, SHE'S GONE.

The first few days that she should be back, I wait for a call that doesn't come. I go to an Internet café and email her. Maybe she decided to extend her trip. Maybe she's having such a good time with her mother and her sisters that she's rethinking this whole Japan thing. But no response. More days pass. I go find one of those bright green public phones outside the local conbini. I feed it ten-yen pieces and dial the number of the expensive mobile that Shinichi got her. It rings, twice, and then a recorded voice comes on in Japanese and talks for a long time, and the connection cuts off. I put in more ten-yen pieces, the same thing happens again and again.

I go to her apartment at the end of the first week. I stand in the street looking around but I don't see any black limos, so I go up the stairs and knock on the door. Nobody answers. I put my ear to the door but I don't hear anything. I call her name through the keyhole, but there's no sign of life. I want to slip a note under the door but I don't want Shinichi to find it. In the end, I leave.

I come back the next day and knock. Then the next. I try her phone a few more times, but the same automated voice talks to me in Japanese and then cuts off. I'm beside myself. I ask the few people from the factory we were both friendly with, but nobody knows. I'm the one who was closest to her. Many of them don't even know she went back to Colombia.

As the days pass, I start to wonder if she even went back at all. Did she lie to me? But why? I can't sleep at night. I lie awake and think about her. I feel like I'm losing my mind. I don't know where to go, how to ask for help. It is so easy for girls like us to fall through the cracks—in our own countries and now in this one.

It is in the third week after she should have returned (and five weeks since I've seen her) that it occurs to me to track down the Nigerian friends she used to tell me about. All I know of them is that they sell hats by the train station. I don't even know their names. When I get off shift, I stand by the train station, my hands shaking in my pockets. I am not afraid in the same way I was when I first got here, but I still don't linger in public, especially not alone. I'm trying to figure out how I can find them, when I see a tall black man in a bright red T-shirt, standing on a street corner. He has a stack of hats in his hand and he's calling out in Japanese to pass-ersby. Of course it wouldn't be hard to find a hat-selling Nigerian man in a sea of Japanese.

When he sees me walking toward him, he gives me a bright smile. "Little sister," he calls out in English, "the shape of your head is perfect for a hat."

I come to a stop in front of him, my fingers tangling and untangling. "I'm looking for—do you know? You were friends with? Risa."

He is caught by surprise, but his smile gets warmer. "You are friends with the little girl," he says, putting his hand at about mid-chest height.

"Have you seen her?"

"Very pretty," he tells me, as if I don't know. "She smiles and mmm, God smiles. Tell her come back to try on my hats. Business is bad without her."

"You haven't seen her," I say, and I feel something sink inside my stomach. I hadn't realized it until now, but I'd been counting on someone knowing something, and now there is no one left.

The Nigerian frowns at me, tilting his head to one side. "For many months now," he says. "Is she in trouble?"

I hear myself say, "I don't know where to find her," and I realize only when I hear my voice that I'm crying. I haven't cried once since I got to this country. Hearing myself cry just makes me cry harder. The Nigerian doesn't know what to do. He starts to say something, then he steps forward and puts his arms around me.

It's been so long since anyone has touched me. And I find that I'm starving for it—the warmth of someone else's body, someone else's kindness. I put my face against his T-shirt and I cry while he pats my head and murmurs things to me in a language that's neither English nor Japanese. The Japanese stream past us and the Nigerian doesn't even glance at them, he doesn't care what kind of a scene I'm making. At last he says, "Come have some tea." I follow him, shaky and dazed, around the corner and inside a small hat shop. There are two other Nigerian guys there, sitting on low stools with their feet up, watching a baseball game on a tiny black-and-white TV.

"Hanshin Tigers," he tells me almost apologetically. His friends glance up at him, then at me with growing interest, but he says something to them and they look away again. He leads me past them into a small room in the back. A year ago, I would never have gone alone with a strange man into that space. But now I'm tired and all the fear I know how to feel is for Risa.

He pulls out a cushion for me, goes to where an electric kettle is simmering, pours us each a cup of tea. He searches around on a back shelf, comes back with some small individually wrapped Japanese cakes, and puts those between us, sitting opposite me. I don't know what my expression is, but it makes him smile.

"Be easy," he says to me. "What's your name?"

"Yuliya," I say.

He holds out a large hand. Long slim fingers, an artist's hand. "Abayomiolorunkoje," he says.

I blink at him. "I'm sorry?"

He laughs out loud this time. "My name, A-ba-yo-mi-o-lo-run-ko-je. It means: People Wanted to Humiliate Me but God Did Not Allow. It's an old name."

"It's beautiful," I say, and mean it.

"Call me Koje," he says, "you won't be able to pronounce the rest of it," and we smile at each other over the tea and cakes. And then he asks, "What has happened with our friend?"

I tell him the whole story. Koje listens until I finish, refilling my teacup from time to time. Then he shakes his head, troubled. "The yakuza are very dangerous," he says. "I knew a Chinese girl who vanished because of them."

"Risa said he would never hurt her," I say, but the words sound pathetic even to my ears. "She was sure of that."

Koje sighs, rubs one long-fingered hand over his face. I wonder if he was an artist before this life, if back home he painted instead of selling hats. I thought of Risa saying to everybody: *How did you get here?* as if this whole new life was a miracle beyond her understanding.

"What do I do?" I ask.

Koje doesn't want to say it, but he says it anyway. "There is nothing to do. If she has vanished, if she is gone—perhaps she has seen something she should not know. Even if you go looking, you would never find her. Perhaps she is waiting for the right moment to contact you. I'm sorry. There is nothing you can do but wait."

I don't stay much longer. We finish the tea. Koje gives me some wrapped cakes to take home. He walks me to the door, past his friends who are screaming at the Hanshin Tigers. In the doorway of the shop, Koje grabs a bright red hat off of a high shelf, and puts it on my head.

"I like bright things," he says, "and your friend was always a bright moment in my day." And he bends down from his elegant height, and kisses my cheek.

AND THEN IT IS MARCH, but still too cold for any real promise of spring. And then April, and the cold thaws gradually, and then May, and May is beautiful. Even in the factory they have caught firefly fever, everybody is talking just like the Japanese about how beautiful the fireflies are, how we should all go see them. Some Japanese-Brazilian boys from work invite me with them to see the fireflies over Tokyo's choked and filthy canals. I say that I'll take the extra hours of sleep over watching insects blink at each other. The boys laugh and pretend to be insulted but mostly laugh. They say, "You have no sense of beauty," but they say it in Portuguese. I am still adjusting to hearing pure thick Brazilian-Portuguese in mouths that look—but are not—so Japanese. It is not that I am making friends in Risa's absence. But the Japanese-Brazilian boys have started talking to me whether I want them to or not, and occasionally they come over to my apartment and bring weed, and we all smoke it together.

May becomes June, and the rainy season begins, and now I have been here exactly one year. I look at myself in a mirror, once, in the back of Koje's hat shop when I'm visiting him. I am thinner, the angles of my hip bones jut. My face looks different too—older, the mouth set, the eyes cold. I look like someone who does not smile in public. And I look like someone who does not feel fear.

June becomes the dead weight of July, and in the third week, the rain tapers off, there are whole days of sunlight and thick wet heat. But still no sign of Risa. Nothing in five months. I replay that last meeting in my mind again and again. Risa's smile and the envelope with money and I'd asked her to call me and she'd promised, she'd promised. . . .

I haven't spent that money. I keep intending to do something with it but then I find myself hesitating, as if I'm waiting for a moment that will make itself clear to me. As August begins, I keep thinking: *Last year at this time* . . . and then images flood me, all of them Risa, sprawled loosely over my bed, my floor, draped against the window, boneless in the heat. And my body, boneless with desire. I ask myself: Did she want me the way I wanted her? Or was I just something exciting, like Shinichi became exciting? Was I so easily forgotten? I ask myself questions that I hate myself for asking, but then I get angry at Risa: *I wouldn't have to ask these if you were here.*

It's in the last days of August that I think I see her.

I'm standing on the train platform with the Japanese-Brazilian boys and we're all a little stoned, heading back home from an excursion on our day off, and then I look across the tracks and there she is.

Maybe.

This person, maybe Risa, doesn't see me. She's standing with her head bowed, a curtain of hair swinging into her eyes, staring straight into the tracks, and the clothes she's wearing are elegant and simple and expensive, blues and blacks and grays, nothing I ever knew her to wear. Expensive sunglasses on her face despite the overcast sky. The kind of sunglasses you wear over a black eye. And the way she holds herself, folded in, protective—if she would move, I could see if she has a limp. But she doesn't move. The moment feels so precarious, like a strong wind could blow and suddenly she would vanish.

It's her. It isn't her. It's absolutely her. Is it? The boys are pushing and laughing, the whole world has changed and they don't know it. I scan the platform behind her. There are men in suits but there are always men in suits, Japan is a country of men in suits, and I can't tell if they're watching her, if they're with her. I don't know what to do. I'm afraid that if I call her name, they'll all turn their heads. Or she'll look up and not be Risa. Or she will be. As I watch her, she lights a cigarette and smokes, without lifting her head. She moves as if she's trying to take up the smallest amount of space possible, trying not to stir the atoms of the air. And this tidal thing rises in me because I'm sure it's Risa, and yet these gestures are so alien to the Risa I knew—the quicksilver, impatient, ferocious girl who kissed me in a Shibuya changing room, who regularly picked the lock and slipped into our apartment, who mocked me for locking the door at all in what was so safe, so *safe* a country.

I open my mouth to call out to her. I can't help it—I have to. And then a train comes thundering between us on my side of the tracks, as swift and merciless as an act of God. The boys jostle me, "Vamos, gatinha"—and I wave them away, desperately trying to catch a glimpse of Risa through the opposite windows of the subway car.

"Not yet," I'm saying to them, "not yet," even though I know it makes no sense to them. They're looking at me like I'm crazy—"It's our train," the oldest one is telling me, like I'm too high to know where I am. But I know exactly where I am. I've arrived at the intersection of six months of stupid hope, six months of unanswered questions, half a year of accumulated fear and resentment and guilt and love.

"The next one," I say, shaking off their hands, craning my neck. "The next one, okay?" I know that if she sees me, she might not recognize me at first. My gestures have changed as well. The Yuliya she knew didn't have friends. The Yuliya she knew didn't go out in public. The Yuliya she knew didn't want to draw attention to herself, wouldn't be running down the platform as I'm running, wouldn't be jumping up on a bench, trying to see, trying to see, trying to make herself be seen, as the train throws itself forward into motion, car after car after car, leaving me behind with my hands in the air, trying to catch something that maybe can't be kept, waiting to see if after all the violent commotion, Risa is still waiting on the other side.

MAUREEN

Maureen hires me because she is young and hot and professional, and she believes in women's voices, and she believes in the new generation of writers, and maybe because I'm green enough that I don't ask for a contract. We meet six months after I've moved to New York, during the span of time in which I'm still sleeping on my cousin Ev's pullout couch, and missing Philadelphia. Maureen has a production company, although she mostly makes documentaries, one of which has been well received. I wear torn jeans to the restaurant, and realize only upon entering that I may be underdressed. Maureen wears a blazer. She makes the decision not to look at my jeans, and I see her make it. She pulls her long limp hair off her thin face, and she smiles. "I'm *so* pleased to meet you," she says.

Over risotto, she explains the job. It's a film. She has an idea, but she's not much of a writer. She'll pay me to write the screenplay. The idea actually came from a dream she had, that she hasn't been able to shake. And she has some characters, she has a concept, but she doesn't know what happens exactly, that would be my job—although she definitely has some suggestions, but really the whole thing would be my prerogative.

Something inside me hesitates. Some tiny voice says, *Pick up this bowl of risotto and walk out onto Sixth Avenue.* Then Maureen says, casually, "Thirty thousand or so."

I say, "Excuse me?" I've been stealing toilet paper rolls from restaurant bathrooms so that I won't have to pay for toilet paper at Duane Reade. I'm straight out of grad school, and my student loans would turn even an iron stomach.

"I mean, if it gets made," says Maureen. "Upwards of thirty-five thousand, if we're doing a percentage, but clearly up-front it would be a smaller fee."

In my mind, I buy nine million rolls of toilet paper. In my mind, I rent a studio apartment in the Village, no roommates, and I put a big oak desk underneath the floor-to-ceiling windows, of which there will be many. In my mind, I pay off all my student loans and I live without preemptively flinching whenever I check the mail. In my mind, I have already calculated how much this risotto will be, with tip. In my mind, I have already started worrying about how much this risotto will be, with tip.

"Oh," I say. "Oh wow."

Maureen takes a tiny bite of her own risotto, which she hasn't touched. It's porcini, and it was more expensive than mine by six dollars.

"I mean up-front we're talking, you know, a thousand," Maureen says.

I'm still reeling from the thirty-five, so it takes me a second to catch up. "A thousand?"

"For the first few drafts," Maureen says. Her nail polish is the color of pearl. Her earrings are tiny gold dots in her perfectly shaped earlobes. "But then once we sell the screenplay to a studio, that's when the percentage comes in."

"Oh," I say. "Huh." Is this good or bad? Maureen says it like it's good. Maureen has a very quiet voice, and you have to lean in to hear her. I read an article once about ways to make people think you're more powerful than you are, and one of the ways was to talk very softly, but the article was written for men. Maybe Maureen already talked softly anyway.

When the bill comes, we split it. I wait for Maureen to suggest that she pay the tip, since hers was more expensive. I try not to look like I'm waiting for this. She doesn't suggest it, so in the end we both leave the same amount of tip.

Outside the restaurant, Maureen shakes my hand. Hers is very cool and her skin is soft. "Give me a call," she says. "I'll be talking to some other writers over the next few weeks but I'd love to know what you're thinking."

I didn't realize she was considering other people.

I didn't realize there was a chance I might not get this.

A thousand dollars is actually a lot, if you don't eat twenty-six-dollar risotto every day. Or even if you don't eat three meals every day. Or especially if you don't eat every day.

I say yes. Of course I say yes.

ZARA IS THE OTHER GIRL who works for Maureen. She works more in the documentary end of things. She's a year younger than me, three years younger than Maureen, and she has two long braids that hang like arrows down her back. The first time I go to the office to meet Maureen, Zara buzzes me in. The office is the second floor of a giant brownstone on the Upper West Side. Zara tells me that Maureen is on a phone call, and she asks if I want a coffee while I wait. I offer to get it myself, and she looks at me oddly, the look I always get when people realize I'm way less sophisticated than anybody else they've ever met. But then Zara says, "Okay, I'll show you where it is, it's just K-Cups." She takes me to the small tea/coffee corner, where a Keurig squats. Outside the giant window, a tree curves and its leaves brush the glass. Light filters in, making the walls soft and elegant.

"This is a cool office," I say, sounding like a preteen. I'm trying not to stare at Zara in a way that could be construed as anything other than professional. She smells a little like balsam wood, I discover, when she leans over to retrieve a mug from the high shelf.

Zara gives me that odd look again. "Well," she says, "I mean. It's not like *office* space. You know?" I don't. "She owns the building," Zara tells me, lowering her voice. As my whole face changes, she rushes to add, "I mean, her family does. But none of them really use it."

"Does she live here?" I ask, amazed.

"No," Zara says. "No, no. She lives with her boyfriend, they have a place in the Sixties, by Lincoln Center."

"Oh," I say. I am suddenly very aware that I'm wearing Ev's button-down shirt because I didn't have any that weren't stained, and it's a little bit too big. Ever since Ev transitioned from female to male, he's been buying larger shirts, and lifting weights in the hopes of filling out all those new larger shirts. Alongside the realization that I look like a slob, is the realization that I haven't been to the gym in approximately my whole lifetime, and then also the realization that my monthly MetroCard expires today and now I have to buy another one, which is just slightly more expensive than a gym pass would be, so there goes the gym, and a life as Maureen's svelte, well-styled, attractive new writer.

"She had this party there once," Zara is saying, low, "you wouldn't believe the canapés, silver tray after silver tray of—and if you went upstairs, you'd see it's like, *wall-to-wall*—" but then Zara's face changes and she says, in a slightly louder and different voice, "There's the coffee!" I turn and the door to a conference room is open, and Maureen stands in it. She's off the phone. I never learn what was wall-to-wall because Maureen says, in her little voice, "It's *so* good to see you. Come in."

MAUREEN IS SOMEONE WHO HAS a lot of ideas. This is something I learn early on. Her ideas do not always go in the same direction, and they don't always build on each other, but they are numerous and seemingly endless. Her boyfriend, I learn, owns a yacht in Connecticut, and eventually his ideas start filtering into the mix as well. By the second day of my employment, Maureen has called me three times. The first time is to tell me she's sent a list of new ideas for me to consider. The second time is because she remembered a dream she thought would be helpful for me to mull over, in addition to the list. The third time is because she and her boyfriend were on the yacht, and her boyfriend remembered a dream, and it felt like something that might be in conversation with where we're going artistically.

"You gotta cut this off now," Ev says. He's sitting on the couch in his boxers, Sunday morning, eight A.M., and I've just played Maureen's three-minute-and-twenty-six-second voicemail on speakerphone.

"I can't," I say. "She's rich."

"She's calling you about her dreams and you've been doing this for less than forty-eight hours."

"She likes to, uh, collaborate?" I try to remember some of what Maureen said at the office on Friday. All I can remember is how Zara smelled like balsam. "She likes to really get in on the ground level with a, a writer, and sort of—like, let the writer handle the text, but let the ideas sort of, uh . . . originate authentically from shared experiences and conversations?"

"And her *boyfriend's* dreams?" Ev scratches the back of his knee. It's hairier than it used to be, which Ev says means the T is working. "That yacht must make for some great sleeping."

"She's either crazy or she's a genius?" I suggest hopefully.

"She's definitely crazy," Ev says. "She *may* turn out to be a genius."

"She said I could make thirty thou off this."

"Uh," Ev says, "maybe."

"I think she'll be fine," I say, deleting her voicemail. "She's just excited to get started."

"Yeah," Ev shrugs, "okay."

————

MAUREEN IS EXCITED TO GET started, but she's nervous about moving past the starting line. Any decision set in stone is a decision that could have been the wrong one. I learn this after the fourth time that Maureen calls me after receiving a set of pages, and suggests that we "reexamine the concept." During this phone call, she suggests that I come meet her so we can talk about it in person—"It's really important to start the right way," she says, her voice languid and wispy. "And I just feel like maybe this isn't the right protagonist? And also can there be a sort of a love story that starts earlier, like maybe the first image is a slow pullback from these two people in bed? I feel like what if there was a guy, and he was in love with the girl, and the girl was the one we were following?"

"Instead of the robot," I clarify, scratching notes across the back of an envelope.

"The girl could be the robot?" Maureen considers this for a moment. "The girl could be the robot but we wouldn't know it."

"Is that sort of . . . ?" I'm not sure how to phrase this, but: "Has that sort of . . . been done?"

A note of impatience is injected into the wisp. "Everything has been *done*. The point is how you *do* it."

"Right," I say, as if that's something I knew already. "No, yeah."

"*Any*way," says Maureen, already moving on, "I just feel like, before you start writing, let's get really focused and specific about the *approach*. I'm not in the office today, but if you want to come meet me in Chelsea, we can kind of just get down to brass tacks."

I'm torn between the desire to remind Maureen that I already started writing four beginnings ago, and the question that I end up voicing: "What's in Chelsea?"

"Oh," Maureen says, "I just moved." She sighs. "Moving is really stressful."

"Yeah," I say, "wow. Sure." A moment. "Are you . . . um, are you shopping in Chelsea, or . . . ?"

"My new place," Maureen sighs again, "my new *place* is in Chelsea. I'll text you the address, just come meet me and we can—I mean I don't have any furniture yet? Or groceries. But we can just—well, there's Seamless. And we can sit on crates. And I just think if we're in the same place we can make some great decisions."

"Great," I echo. "That sounds great. I'm on my way."

MAUREEN'S BUILDING IS A GIANT cage of glass and steel filigree. Her apartment has an upstairs and a downstairs, which I didn't even know was possible in New York, and a roof-deck that seems to belong only to her apartment. Boxes sit around the open kitchen/dining space, untouched. Maureen is curled disconsolately in a deck chair when the doors to her private elevator open and deposit me in the hallway. She brightens immediately.

"I don't have any furniture," she announces. "I think I'm getting a cold? I ordered a juice, do you want a juice? I already ordered mine, but you could get one."

"I'm good," I say, "thank you." Today I'm wearing one of Ev's sweaters that got shrunk in the dryer—salmon, corded—and the same jeans I wore to our risotto dinner. I look like a tiny gay frat boy.

"I got my cards read," Maureen says, still from her deck chair. She takes a sip of a light green juice. "They told me there's a lot of change coming."

"You mean like moving?"

Maureen shrugs. "I was like, 'I just moved and I'm making a movie, do you mean those sorts of change?' The lady was like, 'Worse.'"

"Oh no," I say, genuinely a little alarmed.

"I feel like that's something we could put in the movie," Maureen says, not reacting to my alarm. "I feel like that could be a scene, where the protagonist gets her cards read, and the lady tells her change is coming, and she's like, she asks if it's something good, and the lady just says, 'No.' She could look at the protagonist and just say, 'No.'"

"The robot?" I ask, clarifying.

Maureen looks at me blankly. "What robot?"

"You—this morning, when we talked . . . ? The girl and the boy and the . . . a love story with a robot?" Maureen's face isn't changing expression, and I'm getting increasingly flustered. I briefly wonder if I hallucinated this last phone call. Maybe Maureen has penetrated my dreams. Maybe I am dreaming that she is calling me to tell me about her dreams.

"Oh," Maureen says. "Well. That was just an idea."

"Right," I say, "no, sure."

"It's sort of been done though," Maureen says, a little reprovingly. She shouldn't have to tell me these things—if I'm writing her first film, I should already know this.

"No yeah, totally."

A moment. Maureen climbs off her deck chair. She walks a circle in the open kitchen, framed under the light pouring down from the glass ceiling. She touches the counter, the fridge, the teakettle, and finishes up back at the deck chair, as if she's pulled off some private ritual.

"I've been so anxious," she says. "I mean not in any sort of *weird*— but I just feel like everything is so tenuous right now."

"Oh." I'm unsure what to say. I wait for her to suggest that the protagonist of our movie, whether human or robot, might also struggle with anxiety—but she doesn't.

"I think Joshua is getting tired of this," she says, in that same tone. I try to remember if she's named the protagonist Joshua, if we've agreed on a Joshua—and then she says, "My boyfriend."

"Oh," I repeat. "Tired . . . ?"

"Of this." Maureen makes an encompassing gesture, and at first I wonder what's wrong with walls and ceilings made out of glass, hardwood floors the color of warm honey, an apartment with two levels and a wraparound balcony. Then I realize that her little hand, with its rose-dust manicure, has returned to land on her buttoned cardigan. She's talking about herself.

She sits back on the deck chair. Silence waxes and wanes between us. Then she says, as if we never switched subjects at all, "I just think it's important to think of this as a feminist movie, from a feminist viewpoint, and I have some notes about the, the sort of *male* characters that you're sort of *inserting*."

"There don't need to be male characters," I say promptly, agreeably. I made a list last night about what I will do with the first thousand dollars, when I receive it. The first five hundred dollars are about food. But then I thought I should probably give five hundred to Ev, to offset his rent and apologize for the square footage of his apartment that I have occupied. That still leaves twenty-nine thousand dollars with which to dream.

Maureen is staring out the window. She looks both expressionless and somehow crushed. I wonder if I went too far. Maybe there should be *one* male character. Maybe the male character can be a feminist.

"His ex-girlfriend was in real estate," Maureen says to the window. "She was probably a lot less complex, because she wasn't an *artist.*" She turns from the window to me. "We," she says, "are artists. And that makes us complex." And then she pulls her phone out of her pocket and announces, "It's time to Seamless. I'll place the order, you can just give me cash."

ZARA IS IN THE OFFICE when I arrive, pages clutched in my hand. I've been reading and revising on the subway, trying to anticipate whatever concerns Maureen might have—or whatever new directions she might want to go in. There are twenty-five pages, which is more than enough to establish a beginning, set up characters and hint at themes, and is also the furthest we've ever gotten.

When Zara sees me, she says, "Have you been sleeping?"

This is not exactly what I have fantasized about Zara saying to me. If I have thought of Zara over the past week, it may have involved scenarios in which I'm wearing Dead Poet glasses, and she says, "I stayed up all night reading your screenplay after Maureen left, I couldn't put it down." Or ones in which she says, "There was something distinguished about you from the beginning, I've never known Maureen to have such good *taste*." Or she says, "I guess I always assumed I was straight, but I just can't stop thinking about you."

"You look terrible," real-Zara says. "Coffee's over there."

I make myself a cup of Keurig, trying not to think about the immense environmental waste. Instead, I think about the slender lines of Zara's bra, which are visible through her thin navy T-shirt.

"I've had some late nights," I say casually, as if they're common in my profession.

"Yeah," Zara says, "I bet you have." She lowers her voice, after glancing over our shoulders to make sure we're alone. This moment has also figured in whatever fantasies I may have had . . . but not what she says next. "Is she leaving you the voicemails? Like, two A.M., three A.M.? All the voicemails?"

The "she" in this sentence is unmistakable. "She's left me a few voicemails," I say, "but mostly between eight A.M. and midnight?"

"Oh," Zara says. "Man. Okay. Just wait."

"I mean . . . it's fine?" I say. I'm not sure if this is a test. "Just like . . . general thoughts about the pages?" Maybe Maureen is listening? Maybe she's having Zara report back to her what I say? Or maybe this is just a conversation, a confidential conversation between two people who are gently negotiating what kind of future relationship they might have, but maybe Zara doesn't like whiners, maybe she's not attracted to people who complain, so either way: "It's not too bad," I say.

Zara shrugs. The shrug is world-weary. It says *Okay, chump.* Maybe Zara doesn't like people who are too naïve, who never complain, who get walked all over.

"I mean," I say, "it can get kinda . . . you know."

"Oh believe me," Zara tells me, "I know." A moment in which I see her try to decide if she wants to say something or not. And then she leans forward, her voice sinking to a hush, her breath brushing my cheek, and she whispers, "The thing is, if you aren't careful—"

"Oh hi," says Maureen's tiny voice behind us. Zara pulls away from me as if she's spring-loaded.

"She couldn't figure out the Keurig," Zara says, with cool disdain.

"I couldn't figure out the Keurig," I say, and make a face.

Maureen ignores both of us, and nods toward the pages in my hand. "I've had some ideas," she says, "that I'm excited to share with you, before we go ahead and read those."

THE KIND OF CALLS THAT Zara was talking about start two weeks later. We've reached thirty-three pages, although in the days leading up to the first call, Maureen mentions a number of times that we can't get locked in before having landed on the best possible idea, which implies that all thirty-three could get torpedoed. We have a woman and we have a man (Maureen felt that two women as protagonists might seem "strident"), there are no robots (they were never mentioned again), someone is a graffiti artist in a dystopian world (Maureen has asked me to write a set of pages in which the graffiti artist is a man, and a different set in which it is a woman, so we can see which feels "authentic"), and the scenes with both characters are interspersed with vivid dream sequences taken from Maureen's own dreams. She records them in a tiny blue notebook and in the morning she leaves me voicemails in which she describes the dreams, and I transcribe them faithfully. This has fallen into a pattern normal enough that, when the phone rings at one A.M. and it is Maureen, I'm actually surprised.

Ev ordered in a date from Grindr, and the two of them have been eating Thai food and fucking in his bedroom, so I'm not exactly asleep. But I'm also not ready to reopen the question of whether we have the right "central idea."

Maureen, however, is not calling about the screenplay.

"Do you know how to poach an egg?" she asks.

"An egg?"

"I'm trying to poach eggs and they keep falling apart."

"Oh," I say, "well. Uh. How much vinegar are you using?"

". . . Vinegar?"

I talk Maureen through the three steps of poaching an egg, the second of which involves copious amounts of vinegar. Eventually I have to ask, "Why are you poaching eggs right now?"

"Joshua is staying over," Maureen says. She sounds distracted and a little flustered.

"Oh."

"And I haven't seen him in a little while and I felt like . . . it would be nice to sort of . . . after we . . . sort of a midnight, late-night snack."

"Oh."

"And then all the eggs fell apart." Maureen's voice soars by a few octaves, even though she's keeping it tight and low. If this were anyone else, I would think she was crying. It's hard for me to imagine Maureen in a cardigan, with her rose-dust manicure, clutching her cell phone and whisper-crying in the kitchen. And yet . . . my heart goes out to her.

"I think you've got it now," I say.

I go over to the office the next day. It's not that I think we'll suddenly be best friends, but I imagine a certain warmth between us— a shared joke, maybe—I'm ready to ask Maureen how the poached eggs turned out. But she's as cool and distant as ever, and she begins right away: "I think the man should have a drug problem. He's bipolar and he does drugs, maybe heroin or crack or something, and the drugs aggravate his bipolar disorder, and he goes crazy."

"Oh," I say, switching gears. Maureen hands me a blue Bic pen since I'm not taking one out fast enough.

"I think maybe the girl falls in love with him because he's so crazy, and she thinks he's a genius. But actually maybe he isn't a genius, he's just crazy." This is similar enough to my conversation with Ev about Maureen that I shoot her a look, but she's wrapped up in the pages, margins covered in her tiny precise handwriting.

"And I think we should try the man being the graffiti artist, but the girl is like—an art history major? She really likes art. So that's a point of connection between them, and there can be a scene where she goes to his apartment and the walls are covered with index cards, just *covered* with shit, and she has a realization that he's crazy."

"Is that sort of . . . Did *A Beautiful Mind* sort of do that?" I ask, as mildly as possible. Maureen falls silent. She just looks at me. I feel the misstep immediately. "But I guess we'd do it better," I say. "I mean, the whole point I guess is that *everything* has been done before, but it's *how* you do it."

"What do you think of Zara?" Maureen asks.

I blink at her, taken completely aback. "Zara . . . ?"

"I don't know . . ." Maureen wrinkles her little nose, somewhere between a grimace and a shrug. "I just don't know if she's *committed* to this company."

"She's always seemed pretty committed to me?" I'm aware of the eggshells, and I tread as carefully as I can. "I mean . . . you know her better than I do, but . . ."

"Yeah." Maureen lets the silence hang and then she says politely, "*Thank* you," and I'm aware that I've been dismissed.

WHEN MAUREEN CALLS AGAIN, IT'S TWO A.M., and she doesn't wait for me to say much more than "Hello?" before she launches in.

"I'm having a sharp pain," she says.

"Where is it?"

"In my abdomen? No, in sort of . . . under my ribs. But kind of in my abdomen."

"What side is it on?"

"Left? But sort of . . . but I guess, no, it's mostly on the left."

I bring WebMD up on my phone. "Nausea? Fever? Vomiting?"

"No," Maureen says, uncertainly.

"Any of those things?"

"No . . . but they could start."

"But you haven't had any yet."

"I guess not."

"Numbness? Tingling? Heavy sweats?"

"Like . . . tonight?"

"Yeah," I say.

"Not tonight."

"In general?" I have to ask.

"No," Maureen says, in that uncertain voice, which makes me realize that she is thinking: *But any of those things could start.*

I'm going down another list of symptoms, the answers to which could point us either toward a gas bubble or liver cancer, when Maureen says, "Oh!"

"What happened?" I ask. In my mind, her appendix just exploded.

"It's gone," Maureen says.

"The pain is gone?"

"Yeah."

"Did you—do you feel any kind of . . . ?"

"No," says Maureen. "*Thank* you." And she hangs up.

I LURK AROUND THE OFFICE trying to look unobtrusive until Zara gets back from her lunch break, and then I ask her if she wants to have a cigarette outside.

"I don't smoke," Zara says, looking at me as if I'm crazy.

"I don't either," I hiss, darting my eyes around the room. "Come outside."

Zara walks with me down to the bodega on the corner. When we're far enough from the office that I feel safe, I launch in.

"She's calling me at two A.M. now."

"Yeah," Zara says, unsurprised.

"About poaching eggs, and . . . she had this abdominal pain last night? And then during the day, it's just like—she has questions about the pages. We keep starting over. But she never like . . . acknowledges having called, or anything."

"Right," Zara says.

"Is that . . . I mean, is that . . . ?" I hesitate over the word *normal*.

Zara chooses her words carefully. "I would say that people don't often last here too long. That's what I would say."

"How long have you been working here?"

"A year," Zara says. "Thirteen months, to be exact."

"And she calls you like this?"

"No," Zara says, "no no. I switched carriers. I told her that I was doing a back-to-the-earth thing, where I had a landline in my apartment, and I didn't carry a cell. And I said I live with a lot of roommates. And she doesn't really call me much but she does still email."

"What does she email?"

"She emailed me a list of symptoms that maybe she was having, and she emailed me a recipe that she wanted to know if I thought it sounded right, and she emailed me the link to this online questionnaire she took that was about whether or not you're a right-brain or a left-brain person."

"And do you email back?"

Zara shrugs. "Sometimes I say my email is down?"

"I guess what I'm asking is . . ." *Are you straight? What products do you use that make you smell like balsam? Do you mind if I sniff your hair? Are you currently single? Is Maureen not going to pay me the thousand bucks if I stop answering the phone? Is Ev's increased use of Grindr a sign that he's tired of me sleeping on his couch?*

"What?" Zara asks.

"I don't know," I say. "Forget it."

We're almost back at the office by now. The Upper East Side is sunny and brisk, the sidewalks almost empty except for an occasional hot mom in Lululemon, who jogs past.

"The trick," Zara says, "is don't take anything personally."

"What does that mean, exactly?"

But Zara is already climbing the office steps. "Wait out here for three minutes," she says, "then come in and say you were getting lunch at the deli. Maureen doesn't like smokers."

———

MAUREEN CALLS ME THAT NIGHT, somewhere around eleven, which makes me think it must be a film-related epiphany. In the office we'd discussed Maureen's questions about the characters, which involved her asking about "believability" and "interconnection" and whether I felt like their primary objectives were clear enough to land the themes of the film. At this point everything had changed so much and so often that I wasn't sure what the themes of the film were, but Maureen seemed to feel a lot better after voicing her questions, which made me feel better.

At eleven P.M. on the phone, Maureen's voice is smaller than a bread box.

"Can you come over?" she asks.

"To talk about the movie?" I ask, cautiously.

"I just don't feel so good," Maureen says.

"I live in Astoria? So . . . it might take me a while?" I'm sort of hoping that Maureen will do that thing where she says *forget it, thaaanks* and hangs up, but she says, "That's okay."

"And not all the trains are running," I say, without knowing if this is true. Maureen doesn't strike me as someone who knows which subway lines go to Astoria.

"Can you just catch a cab?" Maureen asks, strained. She's not used to this many obstacles.

"There aren't any cabs out here at eleven," I lie.

"I'm sending you an Uber," Maureen says. "Text me your address and you can give me cash for it."

"I don't have any cash," I say, "but I'll text you my address."

I hang up and sit for a bewildered moment. I'm not sure whether I'm more bewildered by the sudden backbone that has presented itself, or by the part where I gave in anyway. It's at that point Ev stumbles through the living room drunk, his hand shoved in the back pocket of a twink who gives me a nod, and I realize that I might as well get in an Uber.

————

WHEN I SHOW UP AT Maureen's, she's wearing Lululemon leggings and an oversized white T-shirt with the word MARINA printed on it. My first thought is Abramović, but when she turns around I see CONNECTICUT YACHT CLUB printed on the back, and I realize it must be a gift from Joshua. She has a knit scarf pulled around her shoulders, and she's snuggled into it like a little kid.

"Hey," I say, trying to take the temperature. I'm still not sure if Maureen is going to fix me with her flat, calm stare and inform me that she's been thinking about Sherpas in Eastern Tibet, and feels like the screenplay could use a makeover.

But instead Maureen says, despondently, "Joshua needs a new phone, his keeps breaking. I call him and it just goes to voicemail half the time and then his phone doesn't even show him that I called."

"Oh," I say.

"Which is unfortunate, because he's very responsive as a *person*, but his phone basically doesn't work, I mean you'd think a phone in the twenty-first century would work, but his doesn't work. And I've said to him, Joshua, I've said, I will *buy* you a phone. And he says, Oh I'll do it. And he never does it. I think I might just go to the Apple store tomorrow and buy him a phone."

Maureen sinks down on the deck chair, and I notice that she still hasn't unpacked. The boxes are where they were, the place is as bare of furniture as it was when I was here before.

"That's frustrating," I say, when I realize that her silence is weighted with expectation.

"Yes," Maureen says, as if I've chosen the perfect word. "Yes, it is *frustrating*." Into the silence that follows, she says, "Would you like a drink?"

"Are you having one?"

"Yes," Maureen decides. "I am certainly having one." She gets up from the deck chair and pads over to a bottle of scotch that's been left haphazardly on top of an empty planter and a sack of potting soil. I almost expect her to say, "You can give me cash for this," but instead she just opens it and pours a healthy dose—first into a champagne flute, fetched from a half-open box beneath the deck chair, and then into a jam jar, fetched from the countertop.

"Cheers," Maureen says, handing me the jam jar.

"Cheers," I say, and we clink.

THE CHRONOLOGY OF THINGS GETS foggy, eventually. At first we just sit in the sunken, spread-open living room and Maureen keeps re-filling our drinking devices as soon as they're empty. Sometimes Maureen talks about Joshua. Joshua is just wonderful but he doesn't answer his phone and he comes over less and less because he doesn't like the trek from Connecticut and he's very friendly, he has a num-ber of close female friends from the Yacht Club, and Maureen really enjoys getting to know his friends, and appreciates that he's so sup-portive of her by giving her plenty of space to pursue her artistic projects.

I put everything through a decoder, I perform high-grade World War II–style code-breaking, and I come to the conclusion that Maureen is two-thirds of the way into a breakup. Maureen doesn't seem to have come to that conclusion, so I don't say much, and after a while I'm the one refilling her champagne flute every time it plunges precipitously toward emptiness. Maureen also talks about her family, who are equally supportive and who understand her ambitions because they are also very ambitious, very busy, highly directed, involved in a series of international business and philan-thropic projects, far-flung (parents on UWS, cousin in Park Slope). The single salient point that emerges for me: Maureen lives in a world in which nobody picks up the phone except for her employees.

By now, Maureen is slurring, and there isn't a lot of whiskey left. I'm getting a little slurry myself.

"I should head home," I say, hoping she'll call me an Uber.

"Or you could crash here . . ."

I shoot her a look. Maureen is tipped back in the deck chair, eyes closed. With strands of flat hair falling across her forehead, and the little pinch in her mouth relaxed, she looks oddly vulnerable.

"I mean . . . you don't have any furniture?"

Maureen shrugs. "Sleepover," she singsongs. "Whatever."

"Really?"

"Whatever," Maureen says, tipping her head forward into her hands. She massages the paper-thin skin around her temples. She looks both very very old, and very very young, and I construct a story in my head—briefly, in a single flash-pulse that feels close to an epiphany—about her. Her loneliness, her isolation, her desire to participate in the business of life. The way in which making movies—or micromanaging the making thereof—is actually a way to have human relationships. Her nights after her employees leave the offices, night after night in which she sits in this brand-new obscenely expensive apartment with boxes that she hasn't even unpacked, and she waits until she can't wait any longer, and then she picks up her phone and reaches out. Her drive, her ambition, how these things are threatening to a wealthy guy who owns a yacht, whose entire goal in life is owning a yacht. How ambition and drive isolate us all, in a way. After all, my family is in Orange County, and I'm sleeping on Ev's couch, eating eggs for three meals a day and writing the same twenty pages over and over again because I wanted . . . what? To accomplish something?

I see her so clearly right then, and the small threads of commonality strung between us. I see her in a way that Zara hasn't been able to, might never be able to, given Zara's caginess and judgment. Come to think of it, Zara smells more like canola oil than balsam.

So I speak before I think. "Yeah," I say, "okay, sure. Sleepover!"

We curl up fully dressed on Maureen's bed. The bed frame is solid oak, but the blankets and sheets are all weirdly kid-like—printed with flowers and animals. Her bedroom is equally empty, with the exception of a Japanese paper lamp sitting on the floor, plugged into the wall. Maureen collapses on the bed near the wall, already hugging a pillow. I'm going to turn out the lamp but she murmurs, "Leave it," and that touches me even more—this girl going to sleep alone every night with a single lamp burning. The knit scarf is still wrapped around her and tangled into the blankets.

I curl up behind her. I'm not sure if this is a sleepover where we touch or not, but then she scoots back until I'm the big spoon and she's the little one. She grabs my arm and pulls it over her, and passes out completely.

It takes me a while to fall asleep, even with all the scotch in me. I listen to Maureen breathing and I feel the softness of her knit scarf against my face when she moves, and I think about getting breakfast when we wake up, bagels and lox, laughing about the impromptu sleepover, laughing about these stops and starts with the movie. *Listen,* Maureen says over breakfast, *I think we should take the day off from the movie.* And I say, *Yeah?* And Maureen chews her bagel and she says, *Let's go to an art museum.* She says, *I've still actually never walked the High Line, Joshua always said we'd go together and we still haven't,* and I say, *Fuck that, I'll take you,* and I do . . . and we do . . . and . . .

When I wake up, I'm alone in Maureen's bed, and the mid-morning sunlight is bright in my aching eyes.

I scrub my face in the giant bathroom off her bedroom. The sink is the size of a tub, and the tub itself is a pounded-copper basin the size of a small SeaWorld pool. I pull my hair back, brush my teeth with a finger, and venture out into her apartment. It's empty. I search the countertops for a note, a Post-it: *Stepped out / Went for bagels / See you in a few.* Nothing. I sit on her deck chair for a long moment, close my eyes, and pretend that all of this is mine. Nobody is coming home. It's just me, here, in all this space and light.

I start to feel a little bit sad, along with my hangover.

I pull on my sneakers and head out into the blinding morning.

———

I WAIT FOR MAUREEN TO call all day, without admitting to myself that that's what I'm waiting for. I wonder if I should drop by the office, but that seems weird. I wonder if I should call Zara and ask her what to do, but I don't have her number, and she hasn't been particularly useful anyway. I wander around Ev's apartment, from window to window, refreshing my phone. Maureen doesn't email any suggestions for the screenplay. She doesn't leave me any voice-mails beginning with, "I've been thinking . . ." I don't get any links to screenwriting manuals "just in case" I want to read them, with particular attention suggested for certain pages that Maureen has earmarked for me. Eventually I go sit in the Greek bakery on the corner, and drink cup after cup of watery coffee, and still there's no communication from Maureen.

I start to wonder if, in the light of increased mutual understanding (friendship, even?), she has come to realize that the latest set of pages is good.

I start to wonder if she's a little bit thrown by having let someone in, but also, maybe this is the first real friendship she's ever had.

I start to wonder if, post-sleepover, she called Joshua to tell him not to bother with those long irritating treks from Connecticut anymore. Newly empowered by a taste of friendship, she said, "I'd just rather you didn't take up my time, Joshua." Maybe she said, "I just don't find yachts very *interesting*, Joshua. And besides, my friend and I have plans to walk the High Line."

By evening, I wonder if Maureen is dead. Did she leave the apartment too quickly and get hit by a cab? Was she groggy from a deep night's sleep (or a hangover) when she stepped off the subway platform into an oncoming uptown 4/5/6? But Maureen doesn't take the subway. What if she called an Uber, and the driver was some kind of radical militant, and he kidnapped her? "Eat the rich" is tattooed over his heart. "What are you doing?" Maureen asks him. "What have I done to you?" He gives her a cold, steely glare through the cat door built into his basement, then nails a plank of plywood over it, sealing off her last point of contact with the outside world.

I decide maybe I should call Maureen.

Or email, which is less aggressive.

Or text, which is less aggressive but more personal. A text is intimate. A text says: *We slept in the same bed last night, and you told me about your shitty boyfriend, but I am choosing not to reference any of that as I write an economical and brief message about the screenplay on which we're collaborating.*

Instead, I go online and stalk Maureen. She isn't on Facebook or Instagram, so I resort to ancient tactics of intelligence-gathering: I type her first and last name into Google. Eventually I add Joshua's name. I read brief interviews with her about her documentaries. I read a "Personality Profile" that includes her zodiac sign, her favorite color, and the question "What do you like about film-making?" (The answer is "Everything, I guess.") I travel five pages back into Google and find an article about her in her high school newspaper (hometown: Greenwich, Connecticut), talking about how she's been accepted into Amherst and has a promising life ahead of her. I find a picture of her from freshman year of college, women's lacrosse team. She has the same long hair, pulled into a lifeless ponytail, and she's looking at the camera with her lips pulled into a polite rictus. I find all the things I should have found before I started working for her, but I still can't figure out why she isn't calling me, or why I care.

After a dinner of microwaved burrito from the back of Ev's freezer, I email Maureen. I keep it really light and easy. *Hey,* I say. *Looking forward to talking more about the pages I gave you. Let me know when a good time will be.*

It's another forty-eight hours before Maureen replies. Hers is as concise as mine: *Let me know if you can get on the phone in the next hour or two.*

I take a breath, and I call her. When she picks up, her voice is as small and distant as ever.

"Maureen!" I say, "How are you!" and right away, I'm telling my-self to tone it down. I sound jolly, almost avuncular.

"Good," Maureen says. She could be at the bottom of a marina. She could be on the moon. Her tiny voice is almost devoid of inflec-tion. "Is this a good time?"

"Yeah, sure, of course." I immediately wish I'd stopped after just saying "yeah."

"I've been thinking," Maureen informs me, "and I just don't feel that you're a good fit for this project. I appreciate the work you've put in, but I think it's time to part ways."

In the silence, I think, *But we spooned!* a split second before I think, *But I wrote you five sets of thirty pages!*

I'm not sure which one to say, so I settle for: "I guess I don't un-derstand what makes this not a good fit."

"It's just become clear to me," Maureen says, "that it's time to move forward. Aesthetically. For both of us to move forward."

More silence. I want to say so many things but I don't begin to know how. What comes out is, "Do I still get paid?"

"The payment was for a first draft," Maureen says. Her voice sounds a little more certain now—this is more comfortable territory.

"I've written over a hundred pages," I say.

"None of them," Maureen tells me, "ultimately, are usable."

I open my mouth to tell her that none of the beginnings are us-able because she wouldn't let me obtain endings, but: "You should unpack," I hear myself say. "You should get some decorations, and you should just . . . unpack, Maureen."

"Excuse me?"

I've stunned myself into a brief silence. When I realize that was, actually, what I meant to say, the follow-up realization is that I don't have much else to add.

"Goodbye," I say. But I still wait for her to hang up on me—which she does.

———

I SEE ZARA ONE MORE time, in the span of bewildered weeks after Maureen fires me. It feels like a breakup in a way that baffles me, and infuriates Ev. I find myself struck low by strange dizzying spells of sadness. I find myself talking out loud as I fill the dishwasher, as I wait on the sidewalk for the light to change. Every time I hear myself, I'm trying to explain something to Maureen. Why it could have worked, what I could have written next, but mostly, why she shouldn't give up on me. In the end, this is why I reach out to Zara. She's the only other person I know who knows Maureen, and who can tell me I'm not crazy—or that I am.

Zara isn't thrilled to see me, but that's no shock. She's chewing cinnamon gum, and she keeps glancing over her shoulder. She hasn't been fired yet, and I try not to show that I find this surprising.

"You gotta move on," she says, flatly, five seconds into my explanation. "I told you, it's not personal with her."

"But she called me at three A.M.," I say, a little lamely. "She had me come over."

"So?"

"So . . . that's personal."

"No," Zara says, not unkindly. "That's Maureen."

"But she'd email me—like, five, six times a day—"

"Yeah," Zara says, "and *that's* called psychosis."

I'm quiet, stymied.

"Look." Zara takes a breath, as if she's explaining something to a child who is both frustrating and endearing. "Do you like . . . have any friends?"

I blink at her. "Of course I have friends."

"Okay," Zara says, still patient. "But like, who are they?"

So I do a brief tally in my head. There's Ev, who's technically my cousin, and who has started emailing me Craigslist housing ads. There's Kayla, my best friend from high school, who lives in Costa Mesa with her husband (stoic, Air Force) and her first child (loud, constant). I texted her when Maureen fired me, hoping for sympathy, and a day later, she texted me back a picture of her kid covered in poop and said, "Somebody fire me from this." There's Maria, my best friend from college, who moved to Japan to teach English to Japanese businessmen, and who I haven't heard from in years.

I'm still thinking when Zara says, getting less patient, "Who do you *see* every day?"

And the answer, the only answer, is: "Maureen."

"Right," Zara says. "I'm only saying this to help you. You need a friend. You need a boyfriend. You need a job, but not a job where you can, like, fall in all the way. You need a job you don't care about. You need to go to the gym. Okay?"

I don't know what to say other than the simple correction: "Girlfriend."

"Great," Zara says. "Get a girlfriend. It's called Tinder. Do you have an iPhone?" I nod. "Give it to me." She takes my phone. "I'm downloading Tinder, I'm downloading OkC. There might be special lesbian ones, but you need to do the legwork on those. Go on some dates, practice the art of being a human with other humans, and if someone calls you at three A.M., run for the hills." She hands my phone back to me, all brisk efficiency. "We aren't friends," she says, "no offense but I just have too much going on in my life, and Maureen is already more than enough. Good luck."

She turns to walk away.

"Zara," I say. "You are really really good at your job. I hope you don't get fired."

She gives me an odd look and then says, "I mean, not that it matters, but I'm quitting at the end of the summer to work in a talent agency."

I SPEND THE REST OF the day wandering around Central Park. I feel strangely light, untethered from the rest of the city. I sit on a rock for a while and watch people walk by. There are lots of couples, and most of them seem vaguely unhappy. There are lots of dogs, and they seem happier. There's a guy blowing giant soap bubbles from a net, and little kids keep popping the soap bubbles and then both they and the soap bubble guy get upset. I open up the apps on my phone and then it all seems overwhelming and I close them again. I wonder how I could have been in New York for six months without realizing that I had no friends. I wonder if I had any friends in Philadelphia. I had people that I saw, more so than here, but were they my friends? Suddenly Zara has thrown my life into question.

When the shadows start getting longer, I slide off the rock and start the walk back through the park toward the exit that will spit me out by Columbus Circle. I am making lists and tallies in my head: Is the barista who always remembers my order a friend? Is someone a friend if they're nice to you on the subway, when everyone else is shoving you in the kidneys with their book bags and elbows? Is someone maybe not a friend if they need you for things that are unrelated to the things you need them for? Or is friendship a complicated equation, influenced in incalculable ways by things like employment and loneliness and money, and sometimes someone is your friend and then later, a minute later, that same person is not your friend anymore at all?

And if that's the case, I realize, as I reach the subway lights, then maybe Maureen was my friend after all. Briefly. In moments. Not always, but between breaths maybe, or in certain lines of certain emails, or the night I came over, in the space right after she fell asleep and right before I fell asleep—in that moment, I think, in that moment at the very least, we were friends.

And that thought makes me suddenly sad and relieved at the same time, so much so that I have to stop and take several deep breaths, one and then another and then another, before I descend the stairs into the subway.

MAMUSHI

Noriyuki was telling me all about Japanese pit vipers when he noticed the bruises on my arm. According to Nori, who had never eaten one, their meat healed wounds and made even the most flaccid old man into a raging sex addict. "The way you kill mamushi," Nori was saying, "you have to starve them to death. You keep them in this jar for months, the longer they sit there, the more concentrated it gets, whatever special thing is in their body. And then—" He stopped and asked, "What're those from?" and I realized that he was looking at my arm.

I had been copying his homework; I glanced down. From the crook of my elbow up to my wrist, all along my inner arm: soft ripe bruises, like plum blossoms. We were quiet. Then I said, "An accident."

Nori didn't push it. After a minute he started telling me about the snakes again, how his cousin in Hiroshima has been keeping one in a glass jar for three months, in his bedroom. "He can't have sex in that room anymore," Nori informed me. "Mamushi take all that energy and they become these—conduits—of *power*."

"Not powerful enough to get out of the fucking jar, though, huh,"

I said, and shoved his homework back at him. He didn't mention my arm again, although I caught him looking at it.

THE FIRST TIME I GOT Anthony to hit me, we were arguing about something that I can't even remember now. And watching him shout at me, that old predictable line *Nobody, nobody will ever love you the way I do,* I realized that I was bored. He shouldn't be begging for me to love him, not when I was seventeen and he was twice that. If I mattered to him like that, it must mean that he was even more fucked-up than I was. And *that* was pathetic. It must have shown on my face because he stopped yelling. We stood in the sudden silence, late-afternoon sunlight flooding from the open balcony door and the sounds of Roppongi below: A car horn. Somebody laughing. A guy's voice.

I'd wanted to say something mean, but I couldn't think of anything brutal enough, and the stupidity of the whole thing was weighing on me, how laughable and stupid. So I picked up my sneakers in one hand and started to walk out.

Anthony was barring the door before I reached it. "Ancash! Where are you going!"

"Home."

"You go home? That'd be a first. You're just going to find someone else to fuck you."

It shouldn't be so easy for a kid to humiliate an adult, but somehow it is. "It wouldn't be hard," I drawled.

I tried to shoulder past him, but he grabbed me by the wrist, jerking me off balance, and as I stared at him, startled, hit me across the face. The impact couldn't have made much of a sound, but it echoed in my mind like a car backfiring.

He dropped my wrist, took a step back. He was breathing hard, as if he'd been the one who got hit. I put my hand to my lips and when I took it away, my fingertips were tingling too. The pain drained away leaving behind something like anger and something like satisfaction.

I grinned at him.

"Do it again," I said.

In the end, he did. He didn't want to. But I didn't give him a choice—it was either that or watch me leave. Again, across the face, again, and then again. I thought later that maybe I shouldn't have done that, made him do that. Something like that, it can make you strange inside. But I didn't let him stop.

After that, it became part of our whole thing. Part of the routine. And even on the days when I didn't want to look at him, didn't want to talk to him, I'd go back to his apartment. When he was hitting me it was like he wasn't even there at all and I was alone, in the middle of a storm, thunder, hail, fists raining down, and at least I felt alive.

THE DAY NORIYUKI FOUND OUT about Anthony, if indirectly, was the day we skipped out of Tokyo to go a few hundred miles south to Hiroshima. Noriyuki was waiting for me by the udon stand on the corner, two blocks from our international high school.

"I have ichi-man," he greeted me. "We could make it as far as Hiroshima."

"And what're we going to do in Hiroshima?" I asked.

"Help my cousin catch snakes," he said, and smiled.

Noriyuki was just as wild as I was—the only difference was that he was nicer. Everyone loved him. Japanese by birth, he'd spent most of his childhood in Manhattan, and now here he was back in Tokyo. His father was a minister of internal affairs, mine a diplomat. I knew some of the other diplomats' kids hated Tokyo, but given Nori, Tokyo was great. England had been monotonous, Korea was a drag. Tokyo had moments of genuine possibility.

"I don't have that much on me," I said.

"How much do you have?"

I felt in my pockets. "Two hundred yen."

Nori shook his head in disapproval. "That's not even gonna buy you porno manga, kid. You need to start paying attention to the value of money."

"Thanks, grandpa," I said sarcastically. "I gotta make a stop before we leave."

"Home?"

I looked at him incredulously. My allowance was constantly in suspension—there were many things my father didn't appreciate, and my general outlook and behavior topped the list. Nori lifted his hands in self-defense.

"Okayyy, not home. A stop where?"

"Roppongi," I said, and started walking so he'd have to follow.

ANTHONY WAS HOME WHEN I showed up, like I knew he'd be. He worked as a bartender at night at Bar Brasilia, which meant he spent the afternoons asleep. He answered the door with his hair tousled, jeans undone. My knocking had woken him. He was surprised to see me, and pleased, and then suspicious.

"What do you want?" he demanded.

"Good morning, Anthony," I said, ignoring the question.

"Shouldn't you be in school?"

I leaned against the doorframe so my shirt would hitch up a little, so he could see the finger-span of bare skin between the shirt edge and the top of my jeans.

"I'm about to go to school," I said smoothly, "to further my education, but I find that I've forgotten my lunch money."

Anthony gave me that look. A moment of silence between us, sizing each other up. I knew that Anthony would give me what I wanted because he was too deeply in the habit of doing it now, and Anthony knew that he could get something from me, some physical gesture of affection, because he knew how little value I placed on those.

Anthony cleared his throat, rubbing a hand over his unshaven jaw. "How much."

"Ichi-man."

Another beat. It was about a hundred USD, but then again I didn't usually ask Anthony for money. I could see the gears whirring in his head. He wanted to ask me why, and knew in advance that I wouldn't give him a straight answer.

I stretched. Knew what he saw: muscles jumping along my forearms, the finger-span of skin between shirt hem and jeans becoming a hand-span, the top of a hip bone jutting. I dropped my arms and then took a sudden step forward, leaning in. I caught his lower lip between my teeth, held it for a second, then gave him a fast, harsh kiss and stepped back just as quickly. The Germans perfected this technique in World War II, they called it *blitzkrieg*. The Japanese, unfortunately, perfected a different technique—the technique that Anthony used most often. They called it *kamikaze*, and it ended with the pilot crashing his own plane.

Anthony turned and went into his apartment. He came back a minute later, with crisp new bills in his hand. I took them, casually, tucked them in my pocket.

"Why, thanks, Anthony," I said.

"I'll see you tonight," he said, and the warning was clear in his voice.

Nori was waiting below on the sidewalk. When he saw the money he demanded, "What the fuck did you do?"

"Nothing," I said. "Just borrowed from a friend."

"Yeah right," Nori said, grinning. "She must be loaded. And you must be fast."

He shoved me, inviting me to laugh or shove him back, but I knew that Anthony was watching us from behind the curtains of his living room window. I couldn't bring myself to play any more little games, no schoolboy horsing around on the sidewalk. Anthony was already jealous, and the irony was that, of all the people he would be right to suspect, Nori wasn't one of them. I'd never touched Nori-yuki and I never would, not even if he asked me. Which he wouldn't.

ON THE BULLET TRAIN TO Hiroshima, Nori told me more about the mamushi. If they bit you, you died. If you didn't die, you could be kept in the hospital for up to eight months. Also, he informed me, the mother snakes kept their babies in their stomachs and gave birth by vomiting. "That's pretty much what your mom did too," I nodded sagely, ducking his mock-punch. "And you turned out okay."

We got to Hiroshima by late afternoon, and his cousin showed up at the station in a jolting pickup truck. His name was Katsuhiro and he greeted Nori with a grunt and me with a narrow-eyed stare. Nori introduced me in a fast-paced Hiroshima drawl; I made out my name and something about America, and that was about it. After a moment of indecision, Katsuhiro smiled shyly at me, searching for long-forgotten grade-school English.

"I am fain sank yuu ando yuu," he proclaimed proudly, and gestured us into the back of his pickup. Nori climbed up first and checked around before he let me vault up after him.

"Sometimes he keeps things back there," he explained as I climbed up.

"What things?"

"Porcupine babies." Nori shrugged. "Squid."

I opened my mouth but Katsuhiro took off with a squeal of tires and I fell backward into the bed of the truck. Nori, who was hanging on for dear life, laughed at me. His eyes were bright, the way they always were when he was involved in some kind of rebellion. I especially liked being with him in moments like this, watching cool Tokyo Nori laughing like an excited country kid. He noticed me looking and cocked one eyebrow, that old parlor trick. I glanced away, over the edge of the truck bed, and watched Hiroshima City fall into rice fields.

———

ANTHONY ASKED ME ONCE, ONLY once that I recall, if I'd ever loved anyone. He wasn't implying himself; he never asked if I loved him, but rather why I didn't. It was toward the beginning, when he still thought I was twenty-one, and I still bothered to lie because sleeping with Anthony interrupted my daily monotony, and I didn't want to lose it.

I'd taken a shower and I was standing naked in the bathroom, drying off. He was in the doorway watching me, drinking me in with that barely concealed hunger that would have been disconcerting if I didn't almost envy the ability to feel it. And then he asked, like he really wanted to know.

I remember that I didn't know what to tell him. I sat there holding his hair dryer, listening to the whir, and finally I turned it off and said, honestly, "I don't think so."

"Think about it," he'd said. Insistent. "What about when you were a kid?"

I thought about it. England, smoky prepubescence, fourteen-year-olds with toffee-and-tea accents trading cigarettes in the stairwell of Harrow and calling them *fags*, a bit of Brit slang which even then amused me to no end. Later, in Seoul, an older kid with a motorcycle who'd give me lifts back from school. When he dropped me off was the best part of every interminable day, mouths mashed together, fingers groping under jackets. The guy before Anthony—an earnest, quiet German, he gave a great blow job and didn't need to talk afterward.

I unplugged Anthony's hair dryer and put it on the counter.

"Nope," I said.

Anthony was frowning, like he didn't quite understand. He picked up the hair dryer and started polishing off the condensation with the edge of his T-shirt.

"What about a crush?" he said. "Those can feel like love. Being infatuated with someone. Noticing these incredibly minute details.

Appreciating that they make you feel something new, something refreshing—"

I grinned. "Is this where you tell me that you're just a teenage girl under all that hair?"

"You really are twenty-one," Anthony said, disappointed. "But even so, most kids your age—"

"Seventeen," I corrected.

Anthony's eyes widened. "What?"

"Seventeen," I said, slower, enunciating. "I'm seventeen. I've been lying to you."

A longer silence. Anthony laid the hair dryer down on the wet counter, like he was afraid he'd break it. I looked at him and thought that he was more attractive like this, with this muddy sort of roiling on his face and not that slow kind of sadness that made me want to hurt him. This new look, it made me hard.

"Get out," Anthony said at last. "Grab your shit and get out of my apartment."

But of course he asked me back again, later.

As we walked through the narrow paths between the rice paddies, Katsuhiro gave us a crash course on how to find mamushi, and Nori translated. They could be found in the water, between the stones of stone walls, and for some reason they had a predilection for cherry trees. "They jump," Nori added, "sideways, it's incredible." Katsuhiro ground to a stop, pointed at a low wall separating two rice paddies from each other and spoke to Nori in fast Japanese. When he finished he turned around and walked back toward the truck.

"Where's he going?" I asked.

Nori shrugged. "He was drinking late last night, now he's going to take a nap."

"But what about the *snakes*?"

Katsuhiro unloaded a forked stick and a glass jar from the cab of the truck. He gave us a Nikon-moment thumbs-up, then crawled into the cab, shutting the door after him. I stared at Nori. He shrugged again.

"He told us where they are and how to catch them, what's your problem?"

"We've never caught any before, that's my problem!"

"It can't be that hard," Nori said dismissively. "Who's smarter, you or a snake?" Then he studied me, and grinned. "On second thought . . ."

Despite Nori's optimism, the first mamushi took us by surprise, emerging from a crack in the stone wall suddenly and with intention. The two of us leapt backward. "It's *okay*," Nori said, like he hadn't jumped too. But by then the snake was gone, into the water of the rice paddy.

"You know in the fall, the mom snakes shed their teeth," Nori said, watching the water resettle.

"Fangs, not teeth," I said, imagining a pit viper with braces and an underbite.

Nori shrugged. "They bite anything in sight—you know those bamboo poles in the rice paddies? When mamushi pull back, they leave the teeth in the bamboo. You can collect them. Some people grind up the teeth and—"

"Wait," I said, "wait wait. Anything in sight?"

Nori sighed. "Take the glass jar," he said. "I can see we're not going anywhere if you're the one holding the stick."

If it had been anyone else but Nori, I would have said something cutting about how nobody had ever complained about me holding his stick. But I didn't know what Nori knew about me, and I didn't want to risk it. Being friends with Nori was just about the only thing that made me want to get up in the morning, and I wasn't about to throw it away.

"What's your plan?" I asked, like I didn't care. Nori wasn't fooled.

"Snake!" he yelled, suddenly. I jumped backward again, saw him laughing, and flipped him off, but Nori was already halfway to the stone wall. I guess the kid had it in his head that he was going to eat one of these bastards and live forever; personally, I didn't know why anyone would want to.

WHEN WE TOLD THE STORY later, to two of our classmates back in Tokyo, Nori was kind enough to pretend like I'd had an active hand in the snake-catching. We were skipping after-school club activities, grabbing a meal at the ramen stand on the corner. I don't think any of us had plans to go home for dinner that night. Nori was going to the arcade with a girl from the grade below us. Paulo Yasuhara, the Brazilian-Japanese kid of some executive, was headed to the Roppongi clubs with Kaneda, who was as sleazy as Yasuhara but not as sexy. As for me, I was going to Anthony's, but none of the others had to know that.

"—dived after it," Nori was saying, excitedly. "And we've got it trapped with its head in the forked stick, its body is *lashing*, it's going crazy, it takes this *lunge* forward and its fangs like *brush* Ancash's hand, we're screaming at each other—and the snake gets freaked out by all the screaming and it lunges forward *into* the jar."

"No way," Kaneda said, impressed.

Yasuhara lit a cigarette. "Nori says you eat one mouthful and your boner's gonna be raging for weeks," he said, looking at me directly as he took a drag. "You gonna eat a mouthful, Ancash?"

His gaze was always like that—hooded and calculating. The few run-ins we had always felt like the preview to some kind of investigation—one that might involve torture. It made something twist in my stomach, dark and good.

"Yeah," I deadpanned. "You want me to come find you when I do?"

The guys all laughed. The corners of Yasuhara's mouth moved in a murky smile.

"I'll get in line," he said, and the guys laughed again. Nori laughed, but his eyes flickered between Yasuhara and me like he was trying to figure out what was happening. The only way to kill the confused curiosity in Nori's eyes was to take this all the way over the top.

"You better bring a snack," I drawled, "it's one hell of a line," and then I leaned over across the table and grabbed Yasuhara's face, as if I was going to kiss him. From this close, the pale gray of his eyes was strangely mesmerizing. I heard the guys yelling behind me, and when I pushed him away in mock-disgust, I saw that Nori was laughing. My mouth hadn't touched his but I'd felt his breath on my lips, I'd heard the catch in it, and the adrenaline of victory coursed through my veins. I'd heard it, that catch. *Not so cool now, are you?*

The guys were talking again around us, a warm tide of normal conversation. Yasuhara looked at me over his cigarette, one quick flash. The smooth line of his throat. He knew that I knew that he knew that I knew, all the way back to when the first caveman was fighting with the second caveman over a joint of dinosaur meat, and somebody swung a punch and then another, and caveman-muscle met caveman-muscle with sickening impact, heat and sweat—and then all of a sudden the punching turned to pulling, closer, closer, that sweet angry friction, fighting turned to fucking and the dinosaur was forgotten.

Yasuhara's mouth twisted in that sudden brief smile that came and went like heat lightning and I felt my own mouth move in an answering smile.

THE PARTY BROKE UP AFTER THAT. Yasuhara and Kaneda moved off to kill some time in a manga café before dark, and I walked Nori back toward the arcade where he was meeting the girl. Nori said that she was Swedish, had spent the last three years in Tokyo but still couldn't handle Japanese. "But she has pillow-tits," he added. When I burst out laughing, he continued, "I dunno where white guys get the yellow fever from. Japanese girls are skinny and crazy."

I loved how Nori talked shit with his soft mouth and those big shining eyes. "What do you mean crazy?"

"They'll cut your heart out and eat it on rice," Nori said. We skirted a row of bicycles, cutting down an alley. It was evening, and you could smell food cooking behind the lighted rectangles of every window. "They repress and repress and then they just *lose* it. You know Kaneda's girlfriend went for him with a knife once? Japanese are crazy, I'm not even kidding, they do jealousy like nobody else."

I grabbed his wrist, yanking him out of the way of an oncoming motorcycle. "Hey," I said, "watch where you're walking. Anyway, aren't you Japanese?"

"Who the fuck knows," Nori said. Then, "Do you like Japanese girls?"

Caught off guard, I hesitated. I hadn't dropped Nori's wrist when I'd pulled him away from the motorcycle, and now we stood at the edge of the street, practically holding hands, his skin hot to the touch. He didn't seem to notice. I let go of him quickly.

"Sure," I said, "I guess."

"Do you like American girls better?"

I rubbed my hand on my jeans. "They're okay." I flickered a glance at him but his face was open and guileless.

Nori grinned. "Yasuhara says French girls don't shave." He resumed walking. "You know Nicole, from the kendo club? He did it with her." We began to pass the entrance to the JR, and now Nori was hesitating. "I should go home and check on the snake," he said.

"Nori, why the fuck do you need to check on the snake? It's not like you need to feed it."

"I know," Nori said, "but I haven't seen it all day, I don't know. Come back and check with me."

"No way," I said. "I'm not going in your room till that thing's dead."

But I followed him down into the subway anyway, Noriyuki carving a path through rush-hour crowds and me following, my eyes fixed on the curve of his shoulders under the dark blue of his school jacket.

―――――

Even as Anthony opened the door, he was saying, "Where have you *been*, it's been *days*—" He stopped, when he saw me still wearing my uniform jacket. I knew he would. He liked me in stiff button-down white shirts, ironed blazer-pants. Liked me looking like an innocent rich kid who wasn't quite ready to get shoved up against a wall. Everybody wants to feel like they can corrupt someone.

"You're up late, Anthony," I said smoothly. I knew he'd stand aside, and he did.

"Where were you?" he demanded.

"Tonight? All over."

"And the past few days? Where have you been for those?"

I shrugged. "Hiroshima."

He hadn't expected that one. "During a school week?" Genuinely curious now: "What's in Hiroshima?"

Nights like this, it could go either way. We could sit down and talk. He could be kind, he wanted to know things about me, little things. What kind of music I listened to. What I read. Jokes that made me laugh. He could kiss my cheekbones, the edge of my eyes, he could say gentle things. I didn't need that.

"This guy," I said, deliberately. "In Hiroshima City."

And there it was. Slow flush of scarlet. "Oh yeah?"

And so it went the other way.

He fell asleep after we were done. I lay next to him for a few minutes, listening to my ragged breathing, feeling the sticky throbbing in my face. At last I sat up, wincing at the twinge in my shoulder, and walked into the bathroom. There was a mirror against the back of the door. I closed it partway and stood there for a few minutes, staring without seeing myself.

I was remembering a few hours earlier, Noriyuki and that damn viper. It didn't even look like it was hungry yet, coiled in its glass jar, barely moving.

"There are only three dangerous animals in all of Japan," Nori had told me, turning the glass jar so he could see the snake from all angles. "Wild boars, mamushi, and bears."

"We woulda been better off catching a wild boar," I said, tapping the jar lid with my fingernails. "We caught an old lady snake. You eat this bitch, your dick goes limper than udon."

Nori laughed. "That's what you think," he said. "Watch this."

He reached into his pocket, came up with a lighter, and flicked it on. I heard the dull thud of the snake's head connecting with the glass before I even saw it move. It didn't notice the glass was in the way, it just reared back, adjusted its angle, and tried again. Nori held the lighter above the jar this time. The mamushi reared straight up, bashing its head on the jar lid, and I could see that its two little needle-fangs had unfolded.

"Jesus!" I said. My heart was slamming into my ribs. "What the fuck!"

"They hunt by heat sensors," Nori explained. "They can feel the temperature change from a few feet away. When our hands were near the air holes he started tracking us, that's why his tongue was flickering more, he was waiting for us to get closer. The lighter is so strong, though, that he thought we were right there. Pretty awesome, yeah?"

Nori flicked the lighter on-off again, this time to the left of the jar, and the snake tried to rear around. Another failed strike. And all of a sudden I just wanted Nori to stop. I grabbed Nori's hand.

"Okay," I said, "I get it, enough."

He looked at me strangely. "It doesn't hurt the snake," he said. "It thinks *it's* hunting *us*."

Anthony's voice, from the doorway, brought me back.

"What're you doing? Come back to bed."

I looked at him and he flinched and dropped his eyes. I looked in the mirror for real this time. It hadn't felt that different from normal when we were in the middle of it, but I looked like I'd been in a war zone. My lower lip was swollen, blood spattered liberally over my mouth and chin, a bruise darkening along my cheekbone. I turned toward Anthony, genuinely impressed. He was staring at the floor. I was afraid, suddenly, that he was going to cry.

"Go back to bed," I said, fast and cold.

"What're you going to say in school tomorrow?"

"I'm not gonna say anything."

"They'll ask you about it. They'll call you in."

I shrugged. "So I got jumped. It's not your problem, Anthony, nothing that happens outside of this room is your problem."

Anthony was silent for a long time. Outside the apartment, Tokyo whirred on like a neon machine set on "forever." You could hear the beat of club music even from here. I turned on the faucet and started washing blood off my face. We hadn't touched my face except for the first time. Torso yeah, arms, then one day shoulders and back became fair game, but not the face. Well, we'd have gotten there eventually. It's not like it made any difference. The bloody water swirling around the sink basin was dyeing the porcelain a vaguely pinkish hue. I didn't think the color would stick, though, so I didn't say anything.

Into the silence Anthony said, very softly, "It could be different. With us. It could be so different, Ancash."

I lifted my head from the sink and stared at him.

He looked at me. Dripping pink water on the bathroom tiles. Something passed between us, old and weary.

"No," I said. "It couldn't though."

I got Nori's text message on my way to the nurse's office, but I figured in the rush of lunch hour, she wouldn't notice if I didn't show up. The door to the men's bathroom was closed when I got there. I eased it open, and was greeted by the sight of Kaneda, Nori, and Yasuhara crouched in a semicircle. "Ancash," Nori drawled, "better late than never." And then the grin fell off his face. *"Fuck, what happened to you?"*

Yasuhara had been lighting a cigarette but at the tone in Nori's voice, he straightened and looked over at me. His eyebrows went up.

"Let me guess," Yasuhara drawled. "Whatever it was, you lost."

"No big deal," I said. "I got jumped in Roppongi."

Nori was frowning. "Roppongi?" he echoed, and then I remembered stopping by Anthony's place before Hiroshima.

"Yeah," I shrugged. "What's up with the snake?"

Nori kept his eyes on me, but answered the question anyway. "I was showing the guys the heat-sensor thing."

Kaneda moved his hand near the jar, tentatively, but the snake ignored him.

"You have to keep it there longer," Yasuhara told him scornfully. "It's gotta feel your heat." He flicked his lighter on and held it steady over the lid. The snake lashed out as it had before, fell back, regrouped, lashed out again. Kaneda drew back this time; Nori was still crouched there looking searchingly at me. I didn't want him looking at me like that, like he was trying to guess at things he shouldn't know about. The rhythmic bashing of the snake's head against glass was doing something sick to my stomach. I grabbed the lighter away from Yasuhara, burning my hand.

"Enough," I said.

I expected him to say something cutting, but instead he just looked at me, with that pale unreadable gaze.

"You'd think it would have noticed the glass by now," Kaneda said.

"Who gives a fuck about the glass," Yasuhara said, answering Kaneda but looking at me. "It doesn't even notice the glass."

YASUHARA WAS WAITING FOR ME by the ramen shop. He was alone.

"Where's the fan club?" I asked.

The two of us against the early evening light. It reminded me of all those times I stood in Anthony's doorway, framing myself for him like a picture. But when I thought of him it was like thinking of a civilian in a war zone. Yasuhara wasn't a civilian.

He switched my question with his own. "Going somewhere?"

If it was going to happen, why not now.

I looked straight back at him. "I dunno," I said. "Am I?"

WE ENDED UP IN NI-CHOME, at a love hotel that I'd actually been to once, a year ago, before Anthony. The street was waking up, blinking neon, as we came out of an alley and cut across the main thoroughfare. In another hour or so, the crowds would be thick and rowdy.

Yasuhara walked into the love hotel through the discreet side entrance as if he'd been there a hundred times before. We stopped in front of the lit-up display panel of available rooms, and Yasuhara picked one, without asking me. We took the elevator up and followed the blinking red arrow down the dingy little hall to the room. You never have to meet anybody in these places. In some, you even pay at the end, sticking your bills one by one into the money slot; once you pay the full price, the door unlocks and you're let back out. We didn't say anything the whole time.

The door closed after us and the lock clicked into place. We both looked around. A window with the curtains drawn. A big-screen TV. A karaoke machine on the wall, a bathroom. And the bed, huge and remarkably clean for a place where thousands upon thousands of people have fucked in every position and configuration imaginable.

"Love hotels frown on threesomes," Yasuhara said, as if he'd been reading my mind. He dropped his school jacket on the floor.

"Yeah?"

"Yeah. If somebody's watching the security cam and they see three people come in, they'll kick you out. That's Japan for you.

Limited, sanitized perversion." Yasuhara turned to face me, and yanked his shirt over his head. I took him in: the hard flat lines of his torso, the swell of muscle in his chest and arms. A tattoo swam up his ribs, a fine net of dark lines that I couldn't make out clearly. He saw me looking and smiled that thin cold smile.

"Your turn."

I shrugged out of my jacket, dropped it. Pulled my shirt off. Then kicked off my shoes, socks, unzipped my jeans, dropped them, then the boxers. He took me in. I knew what he was looking at. Even in the dim light you could make out the marks.

"Who was it?" he asked, surprising me. When I didn't answer, he started unbuckling his belt. "You don't have to tell me, I know it was that white guy. I've seen you with him."

All of a sudden I wasn't sure what the game was.

"You been following me?" I asked.

Yasuhara stepped out of his jeans, then looked at me with those dark calculating eyes. "You fuck him?"

"Yeah," I said, "I fuck him. What's it to you?"

Naked, Yasuhara walked to the window. He opened the curtain and looked out. "Haven't told anyone," he said. "If you're wondering."

"Don't give a shit if you do."

Yasuhara turned back to me. "Haven't told Noriyuki."

My mouth was dry. "So tell him. I don't care."

Yasuhara sauntered toward me. He stopped a hand-span away, and tilted his head to one side, watching me.

"Yeah you do," he said, softly. "And no, I won't."

He took my face in his hands and kissed me on the mouth, hard but without meanness. It surprised me completely—I don't know why. I pulled away sharply.

"What do you want?" I asked. It had seemed so obvious on the way here, but now it no longer did.

Yasuhara shook his head. He was touching my body now, not answering. My collarbone, ribs, the edge of my hip bone. Outlining the shapes of bruises with his fingertips. The long zipper-line of a cut. That one had been an accident—Anthony forgot to take off his rings. I let Yasuhara touch me. I still had no idea what the game was but it didn't feel bad, his fingertips on my skin. I closed my eyes to concentrate on his strange light touch, but the note of anger in Yasuhara's voice made me reopen them.

"I can kill him if you want."

"Kill who?" I asked, bewildered.

"The white guy. For doing this to you."

I stared at him. "It's not like that."

"Easy to fall through the cracks," Yasuhara said, low and fast. "Hundred thousand people here, one day he'd just be gone. You don't know what I can do. I have friends . . ."

"Don't," I said. The two of us whispering secrets like kids in the dark. "It doesn't matter. He doesn't even want to."

"He shouldn't do that to you." Yasuhara lowered his head to my chest, his lips brushing over the red jag of the cut, down across my ribs. The edge of his teeth, our skin painted red and gold and blue from the neon signs flashing outside. My breathing, ragged now. He stood up in one swift movement and wrapped his arms around me, tight.

"You have no idea what I can do," he said, his lips moving against my neck. "Just ask me."

"Yasuhara." My voice was cool despite the tightness in my chest. "What are you doing."

Yasuhara didn't let go. "I know what you are. Knew it when I met you."

"Yeah?" I couldn't seem to get angry, although I felt like I should be.

"Walking around with Nori, talking all your shit, nobody sees what you are. But I do."

"And what am I?"

He hesitated, and then grinned that small feral grin. "Lonely. Really lonely."

I was pretty sure that wasn't what he'd been going to say, but he kissed me hard. It hurt a little, since my mouth was still bruised, but I didn't push him away. It was bewildering to me, how hot his body was against mine. His skin seemed so hot to.the touch that I wondered briefly if the dim glow in the room was coming from him and not from the neon outside. But still I didn't push him away, and he just kept kissing me, gentler now. It seemed so innocent, suddenly, that I wanted to laugh. The two of us here in a love hotel, secret and naked, and Yasuhara was kissing me like we were at a junior high dance. Like some teen love story. For some reason, then, I thought of Nori.

Earlier that day, the two of us had been in his bedroom watching the snake coiled in its jar. Nori had brought out the lighter but before he could flick it on, I'd said, "Don't." In that one moment, I had this terror that if he sparked the lighter and drew its attention, it would see his face clearly, remember him forever, and then hurt him. He would be asleep and it would move like silk in the dark, it would sink those two needle-teeth into the hollow of his neck where the pulse jumps, pull away and leave the fangs behind.

Nori had asked me what was wrong. I hadn't known what to say. *I don't want anything to hurt you. I'd kill anyone who hurt you.*

"Nothing," I'd said, shaken.

"What's wrong?" Yasuhara's voice drew me back. "Ancash, what is it?"

Nori with the forked stick. Nori with the jar. Nori in the back of the truck and the rice fields flashing by and every rice paddy had mamushi, every stone wall hid mamushi. Nori asleep on the train back from Hiroshima with a jar in his book bag, everyone asleep, the snake and I had been the only ones awake.

"Ancash!"

Nori dodging bicycles. Nori dodging traffic. And me, always five steps behind, following the solid line of his shoulders. *I don't want anything to touch you.* Stupid jokes and sideways glances. *Anything to keep you clean.*

Anthony: "Have you ever loved anyone?"

"No," I'd said, scornful. "No."

"Ancash, talk to me."

I blinked. Yasuhara, shaking me. His face close to mine, that smooth mask disrupted by concern. He stopped shaking me when he saw me focusing on him.

"Ancash—?"

I made it to the bathroom before I was sick.

Afterward, I knelt with my cheek against the cool of the toilet seat. Yasuhara came in, I heard him in the doorway. He stood there looking at me. I wouldn't look at him. Neither of us said anything. Finally Yasuhara swore, in Portuguese, and turned away. I heard him moving around in the other room, then the door opened and closed.

When I emerged from the bathroom he was gone. My clothes were folded on the bed. I put them on and left. It only occurred to me halfway down the street that he must have paid for everything to get the doors to unlock. He must have picked my clothes up from the floor, folded them neatly, laid them on the bed. The folded clothes and the unlocked door, I didn't know what to do, nothing made sense. I'd thought Yasuhara was the same as me. I'd thought he only fucked people who meant nothing.

IT SEEMED AT FIRST AS if Anthony wasn't home. I knocked for a long time and he didn't come to the door, and then I turned the doorknob and the door opened, so I went in. The lights were all on and still the apartment was death-silent, void of any live human sound. I kicked my sneakers off and walked through the kitchen and came upon Anthony, sitting on the couch. He wasn't reading anything, hadn't been asleep. He was just sitting there.

"Didn't you hear me knocking?"

"Yeah."

"Didn't you figure it was me?"

"Yeah."

I tilted my head, trying to see him better. He looked awful. He hadn't shaved, his eyes were bloodshot. I could smell the whiskey rolling off him.

"Are you drunk?"

He laughed, a little thickly. "I made a good-faith effort."

I couldn't seem to put things together today. "Why?"

He stood up then, quicker than I'd expected. He crossed the space between us and grabbed me by the front of my shirt, hauling me close. I couldn't remember seeing him like this before, looking at him and not knowing what he would do. I always knew what he'd do—his predictability was one of the many things I disdained.

"Fuck you," he said. "You can't do this, can't have it like this, can you."

"Anthony, what are you—?"

He hit me sharply across the face. It had never been like this before, that look on his face like he *wanted* to hurt me. I shook my head, startled, and he hit me again.

"You can't make me *do* this," he said, and his voice sounded like he was asking me for something, but then he kept hitting me, over and over again. "You can't *have* it like this, never be able to go back now, never be able, look at myself and it's not the same, I did that for you, you wanted me like that so I, but now I can't, I can't *look* at myself and I can't—"

Dizzy, I pulled away from him, trying to block my face with my hands. The cuts that had started to heal had reopened now, and there was blood on him and on me, and my head was ringing with a deep, old echo, like a stone hitting the bottom of a well over and over again.

Anthony looked at me hard. He was drunk but his eyes were sober. He hated me right then. I didn't blame him. "Don't look at me like that," he said, rage in his voice. "Don't you look at me!"

I looked away.

He was pacing back and forth in front of me. Every so often, he'd slap his palm down on the counter and the sound would snap like a gunshot. I just kept my eyes fastened on the linoleum floor.

"—if you *understood*," Anthony was saying. Lecturing the wineglasses, the refrigerator, now toward me again. "It doesn't have to *be* like—you *make* it like this, you twist things—there's something wrong with you!" And then straight to me, stopping in front of me. "I don't hurt people! I've never *hurt* anybody!"

I looked up at him. I couldn't stop myself. "It's an acquired taste. Don't hate me because you acquired it."

"Don't you fucking look at me," Anthony said, and his voice was as low as mine.

So I looked down again. And because I looked down, I didn't see him pick up the whiskey bottle until he was already swinging it at my head.

I blocked, sheer instinct. It shattered against my forearm and I felt a sharp pain shooting from wrist to elbow. He was already swinging it again, the broken bottom slashing at my face, like a bad bar-fight scene in some movie. I dodged, skidding a little on the broken glass all over the floor. I looked at his face. It wasn't his. I realized quite clearly that he was going to kill me.

I almost stayed. It would have been so easy to just stand there with my arm dead weight and the glass on the floor and let him come at me. Not block that one. I don't think I can explain if you don't already understand, how easy it would have been. But what did it was the thought of Nori, the lid off the jar and the smoothness, the gentleness, two poison needles sliding down into his pulse. I had to tell him to watch out.

I kicked a kitchen chair between us just as Anthony lunged. Even as he tried to stop, he tripped. The bottle flew out of his hand and smashed against the far wall. Glass sprayed like shrapnel. I didn't wait for him to get up. I ran. I heard him yelling my name as the door slammed shut after me.

———

ROPPONGI WAS A WHIRL OF colors, lights, bodies shoving past. Pounding music. I reeled through it. I didn't know where I was going,
couldn't slow down, couldn't think. I fell a few times, got up and
kept going. I had to find Nori. It occurred to me eventually to call
him and the thought was so logical, so supremely precise, that it
stopped me short. Like taking a deep cool gulp of air, I found that I
could think again. My hand was shaking so badly that I could barely
punch Nori's number into the tiny keypad. All around me Roppongi
surged and seethed, and I focused on the thin faraway sound of
Nori's phone ringing. After what seemed like forever, he picked up.

"Ancash, what's up!"

"Nori, I gotta see you. Where are you?"

He sounded distracted. "Shinjuku, I'm at the arcade with Kristen.
What's wrong?"

My legs gave out. I was sitting on the sidewalk, I didn't even
notice.

"Nori, you gotta be careful, don't go home tonight. Or if you do,
turn all the lights on, leave them all on when you sleep. No, don't
sleep. You shouldn't sleep."

"I can't hear you, you're breaking up."

"I said don't sleep! And throw the snake out! Kill it and flush the
body!"

"Kill *what*? Ancash, I can't hear you."

"The snake!" I was getting dizzy again; I shook my head to clear
it, and droplets of blood fell on my jeans. "Nori, we have to get rid
of it!"

"What did you say? Where are you?"

"I'm coming!" I yelled into the phone. "Wait for me!"

Nori started to say something but his phone cut off. I started off
at a run toward the nearest JR station. It was the usual late-evening
crush of commuters, kids, tourists, and they all looked at me,
shocked, and then looked away fast. I cut the line to get my ticket,
and nobody stopped me. They just looked down until I'd passed.

As the darkness flashed by the windows of the train, I stared at my reflection in the glass. I didn't even recognize myself at first. I looked like the echo of a person, like a skin that somebody had shed. I closed my eyes.

Nori in the truck, Nori laughing, Nori's hand in mine, Nori's hand in mine.

I wasn't going to bring him into this, I swore that up and down. Let him have his Swedish girl, I'd never say a word, *keep him safe, keep him safe*, I don't know who I was pleading with, there was nobody on that train but me and the commuters, and the commuters had their backs turned. Everybody in Tokyo had their backs turned, and only the snake was listening.

Behind my closed eyes I saw Anthony again with the broken whiskey bottle in his hand. And then Yasuhara, something feral, beautifully angry—*Just ask me,* he'd said, and he'd folded my clothes. He'd paid for the room. He'd touched my face. He'd folded my clothes. *I know what you are.* What did he want from me? Couldn't he see that I was beyond hope? I couldn't make sense of anything.

I'll make a deal with you, I said to the snake. *Stay in your jar. I won't kill you. I'll climb in. We'll live there together, you and me, with our fangs folded flat against the roofs of our mouths. Our blood will run so slowly that it will freeze inside us. We'll let the world slide by on the other side of the glass, hot and far, flickering neon.*

I opened my eyes and so did my reflection and we watched each other warily, jolting along toward Shinjuku where Nori was waiting, and he didn't understand, he didn't understand, and I swore to God I'd never tell him anything.

SURVEILLANCE

When the headache lasts past a day, I decide I have a brain tumor. Inoperable, probably. Hard to know, but chances are, I'm dead. I look in the mirror. Do my eyes look different? I check my lymph nodes. I can't tell if they're swollen, or if they're just lymph nodes. I wonder how I'll tell this story, when I tell it later. From the hospital bed—or online, a video testimonial of a life cut short, probably intended to raise money for something, or someone, who is no longer me. *I just had a feeling*, I'll say. *I had this headache*, I'll say. *Go to the doctor, kids*, I'll say, *pay attention.*

I meet my friend Agnes for coffee. This is what I do when I think I'm dying, which happens fairly often. I wouldn't say that I'm always wrong, I would just say the jury is still out. There's no special rule that only one thing can kill you. You can have brain cancer *and* Ebola *and* get hit by the subway. One thing may kill you slower and another may kill you faster, but all are operative factors.

Agnes doesn't think she's dying. Agnes thinks people are watching her, and who knows, they might be. The thing about paranoia in the twenty-first century is that, at some point, it's impossible to know if you're crazy, or if you're astute. Everywhere you go there are tiny screens pointed at you like eyes. Every dressing room, every café, every tourist with an iPhone taking photos that implicate you in the background. Every surface is multiplied and reflected, all sight has been turned into fly-sight and bee-sight: triplicate, quadruplicate, hexagonal and multiplying. Are they watching you, or are you just being seen?

Agnes goes on these spirals where she googles things like "NSA" and "Area 51" and "Surveillance" and "How normal people get hauled away to internment camps." I know whenever she's been on a bender because she shows up to meet me with dark circles under her eyes and hasn't yet been to yoga.

"I don't know why you aren't more worried," says Agnes. We sit in a corner, and she holds her still-rolled yoga mat between herself and everything else, like a barrier. "The world is fucked, Sammy."

"I'm worried," I say. I'm not sure how to tell Agnes about the brain cancer.

"I bet you didn't know this," Agnes says, "but . . ." She goes on for a long time, and I listen for the sound of my brain tumor growing. This morning the headache was still there, and the center of my head felt oddly heavier, like there was something malignant nestled inside. Sometimes I don't know how people get up in the morning and make their coffee and go to work, when we live in bodies that are ticking time bombs. Sometimes I don't know how I do these things, and then I want to stop, I just want to stop doing anything at all, and wait for the time bomb to explode.

Agnes finishes, and studies my face to see how I'll react to what was clearly a terrible revelation.

"That's terrible," I say.

Agnes sighs. "I know," she says.

We sit together, in a moment of silence.

"I mean," Agnes says after the moment of silence has passed, "basically we should go off the grid."

"Okay," I say. "Where?"

"The problem is that there's no place left that's *off* the grid." Agnes chews her lower lip. "Not in the U.S. anyway, your phone records all of your coordinates all the time, your camera is basically another portal through which you can be observed, and satellites pass over every inch of everything. You used to live in Japan, what do you think?"

"Definitely cameras everywhere," I say. Agnes chews harder at her lip. "South America," I suggest. "The Andes mountains."

Agnes considers this. We have had versions of this conversation often. It was the first conversation of our friendship, several years ago at the AA women's group. I'd just returned from Japan, arriving in New York to realize that I had no idea what I was doing with my life other than acquiring and nourishing a drinking problem. Agnes sat down next to me on a rickety folding chair, Styrofoam cup of coffee in hand, and asked, "Is there anywhere left that's off the grid?" And I looked at her—gangly, intense, vital with unease—and I knew we'd be friends. "The Andes," I said, and she smiled.

Since then, Agnes has reconsidered the Andes. She feels differently about them, depending on the day. Sometimes they seem like a safe haven. Sometimes it seems inconceivable that someone hasn't gotten to them yet: "By now, even the Andes are bugged."

Today she's in a more hopeful mood. "The Andes are a possibility," she says.

I wonder if now is the moment to tell her that I'm not certain I'll be alive too much longer. I wonder when I should give this information to Oliver. Yesterday Oliver left me three voicemails in fifteen minutes. The first said: "I miss you, are you coming over?" The second said: "Can you bring latex gloves and some more paper towel?" The third said: "Why aren't you picking up, are we okay?" I know he means am I breaking up with him—this is a question that Oliver puzzles over, obsesses over—but the answer might be one he didn't expect. Namely: yes, but brain cancer.

Agnes eyes me over her coffee. "Someone is watching us have this conversation," she says. "Right now? Right this second? Someone somewhere is watching us talk to each other."

We take a moment and dart our eyes around the café. There's a tiny little camera tucked like a bat, sleeping in the far juncture of wall and wall. Last night Oliver buried his face in the juncture of my neck and shoulder and said: "I love you." And then he said, "You don't have to say it back," but it sounded like an accusation.

"Why?" I ask. "What does it tell them, to watch us have coffee?"

Agnes sighs. "If one of us becomes a Dissident Element," she says, "they'll know we know each other and then they'll pick the other of us up off the street, probably in a black unmarked van, and they'll take us somewhere. They're information-gathering."

This morning Oliver called to ask if we could go on vacation together in July. I wanted to know if Agnes could come, to which he replied, "But if Agnes comes, then we won't be *together*." He asked, "Why would you want *Agnes* to come on *our* romantic vacation?" He was information-gathering.

"All information they possess will ultimately be used against you," Agnes warns. "They even tell us that straight up, but nobody really believes it."

I want to tell Oliver that I might be dying, but Oliver wants to tell me something first. I smell a terrible stench before I even get all the way in the door. "Temporary," he's saying, "just for the week," and as my face screws itself up, I come to a halt in front of a giant iguana sitting on his counter. Its cage is open. Its tail is draped across the fruit bowl. I make a mental note to never eat that fruit. The iguana tilts its jagged face to one side and sizes me up, in a singularly hostile manner.

"Izaiah," says Oliver.

"Excuse me?"

"Izaiah the Iguana."

Izaiah and I stare at each other. I think: *botulism*. I think: *salmonella*. I think people have actually died from salmonella, like people with compromised immune systems, like people with inoperable brain cancers. Oliver is excited. He's moving back and forth from foot to foot the way he does when he's overstimulated. With his shirt hiked up and his cargo pants falling down, Oliver looks a little bit like a hyper-caffeinated eight-year-old, and not like someone who is turning thirty.

"Oliver," I say, "*why* are you babysitting an iguana?"

Oliver doesn't understand the question. I try again: "Where did it come from?"

"Oh!" Oliver says. "He belongs to the guys downstairs, but they went to Boston for the week so I said I'd take him."

"Oh," I say, as if this explains things, but it doesn't—in large part because my question isn't really *Where did it come from?* but rather *Why did you think you were the person to look after it?* Oliver is not organized. He's not responsible. I have known him to eat cat food, because he was buying groceries in a hurry and thought he was getting canned tuna fish. Oliver is impetuous, moved by the spirit of whatever moment he is in. Sometimes he feels like smudging the apartment with palo santo. But then he remembers that yesterday he dropped fifty cents behind the bed, so he puts the palo santo down on the counter and goes into the bedroom, but there's mail on the counter, so he lights all the mail on fire. Head shoved under the bed, searching for quarters while the fire alarm starts to shriek: this is Oliver.

When we first met, I found him charming and disarming. I had dropped my phone onto the subway tracks and was trying to calculate my chances of being hit by a train if I went after it. Oliver flung himself past me, down onto the tracks, grabbed my phone, and vaulted back up. I blinked at him, he grinned at me, brown eyes radiating enthusiasm. "I think I touched a rat," he said, and I felt myself instantly drawn in. I am a person who thinks too much, and all of my thoughts instantaneously transform themselves into worries. Oliver's desperate impetuousness seemed like an open door, a blinking EXIT sign, a THIS WAY arrow that might lead me out of myself to safety. Instead, it has led me to an iguana.

"Do you want to pat him?" Oliver asks.

Izaiah looks at me like: *Just try it, bitch.*

"Nah," I say, "I'm good."

"I invited people over to watch him," Oliver says. He's still jig-gling from foot to foot, but less so because he can tell that I don't love Izaiah, and this makes him nervous. Oliver gets upset when we feel different things at the same time, or the same things at different times. He calls this "misalignment," and he says it just makes him very very sad, but sometimes it's the sort of sad where he ends up yelling.

"Watch him, like, you're going out?"

"No, watch him. We're going to sit here and watch him. He's really primal and instinctual and just . . . natural."

"Oh," I say. In my head I wonder if it's time to mention the brain tumor yet. Like: *I don't have time to sit here all night and stare at this iguana, because my time on earth is limited.*

"I don't know how many people are coming though," Oliver says. "I just sort of made a Facebook group and invited everybody."

"That's why I asked you to get rubber gloves," Oliver says, "and paper towel."

"I guess you forgot," Oliver says, and his eyes finish the sentence with *about me.*

I make the decision not to mention my brain tumor.

FOUR PEOPLE COME OVER TO stare at the iguana. One of them is Oli-ver's ex-roommate, an activist named Sofia. She comes directly from a protest, and leaves her placard in the hallway with the shoes. One of them is Oliver's best friend Mason, who has started growing his hair long because Oliver's is long. He is a little bit in love with Oliver, and he thinks Oliver's ideas are generally all good ideas, even when they haven't finished forming. One of them is Mason's recent ex-girlfriend, who comes in large part to punish Mason. She sits directly across the iguana from Mason, and her stony stare could be trained on either him or Izaiah—it's hard to tell. The fourth person is Agnes, who comes because I text her, *HELP.*

Agnes and I stand in the kitchen and confer in low voices, as everybody else sits around the living room in a ragged circle and stares at Izaiah. Oliver is staring so hard that he's top-heavy, leaning forward with his lower lip protruding. His attention is a weight—I know because I've felt it.

"Are they high?" Agnes wants to know.

I say I don't think so, although it's hard to tell sometimes.

"Is the lizard doing anything?"

I risk a glance around the doorframe. In the past half hour, Izaiah has moved from the counter to the top of the microwave, where he now sits majestically.

"Not really."

"It's super weird," Agnes says, also risking a glance. She finds it hard to approve of Oliver. Oliver finds it hard to be disapproved of.

"I know," I say. "I mean who would want to own a fucking *iguana?*"

"You could put a chip in it," Agnes muses.

"You mean like with dogs, like if it gets lost?"

"No," Agnes says, lowering her voice even more. "Like surveillance."

"Like, the CIA?"

She shrugs. "If you wanted access to normal American homes, if you wanted access to everything that was said or ... I mean the pets. Right? American pets."

Oliver chooses this moment to come into the kitchen for water. "Oh hi, Agnes," he says.

"Oh," Agnes says, and makes him wait several more seconds before she says, "hi."

Oliver licks his lips a little nervously. "Are you joining us?" he asks me.

"Yeah," I say, "in just a minute."

"Okay, because that would be really great." Oliver looks just to the left of Agnes's left ear. "You could join us too," he says, as if she might be too shy without an invitation.

"Oh," Agnes says, "no. Thanks."

"Oh," Oliver says, and shifts from foot to foot for a moment, his eyes darting between Agnes and me. The silence is the sound of something continuing to disintegrate. Then: "Well. Okay." Water glass in hand, he goes back into the living room. I always get the feeling that Agnes and Oliver are locked in a silent deadly contest, but I couldn't tell you what the prize is.

As soon as Oliver has retreated, Agnes turns back to me. Before she can say anything cutting and specifically aimed at him, I blurt out: "I have a brain tumor."

Agnes considers this. Then she asks, "Do you want to do the pat-down?"

This is something Agnes and I have come up with. Or Agnes, mostly, has come up with it.

I say, "Right now?" glancing toward the cabal of Facebook Iguana Watchers.

Agnes says, "They're staring at a fucking lizard."

I say, "Okay, yeah." Because I do want to do the pat-down. I need a medical opinion, even if it isn't expert, or even somewhat informed, or even belonging to someone who has a right to have medical opinions. The thing about Agnes is that she's very confident, and I'm a sucker for confidence. When you sound like you know what you're saying, I feel a huge relief fill my entire body. This is because I so rarely feel confident about anything.

"Okay," says Agnes, and I lift my arms above my head. Agnes's hands move down me from scalp to forehead to throat to shoulders. They make a brisk patting gesture, as she goes through the checklist.

"Fevers?"

"No."

"Difficulty swallowing?"

"Not really."

"Bloody vomit?"

"No."

"Bloody shits?"

"No."

Agnes is at my hips now. Her little hands do a pat-pat as she says, "Pregnant?"

"Ew, no."

At my knees she says, "Night terrors?"

"No."

She pat-pats the top of my Chucks, symbolically. "Yeah, you're alive."

"But am I *fine?*"

"You're definitely not fine," says Agnes, with confidence, "but I have no reason to believe you're dying." This time, as she straightens back up, she pat-pats the center of my forehead.

"No brain tumor," she says.

OLIVER CALLS ME TO TELL me of Izaiah's death, shortly after I've discovered that one of my breasts is larger than the other. This, to me, is a clear sign of breast cancer. And if not breast cancer, then a dangerous malformation that signifies bad genes, reckless mutations in my gene pool, DNA strands swapping and slipping around each other until the next kid down the line could just as easily be a frog or a rabbit.

"Izaiah is dead," Oliver says. He sounds very grave. I think he's been crying.

"Was it cancer?" I ask. I'm standing naked in my bathroom, fresh out of the shower. Pools of water are gathering around me as I squeeze my left tit, then my right, then my left again. The right one is the larger one. Is it also warmer to the touch?

"No," Oliver says, startled. "No, he fell out the window and died."

"What was he doing near a window?"

Oliver sounds a little slippery when he says, "He was just sitting in the window."

"Did you *put* him in the window?"

"I thought he might want to see." Oliver is sulking now. "I thought he might want fresh air."

I think my right breast *is* warmer than my left. What generates heat? Infection generates heat. What if, instead of a cancer, I just have a giant infection in my right breast? Like the kind that travels up to your brain and kills you. What do they call that? Meningitis?

"Are you still *there?*" Oliver demands.

"Yeah," I say. "I'm here."

"I can't believe he's dead," says Oliver. "I was only just getting to know him."

Breast-related brain meningitis? Is that a thing? I want to google it, but I'm scared to google it.

"Screens," I say. "You should get screens for the windows."

"I think we should have a funeral," Oliver says. "After I tell the guys downstairs. Maybe we can have it when they're back from Boston. Maybe it could be nice."

"Maybe you should get them another lizard."

"Maybe we can bury him in the garden," Oliver says, a little dreamily, ignoring me. I can tell he's already coming up with a funeral-themed craft project. Oliver likes craft projects. And sure enough: "Maybe I could build a wooden wall, like full of candles, and everybody could light one candle for Izaiah, and say a wish, like a hope or intention in their own lives, and they could dedicate that intention to Izaiah."

I know what Oliver's intention would be: that nobody ever leaves him, not neighbors, not girlfriends, not lizards. I know what my intention would be: to die so quickly, so casually, that I don't even notice I'm dead.

Less than thirty hours later, while Izaiah is still in the freezer waiting for his funeral, Oliver texts me to let me know that he's agreed to babysit a pet rat. "Its name is Wallace," he says.

AGNES WATCHES THE EDWARD SNOWDEN documentary, and comes over. She doesn't call first, in case our phones are being tapped. She brings a roll of black electrical tape with her, and she tapes over the camera on my laptop, and also the one on my phone. "Just in case," she says. She's calm but determined. I wish things that galvanized me into action also made me calm but determined. Mostly, they just make me panic.

I give Agnes my update: "I have breast meningitis, and Izaiah is dead, and also Oliver is babysitting a rat."

Agnes chooses the most alarming thing to respond to first. "A *rat?*"

"Named Wallace."

"Where did he get a *rat?*"

I have learned that there are lots of people in the world who need other people to look after the animals they semi-ironically purchased, and I tell Agnes this.

Agnes is dismayed by the rat's life resting in Oliver's hands. She suggests a moment of silence for Izaiah, which we both obey. Then she turns to the matter of my breast meningitis: "I think probably it's okay."

"They're different sizes," I tell her.

"Mine are different sizes," Agnes says. "Everybody's are different sizes."

"Is that true?"

"Trust me," Agnes tells me. Agnes dates women as well as men, and she's seen a lot more breasts than I have, so I do trust her.

"Are yours really different sizes?"

"Yeah," Agnes says, "a little bit."

"Which is bigger?"

"The left."

"Weird," I say. "Mine is the right." We share a smile—but then the fear rushes back. "Also though, the right one is warmer than the left."

"Warmer?"

"I think so, yeah."

Agnes sighs. I can tell that she's entered her Determination phase, where she solves things. "There's only one way to do this," she tells me. "Whip 'em out."

I stare at her. "Whip what out?"

"Your tits," says Agnes, "take those bad girls out." She's already pulling her T-shirt over her head. As I hesitate, she reaches behind her back to unhook her bra. Agnes stands shirtless in my apartment, entirely at ease. She takes her breasts in her hands. "Left one is definitely bigger," she informs me.

I pull my tank top off, and then my bra. It feels a little weird, but everything Agnes does is probably for the best. Agnes examines my two breasts. She hefts one in each hand like fruit at a market. "Right one is bigger," she pronounces, in the same way that she announced her own. Hearing it said in exactly the same way makes it sound less pathological, and more like a classification.

"And the temperature?" I ask.

"They're both equally warm," Agnes says, decisively. "Now feel mine."

I cup Agnes's tits in sort of the way she's holding mine, like I'm at a farmers' market. Agnes's tits are very small and firmer than mine, so it's like I'm holding unripe kiwis in my hands. Mine are more like nectarines, ripe. I say this to Agnes ("Nectarines, comma, ripe,") and she bursts out laughing.

"No," she says, "I'm like, a kiwi and a crab apple, and you're like, a nectarine and . . . what's bigger than a nectarine?"

"A baby cantaloupe," I suggest, and Agnes shrieks with delight.

"Yes!" she crows, giving my right tit a healthy squeeze. "A baby cantaloupe!"

———————

THIS IS A BRIEF HISTORY of Wallace the Rat: he arrived in a giant wire cage; his coat was brindled, and he had surprisingly large ears and a tail like an earthworm; I would describe his personality at the time as "quirky," "inquisitive," and "occasionally violent"; he liked to roll around in wood shavings; he smelled like musk and allergies and some kind of thick oil, and so did his wood shavings; he liked to be handled, except when he didn't; he was included in Izaiah's funeral ceremony run by Oliver and Mason, in which Wallace sat in a bowl while Oliver smudged his backyard with palo santo and attendees gathered in the bald patches of weed and dirt (all attendees were self-selected responders to a public Facebook event called CELEBRATE THE LIFE AND MOURN THE PASSING OF IZAIAH THE IGUANA); he became known for impulsive decision-making, like the moment in which he jumped out of the bowl, off the table, and made a mad dash across the backyard; he became known for the ability to take on a sudden and unexpected bonelessness, as when he squeezed between the lower slats of the backyard fence; he was an opportunist, he was an escape artist, and he was with us for a very brief period altogether, since the time that elapsed between his arrival at Oliver's and his ignominious departure was thirty-eight hours and six minutes.

AFTER WALLACE'S DISAPPEARANCE, OLIVER IS disconsolate. "I don't understand," he says. "It's like, what's *happening* to me?"

I think about how I might answer the question, and then I think about how Oliver might wish the question to be answered, and those answers diverge so significantly that I don't say anything at all.

"I just feel like, the universe is trying to tell me something." Oliver is sitting very still, arranged in lotus position on the floor of his bedroom. Part of his hair is lying down flat and the other part is sticking straight up. "I think there's a lesson to be learned here."

"What's that?" I ask.

"Things leave me." Oliver turns his sad face my way. It's open and tragic, like one of those flowers that blossoms only at night. Oliver's loneliness has always just been a feature of him, like his dark hair or his stocky build. It strikes me now that this loneliness has intensified, and everything else I used to notice has receded.

"I think the universe is telling me that, if I give them a chance, things will leave me," Oliver says. I want to want to comfort him.

It's directly after this conversation that Oliver takes on the starling.

I WAKE UP FROM A dream in which my body is eating itself. Small mouths have opened on my wrists, behind my knees, between armpit and rib. Areas of my body that were once dedicated to conjoining are now dedicated to devouring. It's three A.M., and I want to talk to Agnes. I want Agnes to tell me the feminist theory behind this dream, or to check me over for tiny mouths, for irregularities, for things that would make me strange and damaged and unlovable. I text Agnes, even knowing she'll be asleep, but the text doesn't go through. I try her again—it still doesn't go through. It would be too crazy to call her right now—even her—so I stay up the rest of the night typing things like "wasting disease" and "consumption" into Google. I start with a regular search, then move on to image search. By the time the sun has come up, I have seen so many horrible things that I'm numb beyond the possibility of actual panic. I fall asleep on the couch and don't wake up until mid-afternoon, when I'm jarred upright by the sound of someone at my door.

The door is jiggling—not the knob, but the whole door—and as I stare at it, wide-eyed, a thick envelope comes sliding underneath. It's wrapped and rewrapped in black electrical tape, and it gets stuck partway. The person on the other side of the door tugs it back and forth, trying to unstick it. It can't be anyone other than Agnes. A wave of relief washes over me. And I realize it's not relief because

I thought someone was trying to break in, but rather relief because Agnes is the only human on the planet that it's a relief to see.

I get up and pull the door open. Agnes is kneeling on the landing, staring up at me. She looks briefly terrified, and then she smiles. "Oh hey," she says, and her relief sounds much more like she thought maybe I'd be an undercover government official.

"Hey," I say. "What's up?"

"I thought you'd be at work."

"No, I had a weird dream and I stayed up all night and—never mind. Did you call me?"

"No," Agnes says, "that's the thing, that's why I was leaving you a letter. I feel like cell phones aren't safe. I threw mine away."

"You what?"

"Yeah, and then I shut down my email account. I think handwritten is the only way you can really be safe and even then I wrapped my letter in tape so you would know if anyone had tampered with it."

"Oh," I say. "Okay." Agnes doesn't look like she slept last night either. "What's the letter say?"

"Mostly what I just said."

Agnes doesn't look like she's slept in a while, actually.

"You should come in," I say. "I'll make us smoothies."

Agnes comes in and closes the door behind her. Then she locks it. She sits on the counter while I put things in a blender. Bananas, cinnamon, milk—whatever's in the fridge, I just sort of add it into the blender—rice, yogurt, I hesitate over a container of pitted olives, but Agnes says, "Go for it," so I put in a few pitted olives.

"So," I say, because Agnes is uncharacteristically quiet, "you don't have a cell or email anymore?"

She shakes her head no, and tells me the Edward Snowden documentary really got her concerned. I ask if there's something specific she's worried the government might discover about her, and she sighs and says, "Information in general is specifically dangerous." Then she asks me how I am, and I tell her what I've learned about wasting diseases.

I want her to feel better, but I don't know how to help. Although Agnes is, by nature, someone my mother would call "particular," I've never seen her like this. I want to ask if she's okay, but I don't feel okay either, so I'm not sure what I'd do if she said no. Instead, I ask her if she feels better now that she isn't encumbered by email and a phone.

Agnes says, "If it isn't this, it'll be something else, won't it. I mean, drones. There's drones. You can't even see them but they're up in the sky." She looks exhausted. She leans her head on one hand, and sips her smoothie very slowly. I sip my own. It's thick and brackish, like pond water. That's probably the olive salt. I ask Agnes if she wants me to make her a different smoothie, but she shakes her head, and then just keeps shaking it, frowning down at her pond water as if she's trying to determine how many people are watching her drink it.

THE STARLING IS NAMED SEBASTIAN. He stalks around his cage like a malfunctioning movie, in staccato jerks and pauses, except for the sudden liquid lunge to take a chunk out of your nearest body part. He shits on everything. The bottom of his cage is covered in newspaper, and it's white with shit. This could also be because Oliver hasn't changed it yet. Oliver thinks that Sebastian thrives on familiarity, and that it would be too much to change both ownership and newspaper in the same period of time. I keep forgetting his name. I just think of him as "the Nasty Bird."

Oliver is bird-sitting for Gina, who is out of town. Gina is at an artist residency in someplace like Mongolia or Berlin or Venice, where she is writing small sad songs on a ukulele and then playing the songs from inside an installation designed to look like a vagina. Or she is collecting paper scraps and creating a collage where the scraps are glued together by her tears as she listens to NPR reports of crimes against women in Afghanistan. Or she is digging shallow symbolic graves with her bare hands, and later photos of her candy-red nails, rimmed by dark soil, will pop up innocently on Instagram. Gina is doing any and every one of those things.

What Sebastian is doing, is pooping.

The other thing about Sebastian is that he talks. Apparently starlings can learn and repeat language, which was not something I knew prior to the Nasty Bird. He already knows how to say "hello" and "how was your day," which are things Gina taught him. He also likes to say, "Go fuck!" If you come in and say, "Good morning, Sebastian," chances are good that he will reply, "Go fuck!" These are the moments in which I almost like him. They are brief moments, but they are real. And then Sebastian clacks his beak and prepares another thick caulk-white stream of shit, and we're back to square one.

Oliver is entranced by Sebastian. The week that Sebastian arrives, Oliver organizes a Bird Viewing through similar methods to his Iguana Viewing and Iguana Funeral, except this time he also places an ad on Craigslist. I attend the Bird Viewing long enough to witness the arrival of several leather daddies, a coke dealer, and three girls who seem like confused hookers—apparently they didn't think he meant a real bird—before I slip out into the night.

It's a hard week for me, because I can't just text or call Agnes whenever the world seems like it's too much, which is sort of how it seems all the time. I drop by Agnes's apartment multiple times, but Agnes doesn't seem to be in, although she leaves me small things outside her door—a note saying *Gone fishing* (which I know doesn't mean she's actually fishing), a Virgen de Guadalupe candle, a Snickers bar. It's possible that she means to convey pieces of coded information with each offering, but I can't guess what they are, so I just eat the Snickers on the walk back to my place, and I put the Virgen candle by my bed and light it.

Oliver and I are arguing more, as well. By the second week of Sebastian's residency, we can't be in the same room without fighting. The fights are like brief explosions, followed by a chain of apologies that happen like smaller explosions, leading back up to a large explosion again. Oliver wants to fight about how uninterested in Sebastian I am; I want to fight about how much Sebastian smells and how loud he is. Oliver wants to fight about my lack of attendance at the event he curated wherein everybody sat around Sebastian's cage and read Poe's "The Raven" out loud together; I want to fight about Oliver's lack of empathy for how lost I am without Agnes. Oliver wants to fight about how I should be that lost without *him*; I suddenly don't want to fight anymore. Then Oliver apologizes, then I apologize, then Oliver apologizes for needing me to apologize, then he asks me if I'm leaving him and we start fighting again.

Gina Skypes Oliver soon after one of these fights. She tells him that she's been offered an extension of her artist residency, and she's going to take it. She asks if Oliver will keep watching Sebastian, and I hear him say that he will, and then he asks how long the extension is.

"Well," Gina says, "it's a funny thing. It's like, six months? With the option of another six, if I can get a visa?"

"Oh," Oliver says. He processes. He processes. "Oh. A visa? Are you . . . like . . . emigrating?"

Gina laughs. It's a light airy laugh, even over Skype. "I mean I think that word is a little bit problematic? It sort of co-opts a *history* of oppression, which is what my work is about, actually?"

"Oh," Oliver says. "I'm sorry. But like . . . are you coming back?"

"I think it's important to finish my project," Gina says thoughtfully, "and art takes time, I know you know that, art takes whatever time it takes."

It's at that point that I go take a shower. I'm still in the shower when Oliver bursts in without knocking, which he knows I hate.

"She's emigrating," he says.

"What are you gonna do with Sebastian?" I ask.

"I don't know! I don't know!" Oliver sits on the closed toilet seat, head in his hands. I can see his shape through the shower curtain.

"Tell Gina you're letting him go if she doesn't come get him," I suggest.

"I can't do that," Oliver says, horrified. Then: "*Can* I do that?"

"I mean, I'm not going to stop you." I turn off the shower and stick my hand around the curtain so he can put a towel in it. I know this tends to upset him, since he believes in the healthy nudity shared by couples who are comfortable around each other. I believe that if anybody sees my body, they will either notice a deformity that I haven't yet seen, or the weight of their gaze will instantly create a deformity that wasn't there before. The only time I have felt differently about this, was when Agnes was weighing my already-deformed tits in her capable hands.

I wait for Oliver to have feelings about my towel request, but he's so upset by the starling situation that he just gives me the towel. "I can't let Sebastian go," he says, pacing a little. "He might die. He might get eaten by something. He might be lonely."

"He's a bird," I say. "He might be happier out in the wild, with the privilege of having all those options."

"She said she was coming back." Oliver is panicking. I rub his shoulder. "I mean . . . six *months*? A *year*? I thought, like . . . a week, I could keep him alive for a week more, or two weeks, but . . ."

I want to say something comforting, but instead I hear myself asking: "Why do you volunteer to pet-sit?"

"My friends need help," Oliver says into his cupped hands. "I like to help."

"Okay, but aren't there other friends—ones who already *have* pets—who could help? I mean—I feel like maybe it's just science, like: there are people with longer attention spans, and they have pets, and there are people with shorter attention spans, and they don't."

"Which one am I?" Oliver asks, genuinely asks. And then he does the math fully, and his face folds in on itself, as if I've kicked him.

"That's not a *bad* thing," I hasten to say. "It's just a thing! I mean, *I* don't have pets."

"You don't want to take care of things," Oliver says flatly. "You don't even want to take care of people."

"What?" I come careening to a halt, realizing we've taken one of those Oliver-y turns in the conversation, and now I'm out of my depth. "Wait, that's not true."

"Oh no? You don't ask me about my feelings. And when I tell you, you change the subject. And you don't feel sad when I'm sad, and you don't want me to *be* sad. And when people have small children, you don't want to hold them!"

I'm torn between outrage and a general agreement with everything Oliver has said. I settle for: "That doesn't mean I don't want to take *care* of people!"

"Oh no?" Oliver is so upset that his whole body is shaking, his balled fists and tight shoulders are shaking. "Then who do you want to take care of!"

"Agnes," I say without thinking, and then find that it's true. "I want to take care of Agnes."

WHEN I ARRIVE AT HER apartment, Agnes has taped newspaper over all the windows so that the whole place is bathed in a weird, hazy gray light. All of her appliances are unplugged, and when I see the row of new locks installed on the inside of the door, I understand why it took her so long to get it open.

"Hi," says Agnes. Her eyes are like bruises.

Glancing around her apartment, I see that she's taped cut-open Trader Joe's paper bags to her wall, and is making a list of pros and cons on them with a Sharpie. The PROS so far read: Power, Privilege, Convenience. The CONS are: Vulnerability, Inconvenience, Death.

I ask Agnes what the list is about, and she says it's about U.S. citizenship on the whole. She tells me that yesterday she made a highly detailed list about the pros and cons of moving to Sweden, but the list was so long that it covered all of her walls, and she ran out of space, so she had to take it down and start thinking more in broad strokes.

"Cool," I say. "When was the last time you ate anything?"

"I'm eating." Agnes gestures to the empty cans of tuna fish in the sink. When I stare at them, she admits that she ran out of fresh food a week ago.

I ask Agnes why not just go to Sweden, see what it's like, and eat some fresh vegetables there. Agnes tells me that she's been watching the part of the Edward Snowden documentary on loop where he's hiding in the hotel room in Hong Kong. She says that the second you go anywhere, your name is on a flight manifest, there's video of you walking through airports, your passport is recorded, your arrival and departure are performed for the viewing pleasure and archival purposes of a million hidden eyes. She says, "It's probably safer to stay indoors." She says, "Tunnels would be better, if there were subterranean tunnels, if I could maybe live in the Catacombs that would be better, if there were a way to get to Paris."

I ask Agnes if maybe she doesn't agree that we should delete the Edward Snowden documentary off of her laptop. Agnes looks at me uncertainly. "It's on Netflix anyway," she says.

"Maybe there are other things you could watch right now."

"That won't help," Agnes says wearily, "it's all still out there." And she sits down on the floor.

I sit down on the floor also. It's kind of nice being close to the ground. There's something calming about refusing to remain standing in the face of hopelessness. I want to capsize, so I do. I lie on Agnes's floor with my face against her cool kitchen tile.

"What are you doing?" Agnes asks, interested.

"It feels better down here," I say.

Agnes capsizes also. Faces half-smushed against the floor, we stare at each other.

"I missed you," Agnes says.

"I missed you too," I tell her. And then I ask her a question that has been floating inside me this whole time, but I don't realize it until I say it: "What's so wrong with being watched?"

Agnes frowns, with the half of her face that isn't attached to the floor. She doesn't understand the question.

I try again. I try to put my thoughts together, but I'm tired too, and they don't seem to want to arrange themselves properly. I say, "I just feel like ... I think there's something wrong with me. It might not be in my brain, or my tits, but it's something, somewhere. I don't know where it is, and that makes me scared all the time. And I guess I feel scared because I feel alone, most of the time I'm alone in my bathroom or my kitchen or even in Oliver's house, pushing at bits of myself and waiting for something to go wrong. And some people believe in God, which comforts them, and I don't know what God really *does* for anyone other than watch them. He mostly sort of just watches them, right? And then they're comforted. And I don't believe in God, but I do believe in the NSA. So maybe I could find that comforting. Like, no matter how alone I feel like I am, somebody somewhere, behind a tiny camera, in some control room somewhere—that person is watching me, and that person will know if something bad happens to me. Even if I never see him or her. There's two of us who care about what happens to me. You know?"

Agnes nods that she hears me. I watch her think about it. And then I think about Oliver, alone in his tiny apartment, being watched by a parade of other people's pets. Lizards, rats, a starling, who knows what else to come—their tiny beady eyes trained on his endlessly forlorn face, in the closest he might ever get to unconditional love.

That makes me sad. It makes me so sad that I want to call him and say, "Keep the goddamn starling." I want to say, "I will never be able to watch you the way an abandoned pet can." I want to say, "I understand you, but I don't love you, and I thought those things could be the same, but they're not."

I say to Agnes, "Or we can just watch each other. And it won't matter who else is staring." I say, "I believe in you, anyway." I say, "Maybe not God, and maybe not the Western medical establishment, but I do believe in you."

Agnes doesn't say anything. But after a minute she reaches across the kitchen floor toward me. I reach out also. And we lie on the floor, with the windows papered over and underwater light filling the room, hand in hand, while the world rushes and pulses and hums somewhere outside of our thin, thin walls.

THE WOLF

When Kryzstof called me and asked me to come over immediately, I did. If I had known there was a dead body on his floor, I might not have. But then again, I might. You never know with me.

He was jittering off the walls when I showed up. Long pool-player hands shaking for a cigarette or a line of coke, his Swedish accent thicker than usual. I was about to ask him what the fuck, when I looked past him and saw the body. It was facedown, in the tiny laundry room—from where I was standing, I could see a pair of shoes poking out past the doorway. "What the fuck," I said. He was glassy-eyed, already in full panic mode. "Oh shit," he kept mumbling, until finally I snapped his name: "Kryzstof!" He straightened up, nose running, hands twitching, and looked at me like a rabbit, awaiting my order.

"All right," I said. "Who else do you know that we can call?"

Kryzstof shook his head and his straw-blond hair flew everywhere. "Nobody, I don't know anybody," he said wildly. "This is Tokyo."

"You know *everybody*," I corrected him. "They're just scum. Think hard."

Forehead wrinkled, fingers interlocked, Kryzstof rocked back and forth gently. I could see him whizzing through a mental card catalog of foreigners—the wiry drug dealers from Paris, the Namibian sex offender with the big grin and the gold tooth, the trio of scraggly Brits who smelled like sweat and evil. At last he said, "The wolf."

I blinked at him.

"Japanese. Always at that little, what's it, Bar Jamaica. You know him, all the gaijin know him."

I shook my head.

"He speaks better English than the English."

I shook my head again. "What's his name?"

"Nobody knows for real, gaijin just call him 'the wolf.' Or Kira."

"Why Kira?"

Kryzstof managed to focus on me for a blank second. "Because it sounds like killer."

"Oh," I said. At the word *killer*, it seemed like Kryzstof was about to lapse back into his hand-wringing head-shaking coma, so I grabbed his cell phone and thrust it at him: "Call him." When he hesitated, I added, "Or you're on your own."

He made the phone call in the bathroom with the door closed. Outside the window, mid-afternoon Tokyo hummed to itself. Sunny, thickly humid, the rainy season tapering off into regular wet heat. All in all, a nice day. Kryzstof finished the phone call and threw up. He flushed a few times before he came out. I gave him a cup of tap water. We sat in his kitchen with his cell phone between us, and the body lay untouched in the tiny laundry room, and we waited for the wolf to arrive.

HE WAS NOT, WHEN HE did arrive, terribly sympathetic.

He was charismatic, I'll give him that. Not remarkable, not at first—another attractive and dissolute Tokyo boy, I thought. Sharp high cheekbones, an earring in one ear, the lines of a tattoo trailing from under the left sleeve of his T-shirt. Yakuza, most likely—

Japanese mafia. Or chinpira—what they called the punk wannabes, full of piss and strut. True, there was something a little sharper about him than the other yakuza I'd met—he dressed simply, there didn't seem to be anything affected in his manner. But it was his English that surprised me. The perfect, scornful, poison-dart sarcasm of the British delivered in that hard-to-place accent that screamed international schools. Kryzstof's Japanese was hopeless and evidently the wolf knew it, because the whole time that he was there, he spoke in fast, disgusted English.

The first thing he said was, "Where is it?"

"In the laundry room," Kryzstof said miserably.

The wolf flickered a flat dark look at me. "And the weapon?"

"No weapon," I said. I would have continued, but the wolf seemed to take that as his answer, and pushed past me into the laundry room. Kryzstof chewed his nails. He looked, right then, like the little blond boys they have on Swedish postcards, doing something naughty. After a moment, the wolf leaned back around the door.

"Do you have any idea how much shit you're in?" he asked.

The body lay faceup. I studied it carefully for the first time. It was the size of a child, although it belonged to a man, probably in his midthirties. Short dark hair, a silk shirt with a bizarrely garish Hawaiian flower pattern, rings on his left hand.

"I didn't kill him," Kryzstof said, his voice uneven. "He was just—we were—"

The wolf knelt down by the body. He muttered something to it, then gently rolled it over. I heard Kryzstof make a sound beside me, as if he was trying not to be sick. I didn't feel sick though. I couldn't look away.

The wolf lifted up the back of the Hawaiian shirt. For a moment, I thought the body was wearing another shirt underneath, and then I realized that his skin was covered in ink. A dragon coiled up his spine, winding around some clouds and daggers, unleashing itself across his shoulder blades. A carp jumped upstream, after the dragon but not catching it.

"Yakuza," the wolf said, into our silence, in case we didn't recognize the significance of the tattoos.

"He collapsed," Kryzstof said weakly. "I swear, I didn't hurt him."

"Irrelevant," the wolf told him. "He's dead on your floor."

I'd been more than willing to bully Kryzstof, but I wasn't about to let somebody else do it. "Hold up," I said. "He called *you* to fix things. So what's the plan?"

The wolf looked at me for a second. Not like he disliked me, or even harbored any sort of annoyance. Just like I was trussed up and he had a butcher knife and was calculating where to make the first cut. I won't lie, it threw me a little. Then he said, politely, "We're going to take away the body. And you will help." Before I could agree, he turned to Kryzstof. "You stay here," he said. "Scrub everything." Then to me: "Get a suitcase."

I looked at Kryzstof. He swiveled his gaze between me and the wolf, like a kid watching his divorcing parents work out the terms of custody. Well. Fine. I didn't need to be the leader of this operation.

"Where do you keep your suitcases?" I asked brusquely.

"Bedroom," Kryzstof replied, still shaky.

I walked past him into the room beyond, and found a giant red suitcase with wheels. In the other room, I heard Kryzstof raise his voice for the first time. "Don't you want to know?" he asked, the anguish plain. "Don't you want to know what *happened*?"

A brief silence followed. And then the wolf said, flatly, "No," and turned away. I took that as my cue to drag the suitcase in.

I CHECKED THE TIME. THE train still hadn't come.

The wolf was on his third cigarette, leaning against the vending machine on the platform. No matter where you get stranded in Japan, no matter how godforsaken it is, there's always a vending machine. And always the usual contents: two kinds of cold tea, three kinds of coffee (too-sweet Emerald Mountain Blend in the turquoise can, something bitter in the dark blue, poor man's coffee in the waxy cardboard box), two sports drinks, one going by the unlikely name of Aquarius and the other by the unfortunate one of Pocari Sweat, and then an assortment of fruit juices.

The pounding in my head reminded me how little I'd slept. I wanted coffee, but if I bought anything I'd have to approach the wolf, and I was willing to let well enough alone. The red suitcase lay on its side next to him, unassuming, deceptive. I'd been called heartless before, but the wolf's equanimity was getting to me. Nobody should be that untouched by a dead midget.

Just as I was beginning to wonder what came next, he turned and came walking back toward me. You couldn't quite call it a walk. A swagger, more like. A lope.

"You gonna cry yet?"

"No," I said.

"Do this all the time?"

"*You* do this all the time?"

He shrugged. "Whenever gaijin pay me for it."

"How come your English is flawless?"

"How come your Japanese is shit?"

I sighed. "That's Kryzstof." And then, in Japanese: "I speak some."

The wolf lifted an eyebrow. "How much?" he asked, switching to Japanese.

"Enough so that men in bars buy me drinks."

"That's not your Japanese, that's the way you dress."

I switched back to English. "So where are we going? And what are we gonna do?" Now that we were talking, I might as well ask the burning questions.

He ignored them completely. "So is he your boyfriend?"

I wondered for a moment if he was referring to our friend in the suitcase. "Who?"

He made an impatient gesture. "The skinny kinpatsu."

Skinny blond definitely didn't apply to the four-foot gangster. "No," I said, firmly.

He jerked a chin at the suitcase. "You kill him?"

"Jesus no."

The wolf cracked a crooked smile. "Then how come you and me are on this platform? You and kinpatsu fucking?"

I straightened up, looking the wolf directly in his serial-killer eyes. "Who I fuck has nothing to do with who you bury."

The wolf's crooked smile widened. "You're not fucking," he decided, and lit another cigarette.

I opened my mouth to tell him off, hesitated at the prospect of being left alone with a body in a suitcase, and then the train pulled in. It was crowded, full of little old ladies throwing elbows with the best of them. The wolf put the suitcase between us and looped one long arm through a handhold above my head, letting his body sway with the motion of the train. When we rounded a corner, his shirt rode up. Before I looked away, I saw the intricate dark web of a tattoo, starting near his hip and stretching up his ribs.

I stared down at my shoes, as Tokyo blurred past. The loop line went in a tight circle, hitting up all the major tourist traps like Shibuya and Akihabara, so either we were getting out somewhere soon, or we were reenacting my personal version of hell. When we stopped next, a bunch of schoolgirls crowded on, giggling and texting. As one of them almost tripped over the red suitcase and shot a dirty look at the wolf, I thought to myself: *There's a lot to be said for an ordinary life. There's a lot to be said for waitressing in LA.*

THE WOLF GESTURED US OFF the train at Shinjuku. He knifed through the crowds dragging the suitcase behind him, and I followed until we got to the gates for the bullet train. There I ground to a halt.

"I'm not taking another step until you tell me where we're going."

"Yokohama," he said, like it should be obvious.

"Yokohama like the port city Yokohama?"

"Do you know another?"

"What the fuck is in *Yokohama*?"

The wolf sighed. "Yuki-chan liked Yokohama."

"Who the fuck is Yuki-chan?"

The wolf gestured to the suitcase.

"Wait," I said, reeling. "Wait. You *know* this dude?"

"Yes." The wolf turned to buy his ticket. I reached out and grabbed his arm, then thought better and dropped it. He turned around nonetheless, and for a moment I wondered if I'd overstepped.

"Yes?" he inquired, courteously.

"Hold it," I said. "You *know* the dead guy. Like—first-name basis."

"Yes."

"And you didn't mention that."

He quirked an eyebrow. "Was it relevant?"

"You don't think—?" I cut myself off, as my voice was rising. I took a deep breath. Then another thought struck me. "Oh shit."

The wolf tilted his head to one side.

"You're going to kill me," I said. My voice was surprisingly calm and firm. "Like a revenge killing."

He stared at me for a second, and then that crooked grin played out over his mouth. "No," he said, with a deliberate seriousness that definitely looked like mockery. "No revenge killing. Do you have any other questions?"

"You're going to kill Kryzstof."

"No."

"Why not?"

The wolf sighed again. People walked by quickly all around us, heads down. A few of them glanced our way, surprised by the sight of a Japanese man speaking fluent English to a gaijin girl, but they kept walking.

"What's your name?" he asked.

"Rachel."

"Rachel," the wolf said. "If I promise not to kill anyone, either here or in Yokohama, can we discuss this on the train?"

"Or later."

"Excuse me?"

"Here *or* in Yokohama *or* later."

This time the crooked grin was back full force. "Right. No killing. I got it."

The wolf bought his shinkansen ticket from the machine, then mine as well. I accepted it warily. "How much was it? I'll pay you back."

"Just think of this as a date," he said, and walked ahead of me through the gates, before I could protest.

THE SHINKANSEN TO YOKOHAMA WAS almost empty. There were four other people in our car, sitting in the front, and although they glanced at us as we walked past, they didn't seem interested.

"You ever been on one of these before?" the wolf asked, as we pulled out of the station.

"Yeah, a few times."

"How long have you been in Japan?"

"Five years in September."

"Coming from . . . ?"

"LA."

"Why'd you leave?"

"None of your business."

A beat. Then: "I bet you don't eat raw fish."

"Sure I do."

"Sea cucumber?"

"There's nothing better."

"Octopus?"

"Pull it out of the sea and I'll eat it."

The wolf leaned back in his seat and studied me. I tried not to sound uneasy when I said, "Hey, can you take your sunglasses off?"

"Why?"

"They make me think you're still gonna kill me."

He took his sunglasses off and continued to stare at me. There was something unnerving about his gaze, and I couldn't figure out what it was at first—and then it struck me. His eyes were pale gray.

"You aren't Japanese," I said out loud. I saw something tighten in his face, almost imperceptibly, and I regretted it immediately. "It's none of my business."

"No," he said. "It's not."

"Look," I said. "Can I ask you something, and then you can ask me something—anything, actually—and I'll answer it?"

After a minute, he shrugged. I took that as consent.

"Are you with the yakuza?"

Whatever he thought I'd been going to ask, that clearly wasn't it. After a long moment that stretched out over several breaths, he shook his head no.

"But—you have a tattoo."

The wolf reached out and curled his fingers gently around my throat, palm over my pulse. I froze, but before I could react, he'd retracted his hand. "If you're scared of me, why do you keep asking questions?"

"Who said I was scared of you? At the most I'm nervous."

He reached out again, his fingertips against the curve of my throat. "Nervous is like this," he said, and his fingers beat a gentle ta-dum ta-dum rhythm against my skin. "Scared is this," he added, and the rhythm sped up until it was matching my heartbeat.

I blinked at the wolf, suddenly aware of how close he was. He dropped his hand.

"There are many young people in Japan who have tattoos and aren't yakuza," he said reprovingly, as if we were just continuing our conversation.

"But you know Yuki-chan."

"And you know Kryzstof. That doesn't make you a dealer. Or does it?"

"No," I said, annoyed. "I don't fuck around with that shit."

"I get to ask you a question now," the wolf said. "Do you have a boyfriend?"

I blinked at him, half-startled and half-outraged. "*That*'s your one question?"

"Yes."

"No," I said icily. "I do not. And neither am I looking."

"Why not?"

I was going to tell him that he'd already asked his question, but instead I said, "Because now I date women."

Both of his eyebrows went up this time. "You *like* women, or you *date* women?"

Fine, if all bets were off: "Are you half-Japanese?"

"Do you have a girlfriend?"

"What's your other half?"

"Why no girlfriend?"

"Because I don't *like people*." I stared him down.

The wolf smiled. It wasn't the crooked smile, and it didn't seem mocking. I hadn't seen it before. He held out his hand, Western style.

"They call me Oukami Yasuhara," he said. "You know what that means?"

"Yasuhara the wolf," I translated.

"My friends call me Paulo." His mouth moved in something like a smile—a concession to my earlier question. "You can call me that."

"Are we friends?" I asked.

Yasuhara the wolf kept his hand extended. "Just for today."

I took his hand. He held on for a beat longer than a handshake, and then released it. "Hajimemashite," he said, with mock-formality. "I'm so pleased to meet you."

YASUHARA WAS MORE WILLING TO talk about Yuki-chan than about himself. Yuki-chan was low-level yakuza, drugs and girls mostly, took orders more than he gave them. He was reliable and he got the job done. The wolf said that a few times: *He got the job done*—which made me wonder if he was a hit man as well. People didn't take him seriously at first, but by the end they always did. (That line convinced me that Yuki-chan was a hit man.) Yuki-chan could be cold but in general he liked to laugh. Things were funnier when he was around. For example, one night they were out drinking and they picked up two gaijin girls, German tourists, and managed to convince them that Yuki-chan was the guy who played R2-D2 in the original *Star Wars*. Shit like that, the wolf said. Funny.

I asked how they met, and he told me that Yuki-chan had gotten him out of a bad situation ten years back, just after he'd finished high school—but he didn't tell me what the situation was. He said that they never worked together, but they'd drink together and Yuki-chan would tell him jokes. "Jokes?" I asked, and the wolf nodded and smiled and patted the top of the suitcase.

"Jokes," he said, "he liked jokes."

Whenever I tried to steer the conversation back to him, he'd shut up, stare out the window. Finally I just gave up, and asked him why we were going to Yokohama. "Are we going to bury him there?"

Oukami Yasuhara glanced at me as if I'd said the stupidest thing in the world. "Bury him? In Yokohama? Of course not."

"Then what are we going to do?"

"We're going to show him a good day, the best day of his life. And then I'll take care of the body."

I must have looked like a cartoon version of bewilderment, because he laughed out loud. He reached across and touched my jaw, closing my mouth. His fingers were cool, but the touch burned, and he left his hand there.

"Daijoubu," he said, "your job is very simple. I'll take care of the hard parts."

"What's my job?" I asked against his fingertips.

He retracted his hand too quickly, as if the feel of my lips moving had burned him as well. "Yuki-chan had bad luck with women," he told me. "Women are shallow, they didn't care if he was funny. All he wanted was one nice date, but girls just laughed when he asked them out. Tomorrow would have been his birthday, so today you'll be his date."

Two thoughts occurred in my head simultaneously. The first was to jump up, run to the door, and fling myself off the bullet train. The second was that this was the first thing I'd seen in years that could honestly be called "sweet." Oukami Yasuhara wanted to give his friend a nice date before he stuck him in the earth. I wondered if I knew anybody who'd do that for me. And yet . . . it made me think about those news stories in which unwitting Indian wives got burned on their husbands' funeral pyres. If I didn't return, only Kryzstof would notice for at least a few days. And Kryzstof was useless.

The wolf must have seen these warring impulses on my face because he said, with some disgust, "Unless you're too good for him."

"Look," I said, stung. "Ground rules: I'm down, but I'm not gonna kiss him. No offense, but he's dead. Also, I get returned to Tokyo afterwards. No scrapes, no dents, nothing that's gonna get me deported."

The wolf listened with that strange smile on his face, the one that wasn't mockery. It came and went so fast that I couldn't figure it out. "Anything else?" he asked politely.

"Yeah. No more questions about boyfriends or girlfriends. I'm your friend's date, not yours, get it?"

The wolf's gray eyes widened a little, and then he laughed out loud. "Got it," he said.

YOKOHAMA, CITY OF JAPANESE SOAP operas. The bay, the lights, the ships, the countless TV heroines who have been dying of leukemia and have leaned out over their hospital windowsills to see the Yokohama Ferris wheel sparkle and glow. We joined the summer crowds walking by the harbor; Japanese girls my age, some of them in summer yukata, clutched their boyfriends' arms as they hobbled along on six-inch stiletto heels. When we stopped to buy sweet ice kaki-gori, I remarked to the wolf that I'd never understood the Japanese female addiction to S&M heels, and he looked at my scuffed black Chucks and shook his head a little.

"Yuki-chan liked girlier girls," he said.

"Yuki-chan better appreciate what he's got."

"Yuki-chan liked expensive girls," the wolf said, turning away to pay the vendor. "You're more my type." When he turned back to hand me my sweet ice, his face was expressionless. I didn't know whether I'd been insulted or not, so I just followed the wolf and Yuki-chan through the streets, eating my kaki-gori.

And yet, it wasn't a bad first date. A better one than most. We stopped in Yamashita Park, sat in the sun. We went to the Landmark Tower, walked around the observation deck watching Yokohama sprawl out beneath us. We wandered through Chinatown, ate street-vendor pork and sweet sesame balls. I didn't worry about eating too much and looking like a pig, and for his part, Yuki-chan was a perfect gentleman. He was quietly appreciative from within his suitcase. He didn't brag about himself, comment on my appearance, drink to excess, try to cop a feel. The wolf himself was a gentle facilitator, never once overstepping his bounds. He didn't even talk to me much. After all, I was his friend's date, not his.

It was early evening when we ended up back by the harbor. The wolf bought us three cold teas from a nearby vending machine, and we sat on a bench, the red suitcase between us with a green tea tucked into its side pocket, and the wolf and I drank ours and watched the sky darken to frame the glow of the harbor lights. The silence was strangely companionable.

When he'd finished his tea, the wolf sighed and patted the suitcase. He muttered something to Yuki-chan that I didn't catch, and then to me, "Tobako katteku, iru?"

I noticed that he'd spoken to me in casual Japanese—no mockery, just an easy invitation. But I shook my head—I didn't smoke. He nodded, then stood and walked down the quay toward the cigarette vending machines. Left alone with Yuki-chan and the harbor lights, I panicked at first—what if a cop came and asked me to open my suitcase? But then I relaxed. There was no one in sight, just a few couples walking far up the quay. The breeze off the water was gentle, it smelled like salt, it smelled like faraway promises of faraway places.

"Yuki-chan," I said experimentally. I stopped. The silence was a listening one. I imagined him, curled up like a little fetus in the red suitcase, tattoos and track marks, waiting to be reborn. "What's up?" I waited—still the listening silence. "Hey listen, man. I'm sorry you died on my friend's floor. I mean maybe you don't care. Maybe an overdose isn't a bad way to go. You're just chilling and then you're floating and then you're gone. I don't know. But I hope you've been having a good day."

Yuki listened. Inside the suitcase, he shrugged a little. Tilted his head to the side. Waited for me to continue. So I did.

"Look, you've been a gentleman. You should know that. And if I die—when I die—I'd like something like this. Lights and the ocean and a Ferris wheel. I'd really like that." I hesitated. But only Yuki-chan was listening, so I plowed on. "I've been in Tokyo for five years, I don't know anyone who'd do that for me. Anyway." I took a deep breath. "That's not your problem. I guess the point is, I would've dressed better if I'd known."

A sudden tightness in my throat surprised me. Inside the suitcase, Yuki shook his head a little: *Don't worry about it.*

He wanted to know if I was doing okay.

"Yeah man, it's been a good day. Better than most, actually."

He inquired gently if I was homesick. But I didn't know how to explain it right then. If I'd had the words, I would have said that it wasn't about missing another place, so much as no longer being able to extricate myself from this one. How your shape changes, here. How the language changes and the silence changes too, there's so much more of it, and if both the words and the space around them are different, then after some time, you become different too. And after enough time has passed, you can't remember a way back to your old life—and if you did, if you somehow did make it back, you wouldn't even fit there anymore.

But I didn't have those words, in either his language or mine, so after a moment I said, "Gaijin lose it in Tokyo. We just . . . down the rabbit hole. Kryzstof, he's gone. Goodbye Krzystof. He'll never make it out alive. You know he tried to leave? Three times. Came back each time. Started dealing the last time. He just got lost. You know?"

Yeah, Yuki-chan said. *I know.*

And I thought: *Of course you do, to die the way you did.* But I didn't say that. I didn't want to be rude.

We were sitting in thoughtful silence when the wolf returned, a packet of Larks sticking out of his hip pocket. He looked a little surprised to see me there, which made me wonder if he'd expected me to bolt the second his back was turned. He sat down on the bench, a little closer than before, lit a Lark, and took a long sweet drag.

"Hey," he said in English. "You wanna hear a joke?"

"Sure."

"A murderer walks into a forest with a little girl. The little girl says, 'It's dark, I'm scared!' The murderer says, 'What are *you* scared of? I'm the one who's going to be walking out of here alone.'"

I blinked at him. "That was terrible."

"Yeah," he agreed.

"Did Yuki-chan laugh at that shit?"

"I got it from him," the wolf said, and grinned.

I hadn't seen him this relaxed until now, sprawled out easily over the bench, his whole body one long loose line. In the harbor light, he looked younger. I imagined him as one of the junior high boys riding the subway as I went to work, making faces at each other's reflections in the windows. I imagined him playing baseball, riding his bike to the gas station, falling in love, doing something other than burying bodies.

"What," the wolf said, a little self-consciously, and I realized I'd been staring. I looked away fast.

"Nothing."

He finished his cigarette, flipped it onto the pavement and crushed it with the toe of his boot. Took another cigarette, tucked it into the suitcase pocket next to the bottle of tea. I could almost see Yuki relax, shift, inhaling the sharp-sweet tobacco smell through the fabric of the suitcase. There were so many questions I wanted to ask right then. If the wolf died, was there someone who would put him in a suitcase and take him down to the harbor? And that made me wonder again—who would do it for me? And I felt sad, a sort of sad I hadn't felt in years. You go to work and you come home and you sleep and then you do it all again, and you forget how vast Tokyo is, how implacable. It sleeps its strange cold sleep and dreams its vast glass-and-neon dreams and there you are in its heart, tucked away with all the other dreamers, and each of you is alone.

The wolf touched my wrist. I jumped—I hadn't realized how close we were. I realized he was tracing the thin faded lines, a crisscross over a decade old, climbing up my inner arm. I looked at him. I didn't say anything and he didn't say anything, but I could see in his eyes the same double vision I'd had of him just moments before. He'd seen me one way, all day, and suddenly here was a glimpse of potential past lives spiraling out into infinity.

His fingers reached the top of my inner arm. The faded lines went past that, up under the sleeve, but he didn't chase them further. After a moment he started tracing them down again, and when his fingers reached the inner cup of my hand, he stopped. We sat, fingers tangled, not quite holding hands.

It was thick night, now.

I don't know how much time passed. I thought about asking him any number of things. I didn't. At last the wolf shifted, and I realized my body was stiff and cold, aching from however long we'd sat on that bench.

"We should go back," he said.

"Back?"

"Before it gets too late."

"Oh," I said, like a dreamer waking up. "Back."

WE DIDN'T TALK ON THE shinkansen home. I fell asleep briefly, woke up a station before Shinjuku with my head on the wolf's shoulder. I thought at first he'd fallen asleep as well, but then I saw that his eyes were open and he was staring out the window, his face expressionless. He didn't wake me up or try to move me. When I sat up, he glanced at me as if he'd forgotten I was there. I don't know why I said it then, I hadn't said it the whole day. But: "I'm really sorry about your friend."

He stared at me for a moment, and then he said, "It would have happened. In Kryzstof's place, or somewhere else."

"What do you mean?"

"He had a darkness." The wolf touched his chest. "Here. He liked to laugh, but his heart was dark. It would have happened sooner or later."

I heard myself ask, "And you?"

"And me what?"

"Don't you have it too?"

I thought he wouldn't answer at first. The night slid past, shadowy fields replaced by Tokyo lights, closer, closer. And then the wolf said, quietly, "Don't you?"

We pulled into Shinjuku, got off the train with Yuki-chan. I kept feeling like there was something else I wanted to tell the wolf, but I couldn't think what it was, so I followed him and the red suitcase through the thick crowds. I hadn't realized how thin he was until now, walking in front of me with all of his rib bones under the taut fabric of his shirt. I wondered if he lived alone. If anyone cared if he ate. If Yuki-chan had cared. I imagined the two of them, eating raw octopus and mackerel in a dodgy side-street izakaya. I wondered if either of them had other friends.

"You know how to get home from here?" Oukami Yasuhara asked.

I looked around. We were standing at the southwest exit of Shinjuku Station, and a light rain was falling. Street musicians were playing, an assortment of Japanese teenagers with guitars and torn jeans.

"What about Yuki-chan?"

The wolf tilted his head a little, the way I was starting to realize meant that he was surprised by something. "I'll take care of him now," he said.

We hesitated, and then the wolf nodded to me. "Thank you for today."

His tone was formal, and I thought how we'd look to the people walking past—a Japanese man and a foreign girl, saying good night. People might assume we worked together at the same company, perhaps. But we had sat for hours by the ocean with a body between us.

"Kochira koso," I echoed, a formal thanks, and my voice was as distant as his.

We nodded to each other again. He turned to go. Tokyo would swallow him back up. The earth would swallow Yuki-chan—or fire, or water, whatever one did with bodies that no one wanted discovered. And I thought: *I'll never see him again. Tomorrow it will be as if this never happened. By next week, even Kryzstof won't talk about it. It will be my dream, me alone, tucked away in my little cell in a city of cells, all of us dreaming in silence.* And I imagined the wolf, tucked away in his little cell, dreaming black and silver dreams, but somewhere in them, the glitter of the Yokohama harbor at night, the flash of a bright red suitcase.

And so I called out to him, without intending to. "Oukami Yasuhara!"

He stopped and turned back, and I could see the surprise clearly in the lines of his body.

"If you die," I said, "let me know. I'll take you somewhere fantastic. Okay? It'll be the best date of your life."

A moment in which his face was blank, utterly blank, and then he smiled. It was radiant, it transformed him completely. It was as if a new person had walked into his skin and was smiling out at me from that smooth cold face. And I smiled back at him, something in me glowing out at something in him, two sleepwalkers shining flashlights down at each other from opposite windows.

"Tanoshimi ni," the wolf said. *I'll look forward to it.*

Safe journey, I thought to Yuki-chan. And Yuki-chan gave me an Okay with his thumb and forefinger together, bumping along in his red suitcase, unfurling like a flower, reaching his roots up toward the sky.

THE PIKE

Later it will seem remarkable to me how innocuous they were: both of those first meetings. Snow had fallen in the kind of thick gathered layers that only a New England winter can roll out, snow like muddy wool, snow like two-day-old cake frosting. I was reeling from an eight-hour bus ride turned eleven by the weather, hauling a backpack and battered guitar case into the main outbuilding of the artist colony. I remember the thrill of anticipation—this was a place where the relentless onslaught of our lives yielded a little, where peace seeped in and changed us over the days and weeks of working alone. I was ready to be changed. I was primed for transformation and heavy with exhaustion, and then Camilo was there.

He'd just come in from the outside, where a car stalled with his boxes of darkroom chemicals. I remember taking him in and not taking him in—spiky black hair, slight frame, bare inches taller than me, his obvious nervousness, a women's coat that made him look like Little Red Riding Hood. ("I don't buy clothes," he would say later, a statement of purpose. "I only wear things that have been given to me.") He glanced anxiously at me, and I smiled, and turned away again; I wanted the keys to my studio, I wanted to be alone.

Months later, almost half a year, Camilo would say: "That was when I fell in love with you." He would say: "You were so confident. You shook my hand. You looked me straight in the eyes and you said 'Hello.'" This must have happened, but I don't remember it because in that first encounter, he didn't matter to me at all.

I met Corah two weeks later, also at the main hall. I was determined to do laundry, so I didn't notice her until my second trip up from the basement, and then there she was: an older woman, long tightly curled black hair, perched stiffly on one of the leather couches. A book in hand, I think, a glass of whiskey, some prop that declared: *I belong here*, the prop that every new arrival needed in order to feel like they could sit on the leather couches. I remember her plunging neckline, a strand of elegant pearls, heels, and I remember thinking: *heels, winter, New England?* She said hello, I made a joke about laundry and continued on. Nothing about her struck me too deeply, except maybe her sad eyes, trained on you in an unyielding direct stare, even as she discussed the snow—when did it start snowing, when will it stop, the snow is so bad this year. Later everyone would say this about her: "She had such sad eyes." Later than that, she would describe herself as having sad eyes. Much later I would realize that her exquisite command of her own details threw them all into question—what was manufactured? What existed on its own? What could be trusted?

When I think about each of those meetings, I envy myself in them. Neither meant anything to me, and so I continued unscathed.

I WAS READING SYLVIA PLATH's diaries that winter, Ted Hughes's letters, and both their poems. I was finding their bodies of work as intertwined as their lives had been, a conversation that continued even after Plath's death. I had recently ended a long relationship with an artist whose work I loved as fiercely as I loved her. Although I tried not to read either of us into that legend, I found myself raw, strangely moved by the convergence of the two poets' work. Hughes's later poems from *Birthday Letters* intentionally riffed on earlier ones of Plath's; some of Plath's earlier poems were written on the backs of Hughes's drafts. I couldn't have explained what I was looking for in all those papers. Retelling their relationship lends itself to reductive cinematics: the young poet lovers, the mad broil of art, Plath's jealousy, Hughes's great and wandering eye, an older woman seductress, a betrayal, a rush of rage and fevered genius producing *Ariel*, finally Plath's suicide. It's ripe for the picking, easily distilled, too easy. What attracted me most that winter weren't the reductions but rather the complexities—how headlong everybody was, how hungry and shipwrecked on each other, how impossible to tell right from wrong.

Assia Wevill was the figure at the heart of it, the mysterious and powerful Other Woman—and yet there was so little written about her, in comparison to the volumes and volumes on Plath and Hughes. Assia was a mystery, gathered in snatches of detail, a passing mention here, a blurred photograph there. I discovered that she was a Berlin-born Jew who'd fled Nazi Germany for Palestine, lived in England and Canada, married three times, had passionate affairs about which she spoke candidly and multiple abortions about which she also spoke candidly. In 1961, she and her husband, the much younger poet David Wevill, sublet a London flat from Plath and Hughes, who'd relocated to a farm in Devon they called Court Green. The Wevills were invited to visit Court Green; on the eighteenth of May they did visit; over the course of a night and a morning, Hughes and Assia fell into the sort of passionate affair that Assia excelled in.

I was haunted by the poetic irony of this, the Greek tragedy–like invitation of destruction into one's midst. It was so easy to imagine how a different story could have unfolded: if only a different tenant, if only no dinner invitation. I found myself imagining the innocence of that first farm meal: the long wood table, both couples laughing, faces flushed from wine, candlelight, beef stew, dark gingerbread. So tempting, to try and conjure the seeds of all that destruction planted right there, in a glance that held too long, shadow on cheekbone, light on a wrist. How can we know what will come of the strangers we bring close? And who can resist a story in which the price of unknowing is so high?

IN THE TWO WEEKS BEFORE Corah arrived, Camilo tracked me with the patience and single-mindedness of a bloodhound. When I got to the Hall, he was there smiling. When I left, he was actually going back to his studio too, why didn't we walk together. When I headed into town, he needed some supplies, he might as well come. When the resident artists gathered in someone's studio for a night of drinking, wherever I was sitting or leaning was where he also happened to be.

I didn't fully realize it at first. He was just there, someone I didn't mind talking to, despite an unwavering directness that was not always kind. When he asked what I was working on and I told him the subject of a human interest piece I had been paid to write, he said in his flat objective way, "Why are you writing that? It's unoriginal." I found myself stammering a little, trying to explain that it wasn't my idea, I was getting paid to execute it. But—"That's silly. Why are you writing something you don't want to write?" Surrounded as I had been in New York by a scramble of other young artists desperate to make rent, this seemed like an entirely naïve— but also new and suddenly fascinating—perspective. Why *were* we doing things we didn't want to do? Money must be too simplistic an answer, if Camilo hadn't even considered it.

In another conversation, he said that he was undocumented. "I came to the U.S. when I was thirteen. I don't have papers." At first I thought I misheard him, or had misunderstood. When he saw the blank look on my face he said, "I'm illegal."

"Oh," I said, uncertainly.

He shrugged. "I'm getting my green card through my wife. We married in the fall."

"Congratulations!"

"It's just for the green card. She's a friend. But thank you."

"She's a good friend," I said, awkwardly, "to do that for you."

Camilo sort of smiled then. "She has projects," he said. "I'm one of them."

The first time we slept together was something of a surprise. It had never occurred to me to find him attractive—I'd been dating women for the most part, and besides he looked nothing like the men to whom I was drawn. He looked more like a child, with his large sober eyes, unruly hair, the bright primary colors of his scavenged clothes. And so when he invited himself back to my studio and then, sitting close on my narrow twin bed, asked, "May I kiss you?" I felt both a shock, and then also a recognition. *Oh this is what this is. This is what's happening.* And it was February, and the woods and the snow dampened all sound, changed all color and texture, everything that happened here could so easily never exist at all, so I said, "Okay," and then he kissed me.

SOMEHOW IT WAS ASSIA ON whom I fastened. She kept diaries too, I discovered, but they'd mostly been destroyed. Some of her watercolors remained—ink drawings, featuring exotic birds and strange plants. She had a steady hand and an eye for beautiful things, and both showed themselves in her affair with Ted Hughes. Hers was a quick wit, and a sharp one. Men found her irresistible, women as well. She knew how to make a mark, how to be the only one in a room that anyone would remember long after. And she was someone without family (nearby), without home (-land), whose self-description as an orphan and a refugee made her both infinitely sympathetic and utterly exotic. But more than any of that, she was desperately hungry. She couldn't stand to be alone and so she lined up her husbands carefully, making sure to have the next in place before she left the first. If all eyes in the room weren't on her, she couldn't be sure that she existed.

CORAH'S ARRIVAL KICKED WHAT HAD been a sleepy working colony into high gear. She showed up with a handle of whiskey that she placed by the leather couches—"for late nights," she said—and tea drinkers converted themselves immediately. At dinners in which the rest of us were in jeans and fleeces, she wore bodice-plunging silk dresses, heavy mascara, once a contraption that looked like a corset. She came from wealth, and she made that clear in a way that was equal parts ostentation and defiance. Corah didn't find women terribly interesting, I discovered, but in rooms with men, she blossomed. She became vivacious, aggressive, she said provocative things and then leaned back and sized everybody up. Her first night after dinner, she announced, "Well, my husband and I divorced recently. I guess I'm here to find a new husband." She laughed, inviting the rest of us to laugh, adding: "We didn't have enough sex, you see. Sex matters much more to me, and so I was always unsatisfied." She made light eye contact as she dropped the words, her liquid gaze flitting from the composer to the sculptor to the novelist to Camilo, who was sitting next to me, clutching a slightly incongruous hip flask. ("It was given to me.") On the path from the composer to Camilo, her eyes stopped on mine for a sheer second by accident, and we looked at each other, and then she moved on.

Corah was there to work, and she took it seriously: there is no work greater than either finding the next love of your life, or getting the taste and feel and smell of the old one off of you. I still thought my own work was much simpler: the article, which I hadn't touched since arriving—and maybe also Assia, about whom I now knew a startling amount of unhelpful detail, and none of what I actually wanted to know. I hadn't realized or couldn't admit that my work was similar to Corah's, even if I masked it better.

CAMILO AND I HAD BECOME inseparable by then, as time blurred into what felt like one long day, punctuated by nights. We worked together, sharing the long table in his studio as he played South American folk music and I put new logs on the fire. We ate our lunches together out of the picnic baskets in which they were delivered: thermoses of hot soup, large still-warm cookies. We walked together, long loops through the woods, snow sometimes sinking us thigh-deep. We slept together, yes, but more than that, we woke together.

He told me secrets late at night—about his mother, who had abandoned him as a child while she went to America, and how her sporadic returns bewildered him: "I followed her through every room of the house, and she still left me again. I wouldn't eat, they had to call her in America and say: Camilo will not eat." He told me about how lost he felt as an artist: "This is the first time since I left art school that I've made work. I don't know if I'm even actually an artist." He told me about his legal wife: "Her mother said, 'Do not marry him, he will steal all your money'—and that was why she married me, I think." But mostly he talked about his own mother: "Now she lives in Florida, I spent three hours on the phone with her electric company, they overcharged her but she wouldn't argue with them, she makes me take care of her even from here." Camilo spoke of his mother with anger, bewilderment, confusion, longing, occasional tenderness. He wrote letters to her that he never sent, but sometimes he would read them to me, in the dark studio with the fire leaping.

In service of keeping my focus on my work, I'd had a series of conversations with Camilo that began with, "I'm not looking for a relationship, you understand," and had invariably ended with us naked, woodsmoke and blankets and decadent mid-afternoon sunlight, all of that bright, blinding incandescent snow, so bright you couldn't see properly, maybe, exactly what it was you were doing.

Camilo was as receptive to these conversations as he was to everything else. "I understand," he always said in his dispassionate tone, and I took this as a great, overarching, broad-ranging understanding, the kind of understanding that took in my recent breakup, subsequent unease, conflicting desire to be happy, and how all of these contradictions could propel us together, result in an unending night-after-night that had begun to feel like intimacy. "I understand," he would say, and eventually I incorporated that into my understanding as well. Calling my best friend, I said, "It feels complicated, but Camilo understands."

"What does he understand?" my friend asked, and before I could consider my answer, maybe study it a little longer, I'd already replied: "Oh, everything."

THE FIRST AND ONLY NIGHT that Assia and her husband stayed at Court Green, she had a dream about a giant pike with golden eyes. Within each golden pike-eye was curled a human fetus. It was a fascinating, exotic dream—she expected no less from herself—and she told it with flair at the breakfast table the next morning. I imagine the scene: Sunday, a cool English spring, a hot mug of coffee thick with milk, Assia with her hair artfully loose, just awoken. She clasps her fingers around that mug, her voice is husky and warm, just low enough that you have to lean in. She sees herself reflected in Sylvia's wide eyes, while Sylvia listens "astonished and envious" as Hughes later described her in a poem.

Later, Hughes would write the infamous epitaph to the scene: "That moment the dreamer in me / Fell in love with her, and I knew it." The day would build to Assia and Ted alone and laughing in the kitchen, Sylvia rising stonily from where she sat with Assia's husband, asking the Wevills to leave, ending the visit abruptly. But the dream would linger—not the fish itself, but the spell of it, I think, the sensation of being caught in someone else's vision told to you at your breakfast table, transforming your breakfast table, transforming your breakfast, transforming you.

—————

THE FIRST TIME CAMILO MENTIONED Corah to me, we were naked. "She wants me," he said, as if we were discussing the weather. "If I slept with her, would you mind?"

Lying against him, our skin sticking a little to the leather of his studio couch, I turned the question over and over in my mind— the betrayal of it, but also the way it had been asked so matter-of-factly. Did this mean it was not a betrayal? Was this, in fact, a reasonable conversation? He sounded reasonable. This must be reasonable.

"Do you want to sleep with her?" I asked.

"She's very attractive," Camilo said, without hesitating. He could have been talking about a tree or a horse or somebody's painting. "Don't you think so?" In my silence, he added: "She has sad eyes. And she has a difficult time with her mother."

"How do you know that?"

"She gave me her memoir, I'm reading it."

"Her memoir?"

"About her mother." Camilo shifted a little. We'd gotten off topic. "So—if I have sex with her, how do you feel about this?"

Called upon for a sudden answer, I hesitated. Camilo was clearly a free spirit, I felt required to be just as free. And yet . . . "Look, if you want to be involved with somebody else, this—what we're doing—it needs to stop. No hard feelings. But it's just—too complicated, to sleep with you if you're sleeping with her."

"Do you not like her?"

"It's not really about that." A moment, and then I heard myself add, "She's slippery."

"She has suffered," Camilo defended her. "My mother, she has also made me suffer. Corah understands these things. I read her my letters to my mother yesterday, and she said—"

I sat up. "You know, I think let's just call this quits."

"No," Camilo said, fast. "I want to be with you."

"Think about it," I said. "You should probably take some time to think about that."

"I don't have to think about it. If it's a choice, I choose you."

"Okay," I said, and I won't lie, of course it felt like victory. Of course I felt like I'd won something.

TED HUGHES SENT ASSIA A note in London: "I have come to see you, despite all marriages." And, the story goes that she took a blade of grass, dipped it in Dior, and sent it back to him. No words. She knew how to craft an image, Assia. She knew how to stand in doorways. Sylvia was a poet, so Assia found a weapon stronger than language.

Meanwhile the pike, well, I think it twisted and turned, golden-eyed and restless, swimming under everything, creating ripples every time it got just a little closer to the surface. Meanwhile Sylvia, sleepless in circles, suspecting everything, sparrows and ants and tree branches, sudden gusts of wind, anything that could snatch him away. I read her journal alone in my studio, one of the few times that Camilo wasn't dozing on my twin bed, or writing to his mother on my floor. I wanted to say to her: *Things come to us and then we lose them again.* I wanted to say: *It's all on loan, don't you know this?* I wanted us to sit together at a long elm-planked table, drinking her Nescafé, and I'd tell her this thing: part warning, part absolution. But the truth is, I was starting to forget it myself. A strange but constant presence in my life, Camilo was becoming something I didn't want to lose.

WE HAD ONE REAL CONVERSATION in the time that I was there, Corah and I. I say "real" because only the two of us were there, not because I was any more or less assured of its authenticity than at any other time. It was a snowy pine-bound morning; I came in at the end of the breakfast rush and found the communal dining room empty. I'd left Camilo asleep in my bed, planning to bring back a thermos of coffee for us both, but when I found the room so empty and bright, I sat instead of hurrying back. I poured the coffee from the metal bullet of the thermos into a chipped yellow cup and wrapped my fingers around it, letting the steam rise damply to my face. I stared at myself in the bright windowpane, snow framing me and my reflection both cradling our coffee cups, our eyes meeting in a bold, direct gaze.

Corah broke the peace with her sudden arrival, stamping snow off her fur-lined boots, hair down, cheeks flushed. She scanned the room as she entered, and her eyes lit on me. I kept my stare fixed on my coffee cup, so we could slide past each other unhindered, but she sat down at the end of my bench.

"Late breakfast," she said with a wry smile, and I couldn't tell if she meant for me or for her, so I nodded and smiled. "Late night," she added, and then I realized she meant for her, and I nodded and smiled again.

"How's the writing going?" she asked. I shrugged, but she waited, so I risked a neutral, "It's okay." Then, "How about you?"

I expected a polite nonanswer; something to pass the time. Instead, Corah made a face. She looked out the windows, scanning the far distance for the truth, then turned back to me. Caught in the high beam of her stare, I found myself sitting very still, shoulders straight.

"It's hard to be alone sometimes," she said. "It can be . . . urgently lonely, actually." I lived inside the green flecks of her gray stare. I tried to brace a little against it—I could feel her searching me like an X-ray, that stare rummaging inside my pockets. "But maybe you don't find that?"

I didn't know if she knew about Camilo or not. Suddenly, I didn't know if I was supposed to be keeping it a secret or not—if Camilo was keeping it a secret—if he shouldn't be, if he should be. I was filled with an intense unease.

"Maybe sometimes," I said.

"I thought it would be easier to be here," she said. "We think that all we need is to be alone, in order to work everything out. Sometimes when I'm alone, it all just comes crashing down instead." She smiled. The smile was so adept, so skillful, that I felt my whole body leaning toward it before my mind had caught up. I stood quickly, in a strange lurch. She didn't seem to notice—she'd turned back out to the windows again.

I almost sat back down. And yet, the image was arranged for me cleverly—her face framed by morning light, the artful lowering of her chin. Even the phrasing—*urgently lonely*—was this something one just thought and blurted, or was this a phrase one turned around in one's mind, shaped like a missile, and then delivered?

"I should get back," I said, clutching the thermos. "Have a good breakfast." And something flickered over her face—was it interest? or disappointment? or neither—and then she shrugged. I realized, when I was back in the woods, that I'd been holding the now-empty thermos so tightly that my fingertips were tingling even before the cold hit them.

WE STARTED READING CORAH'S MEMOIR together in bed. It was a strange time. Camilo liked to read out loud, in his singsong lilt—the white of the comforter and the white of the snow and the white of the moonlight, and the unfolding saga of Corah's mother.

When he first started this, it occurred to me to stop him. I almost asked if he was joking. And then I didn't. I'd become fascinated with her too. I, too, wanted to know how her mother had plucked her from a rib and molded her into a voluptuous, sad-eyed woman, who sat at the dinner table pouring expensive red wine down her long throat (and she arranged the image so that you didn't notice the folds of skin, the slight wattle, you just noticed that length of throat), saying things like: "Well we used to have an open marriage, the agreement was that I could sleep with whom I liked, and so I did, there's nothing hotter than a new lover, there's nothing quite like desire." And her eyes flickered over Camilo, held, as he blinked at her, transfixed. We all were by then. We all were.

THE NIGHT BEFORE MY RESIDENCY ended, Camilo and I watched *Into the Wild*, projecting the movie onto the giant white wall of his studio. The colors were washed out and the sound was faraway, which intensified the feeling of being in a universe apart from all other universes. Partway through the movie, Camilo asked, "Will I see you in New York?"

"Sure," I said.

He smiled, then: "I have a question." He took a breath. "I would like to continue this. Spending time with you, seeing you." He hesitated. "Also sleeping with you. Also, being with you."

I laughed. Only Camilo could have made all four of those separate, equally laden things. "That's not a question."

"Would you like that as well?"

"Yes," I said, "I would."

And he beamed, one of his sudden, astonishingly bright smiles. "You are very special to me."

I stared at him, disarmed. "I am?"

"Yes," he said, "you are."

We smoked a ball of hash after that. He'd been saving it in a tiny plastic ziplock. We couldn't figure out exactly how to do it, so finally he just lit the thing on fire and put it under a cup, and we took turns lifting the cup edge and inhaling the rich musky smoke. When it hit, he lay down on the floor, and eventually I lay down next to him, holding his hand. I could feel wings growing under my skin, just where my shoulder blades had been. "There are wings under my skin," I said to Camilo, my voice hushed and awed. But he was in his own haze, staring up at the vaulted studio ceiling, the raw wood beams. I stared up as well, the cold tiled floor making shapes in my bare back, great wings preparing to lift.

Later I asked, "Where did you get that hash anyway?" and he said a woman had given it to him during Occupy: "She smuggled it out of Morocco, in her vagina."

TED HUGHES WENT TO LONDON for Assia. He couldn't stay away. And Assia was luminous, people reported in their unkind memoirs of her, backlit by victory. But more than victory, I think, Assia was backlit by love. She had fallen headfirst, no shock there, falling in love was one of her great skills. But what she found at the bottom of it startled her, and her transformation startled her friends. She began to sleep badly, couldn't eat, seemed both triumphant and frightened when she told friends that Hughes smelled like a butcher in bed, that she wouldn't see him again, that she had to see him again, that she couldn't live without him.

This is the part where what once read like a romance now starts to read like the Bluebeard legend, depending on the narrator; this is the part that her friends scribbled down in their diaries with jealousy, fascination, or scorn, and this is the part that bewilders me. For someone so skilled at writing her own narrative to be utterly at the mercy of a new story? ("We don't pick our obsessions," said my best friend, when I told her about this turn. She was in the throes of Facebook-stalking her ex. "They pick us when we're weakened, and then we let them in.")

I went back to New York. It was a wildly disconcerting reentry into a too-loud too-bright world of subways, taxis, buildings packed shoulder to shoulder, everybody yelling. I'd walked out of the snow and here it was spring; it seemed like not just another world, but also another season. I was a sleepwalker bewildered by sudden awakening. Camilo emailed at first, a few sentences here and there. *I miss you. I can't sleep. I lie awake all night. It is so strange here without you.* And then radio silence. But I prided myself on understanding the kind of hermetic seal that an artist colony provides—the distance from outside life permits calm, permits art.

Hughes and Assia took up in London, less and less discreet, and then not at all. Crowded bars and pubs and poets' parties, the back-room intellectual chaos of the early 1960s, smoke and alcohol and Assia like a gem, fixed to him like a gem, glittering out at everyone from the back of the darkest room. The images of her, recorded in gossip and diary, are a little breathtaking—she's flushed and myste-rious and even as she holds his arm, she's afraid he's slipping away, and the fear makes her feverish, and the fever makes her glow brighter than an insect or a lamp or a star, and every poet who con-fessed on record confesses to desiring her.

Camilo returned out of the blue, out of the silence, landed on my doorstep like an asteroid. He'd biked from Brooklyn, his hair longer now. Seeing him in the unforgiving glare of a New York afternoon, he looked like a complete stranger: bike helmet in hand, ill-fitting Little Red Riding Hood jacket, nervous and blinking. We hugged and it was awkward, I invited him up the narrow flight of stairs, I made coffee in my tiny kitchen while he fiddled with his helmet, a cup, loose pens on the tabletop. Finally we sat across from each other, staring at each other, and I kept waiting to feel that great magical connection. He'd gained some weight. He'd shaved. His voice was higher and more nasal than I remembered. As I poured our coffee, he said, "I have to tell you something."

I handed him a cup. "What?"

"I have slept with Corah."

"Oh," I said.

"And two other artists."

"Oh."

"You see, all four of us slept together."

"Oh . . ."

"You see," he said, in his entirely reasonable way, "Corah sug-gested that we all go back to my studio, since there were four of us. You know how large my bed is, so it made the most sense."

I heard my voice from faraway saying "Yes."

"So, the four of us were sexually engaged. This happened a few times. I thought perhaps I should tell you that. Honesty is very important to me, you know my mother has always been dishonest and I've found this very harmful." A silence, while I sipped my coffee. "What are you thinking?" he asked.

"Did you also sleep with Corah alone?"

He hesitated, but only briefly. Then he said, "Yes."

"You did."

"Yes."

"More than once?"

"Yes."

"Oh."

The silence stretched. I was thinking: *Is this a betrayal? If it sounds so reasonable, perhaps it's reasonable.* I was thinking: *But there were wings under my skin, there was light pouring in from everything, off everything, and you were part of that.* I was thinking: *I don't want to lose that just because you fucked it up.*

"Are you angry with me?" He sounded childlike.

"I guess I don't understand."

"Oh!" He brightened. He could explain. "Well, we were sitting on the couches, it was after dinner, we had all been drinking, and Corah put her hand—"

"I thought I was clear that if you wanted something real with me, it meant not fucking everybody else minutes after I left."

"It wasn't everybody," Camilo said, "it was just Corah, and Gina, and they were engaged with Ivan, who had joined us at some point, but *I* . . ." He trailed off. Then: "I don't think this should come between us. It meant nothing to me."

"If you're telling me, though, clearly you knew it would mean something to me." That silenced him. Into the hush, I had to ask: "Was that how you felt about us? That it meant nothing?"

"No," he said, stricken. I'd never seen his eyes so wide or so dark. "You matter to me. I told you so that we could begin from a place of honesty." More silence. "I want you to trust me."

"*Trust* you."

"Yes," Camilo said, radiating sincerity from his tiny body, and I could have sworn he was quoting Corah when he said, "Trust is the lifeblood of every relationship."

AFTER PLATH'S DEATH, THE SCANDAL machine turned and pulsed. Suicide, the gas oven turned high, bread and milk laid out for her children when they awoke. This image has become a Polaroid, even for people who know nothing about Plath or Hughes or their work. Plath engraved herself into history as "that poet who killed herself," Hughes was forever cast as "the man who made her do it," and Assia was erased from the image entirely.

By mid-February of 1963, only days after Plath's death, Assia was spending most of her time in Sylvia's flat. As the long dark days passed, Assia was free to roam through Sylvia's things, reading the *Ariel* manuscript and her diaries, which Assia called "most incredible." She slept in Sylvia's bed, leaving books, papers, even knickknacks as Sylvia had left them. By the time that Ted invited her to move in and help care for the children, Assia was accustomed to living willingly, even hungrily, among the shards of Sylvia's life, and Hughes noticed but couldn't understand her growing fascination with his dead wife. He later wrote to Assia's sister: "I knew Assia had some odd bits and pieces of Sylvia's. I don't know why she bothered to do that sort of thing—I know it used to help to depress her."

There are some records, snippets of conversation that friends diligently recorded. Teas with Assia in which she talked of Sylvia obsessively—her books, what she had once underlined in gentle, ghostly pencil, how Assia was now reading those same books. One supposed friend, Anne Alvarez, told biographers Yehuda Koren and Eilat Negev well after the fact: "She was so beautiful, and kept on talking about Sylvia. . . . For her own good, she would have been much better off not to sleep in Sylvia's bed."

Hughes didn't understand, or he didn't want to. But obsession is like a foreign country. People back home can't quite comprehend what it is you're seeing day after day, the words that you're using. There's no way to describe what it's like to dig yourself down into soil they've never touched. And so Assia dug, and Hughes tried to reach her, he said—long-distance calls over wavery wires—but she wouldn't be reached.

I imagine she heard him. I think she did. She just heard Sylvia louder and more clearly.

We continued to see each other, Camilo and I.

I remember it like walking down a narrow, long hallway. You don't think to turn around. Your only thought is that something magical must be waiting at the end, to make up for the hallway being so long.

And so spring became summer. There were moments that were good. Nothing quite approximated the rush of February light, the sound of our voices reflecting across a silent forest, our footsteps in snow. But there were moments in which I was reminded of having felt how I had felt. *Liberated,* was the word that stayed with me, long after it no longer applied. The wings just ready to rise, the feeling of lift-off.

Camilo was in love. He hadn't ever been in love before, he said, not really. And now he was, and the Camilo who was in love was not the Camilo who had helped measure the winter days with his heartbeat. The Camilo who was in love was prone to drastic mood swings. He would write me notes that ran the length of a twelve-by-eighteen sketchpad page, that read: *I love love love love love love love love love you, I love you, I love love love . . .* Half an hour later, he would be shut down, silent. I didn't have enough time for him, he would say, if pressed. Why wasn't I willing to make time for him in the same ways he would make time for me?

He was semi-employed by that point, left with whole days of free time extending into open Brooklyn nights. My days started in the morning and on the nights I was lucky, spat me out at eleven—

more often, midnight. Camilo first suspected that my love was being diverted away from him toward my ex, but over time he came to the conclusion that my work also diverted that love, and my friends, and then finally my writing. He decided maybe he wanted to be a writer too. Maybe we could be in the same rooms at the same times, and talk to the same people, maybe we could write *together*, maybe our work could be intertwined. For someone who had once preached a mantra of openness and fluid boundaries, he kept surprising me with what seemed like jealousy.

I would take the long train into Brooklyn late at night as a token of compromise—*It's late, but here I am.* And at first, that was good enough. He'd run me a hot bath in the aging porcelain tub on the top floor of his old house, ask me about my day, offer stories from his. But our conversations ground more and more into silence. Anything I talked about was something that excluded him, I was part of a world that was not his world, and it ate at him. He would grow quieter and quieter, more and more sullen, and finally the conversation would veer sharply into an interrogation of how much I loved him, how much did I care, what might I additionally do to show him that I meant it.

More and more, when I looked at him, I saw a small boy with giant eyes, hair well past his shoulders now. It became autumn, and when we slept in the same bed I wanted to keep my clothes on. I didn't want him to touch me. I said it was cold and his house was unheated. I said I was tired, we'd been up so late fighting, fighting. This was the greatest rejection of all and he felt it deeply, and didn't hesitate to make that known. So finally I gave in—it was less exhausting than the fighting, and when it was over, I could go to sleep. Weeks passed like this. The leaves had barely changed color but I dreamed of winter, all the time, snow covering everything, tree-silent, world-far. Another month passed. I started to think of myself as someone without a body. I thought of myself as a pair of eyes.

I thought broken trust could be willed whole. I began to learn what I hadn't known: there is no such thing as broken trust, there is only trust and its absence. The absence of something can't be repaired: the thing is simply gone. And if we choose to stay in its aftermath, we live in the hole it has made.

THE NATURAL QUESTION IS: WHY didn't I leave? The answers are all unflattering in the extreme. One answer is that I tried—I broke up with him a handful of times over the late summer, and into the long bleak fall—and that answer is the weakest, because I didn't stick with it. Another answer is that I thought things would get better, they couldn't get worse—and then another week would pass and every time I arrived at that freezing ancient house there was a fight. Midnight, one A.M., two A.M., it was three A.M. and the bathwater was cold and he was sitting in front of me crying: *I love you, I love you, I love you.* Maybe the worst answer is that he painted a picture of me and I started to believe it: I was selfish, I journeyed to places he couldn't go, I was callous in my abandonment of him, just like his mother.

And here is another answer, and to this day, now returned from that strange foreign soil, I don't know what to make of it. I stayed because of Corah.

ASSIA WAS REMARKABLY CLEAR-EYED ABOUT herself. That was the thing. She wasn't blind. She'd moved onto a little island, she'd chosen the one that had no boats or planes or means of leaving, and she knew it was territory that would devour her. She continued to sleep in Sylvia's bed, use her linens, eat with her utensils, and she wrote in her own diary: "A strong sensation of her repugnant live presence." In letters to friends she called their flat "the ghost house," and, as Hughes concentrated his energies into editing and compiling the *Ariel* manuscript, Assia wrote: "Sylvia [is] growing in him, enormous, magnificent. I shrinking daily, both nibble at me. They eat me." Later, another diary entry: "[S]he had a million times the talent, 1,000 times the will, 100 times the greed and passion that I have."

Obsession is comparison, fueled by jealousy: *Who is this person, what do they have that I lack?* But it's also compassion of a kind—or perhaps, more accurately, it's empathy. One seeks to put oneself into another's shoes. One seeks to feel what another has felt, to understand another down to her bones, to her DNA, down to the spinning heart of her atoms. Obsession is, ultimately, the compilation of narrative: it is uncovering a story, attempting to piece together what it would be like to be the person who lives inside. The line between biography and obsession, I think, is perilously thin. Sometimes there is none at all.

A FRIEND HAD BEEN AT a different residency with Corah, and over coffee, her name came up. They'd slept together, my friend said— he'd liked her a great deal, but had eventually discovered himself to be part of a long list that Corah was working down. Those on it were replaced quickly enough—a young composer, then a writer. Months later, another friend: they'd been at an artist colony as well, Corah had been drinking heavily, she'd made advances to a novelist who rejected her in reluctant loyalty to his fiancée at home, Corah had wept. This startled me. Had she actually wept? Was a half-stranger's rejection enough to actually wound her?

I thought of her. I didn't want to, but I did. More through the grapevine: *She's like a tornado, everything she touches ends in destruction.* This from someone who watched her sleep with two friends at different times, then wait, breath held, for the moment in which they told each other. She became a myth of sexual weaponry. She became more interesting than Camilo, who was constantly sullen now, who clung at my sleeves, who grew younger every day, who was waiting in a closet, who needed me to come let him out. She was an unapologetic missile, a god of destruction. "Pathological"—

this from a writer—"just pathological, she's not at home anywhere unless there's absolute chaos."

By the winter I was reading another of her memoirs, but I hid it from Camilo. I couldn't explain my obsession. If it was jealousy alone, it would have been something I could name and then admit to, but it was something I didn't have words for. The book was as lurid and tell-all as one might have imagined: everybody was sleeping with everybody and screaming at everybody and doing drugs with everybody and never forgiving anybody and then rushing off somewhere with someone new, and then it started all over again. Nobody was sitting on the third floor of a Brooklyn brownstone, sadly folding socks and waiting for someone to come home. Nobody was leaving resentful voicemails about how perhaps somebody was too busy to step out of work and call them back. Nobody was comparing everybody to their absent, much-hated, much-needed mother; instead, somebody was a Molotov cocktail, doing coke with married men and eager to detonate. It was her unstoppable plummet that held my attention. It was her inexorable vitality, in stark contrast now to Camilo's sullen stillness.

WHEN WE FIRST STARTED DATING, Camilo had mentioned Corah often, as if completely unaware that it would hurt me. She'd given him a book of photographs, and he leafed through it, impressed by her knowledge of art. I hadn't known that she had children until he mentioned it—she was taking her eldest to look at colleges. "She's such a good mother," he said wistfully, and the thought struck me that he wasn't much older than her own son. Another time he mentioned how she'd pursued him—"from the beginning," he said, with the awe and pride of someone wholly unused to being pursued. Once she'd come over to his studio with a bottle of wine in hand, and had given him advice about his mother while they drank. This was while I was still there, he said, but "nothing happened." Later, it came out that he'd invited her to take a bath with him—"I thought

I told you that already. Anyway, we didn't do it." Every revelation shifted the uneven ground on which we were standing. Every revelation changed our story of the snow and the wings and the glorious space, and made it smaller, stickier, increasingly absurd.

Eventually he spoke of her less and less, but her presence remained. Most obviously, in a low-grade paranoia that ran like a fever through our every interaction. Every time he hesitated before speaking, I put the next sentence in his mouth: *I have something to tell you.* In the beginning, I flinched from this sentence. By the winter, I willed it. What else could he give me of Corah? What had she said, what had she meant, what had she revealed to him in an unguarded moment?

But now he didn't want to talk about her anymore. He was suspicious of my persistent interest. I wanted to know if he thought she was happy. I wanted to know if he thought she did things just to write about them, or if she wrote about the things she did in order to understand and then escape them. What was story and what was Corah? What does escape look like, if you don't know the way out?

"Let's not talk about her," Camilo said. "That doesn't matter now."

"Why do you want to talk about her?" Camilo asked. "You don't like her."

"I don't even think of her anymore," Camilo said. "I think only of you. Why aren't you thinking of me?"

It was early December, by now. Almost a year had passed since meeting Camilo and it was the coldest winter on record—something called a "polar vortex" swept in like a knife, straight from the Arctic, and rendered us raw and miserable. I seemed to be sick all the time. I was always cold, never hungry, most often nauseous. I'd lost fifteen pounds, although I couldn't have told you where they went. Skinny enough at the best of times, now I watched water bounce off my rib bones when I showered. Camilo told me I wasn't taking care of myself, I was careless with him and careless with myself, why couldn't I be less careless.

And again through the grapevine: the divorce hadn't been a reasonable mutual decision, Corah's husband had simply decided he couldn't take any more, and had left. She wanted him back, he was unyielding. She fled from artist colony to artist colony. Her children were resentful, old enough to understand betrayal, the unspoken kind most of all. Everything at home had spoiled, but as long as she stayed in the woods, whichever woods they were, the dream remained good. I knew how that felt. I'd left the woods, and look what had happened to my good dream.

Camilo was sad, and the snow was gray, nothing was or could ever again be new, I weighed as much as a twelve-year-old boy, and it was almost the new year.

ASSIA WROTE IN HER DIARY that Hughes was having nightmares all the time, dreams of Sylvia—ones in which her hair grew shock-white, or in which he shot the cat they'd once owned together, but it wouldn't die. Assia's waking dream was Sylvia. In her diary again: "I'm immersed now . . . forever in the burning shadows of their mysterious seven years." And then: "What insanity, what methodically crazy compulsion drove me . . . to this nightmare maze . . . and Sylvia, my predecessor, between our heads at night."

THE ONE CONSTANTLY SURPRISING FACT that I keep learning is that things come to an end. They carry themselves as far as they can, but eventually momentum runs out.

As the polar vortex sharpened days to a point, I read the few books I could find that contained excerpts of Assia's diaries, Koren and Negev's biography being the best. By September 1963, she was living alone in London, in Sylvia's old flat, and Hughes was living with his family at Court Green. Although she joined him there for a period of time, his parents couldn't forgive her for the death of Sylvia. In 1965 she had a daughter, Shura, whom she identified as Hughes's but whom Hughes would not claim. By 1967, she had returned alone to Plath's flat in London, and she and Hughes were exchanging long, fraught, argumentative, passionate letters. She wanted them to move in together, marry, find a house that would fit all three but leave no room for ghosts. Meanwhile, Hughes was split between his elderly parents, Sylvia's estate, his depression, and multiple other women carefully spread out between Devon and London. Assia didn't permit herself to think of these women, but she knew and the knowing fed her fears and insecurities. Phone calls devolved into shouting matches. By the time the harsh winter had descended, the kind that Plath struggled through seven years earlier, Assia was exhausted, depressed, and entirely alone, save for Shura and the ever-presence of Sylvia. And so Assia continued trying to reconstruct her, trying to resurrect the meat, the bone, perhaps so that Assia could understand the parameters of this invisible and implacable barrier. In her diary, at various points she wondered if Sylvia's elbows were sharp, if her hands were large-knuckled—what shape did brilliance assume? She might have kicked herself for not noticing, that weekend so many years before. She might have wished to go back in time, although even I can't guess for what: to do it differently, or just see it all more clearly?

In December, Camilo came to my apartment. I was sicker now; walking up subway stairs took twice the usual amount of time, and I had to rest partway. I just wanted to sleep, and then sleep, and then go back to sleep. I made dates and then missed them, agreed to meet Camilo for breakfast, and then canceled. Even his anger and hurt couldn't penetrate my thick weariness. We'd broken up, come together, broken up, come back together. And then he came to my apartment late that night. He'd come to take care of me, he said, to put all the madness and fighting aside for a moment and just be there for me. And as I made us both tea, handed him a mug, he said, "I have to tell you something."

IN THE SPRING OF 1969, Assia accompanied Hughes to Manchester, for a television reading that he'd agreed to do. They went to dinner afterward at the Elm Hotel, and Hughes, probably exhausted and definitely drunk, was goaded into admitting that he could see no chance of a life that they could share. That evening Assia quoted him in her diary: "It's Sylvia—it's because of her" and finished with her own addendum: "I can't answer that. No more than if it were a court sentence." Assia returned to London feeling as if, for better or worse, after so much time, she had her answer.

THE NEW GIRL SOUNDS FINE. Sweet, optimistic, also Colombian. She participates in a book club with him. She smudges sage around the room to keep out bad spirits. She understands his situation with his mother, Camilo told me, and her understanding is healing. She came over just the day before and cleaned his room for him, sorted all of his clothes. She says kind things to him in his mother tongue, that his mother never said. She's married, but it's recently become an open marriage. And he just felt that it was very important to be honest because he loved me, he had hopes for our reunion, after all his relationship with her was an entirely separate thing. Then he asked if he could borrow five hundred dollars, for his rent.

I asked him to leave my apartment.

And in hers, Assia dismissed her nanny, held her sleeping daughter, turned up the gas, and went to sleep. "Life was very exciting at the beginning," she wrote, "but this living death was too much to pay for it. . . . Please don't think that I'm insane, or that I have done this in a moment of insanity. It was simple accountancy."

There is no more waiting. There is nothing left to turn over, assemble, uncover. There is no more story.

———

I SAW CAMILO ONE MORE time after that. Early summer. I felt like I'd come out of something much longer than just a winter. I'd gone to San Francisco for work, lived in a high sunny studio with a courtyard in the back. Nobody else in that space but me; no ghosts, just sunlight. I'd gained a little weight by then, laughed more easily, slept better. I returned to New York and fell, unexpectedly but entirely, in love with someone whose gentleness, generosity, and consistency were in every way antithetical to the madness in which I'd been living. Someone who moved in easy strides through the world, whose quick wit went hand in hand with an unshakable loyalty. It wasn't that anyone had built a bridge to my island, rather that I'd dived into the shallows and started swimming.

Camilo met me before work. He'd chopped off all his hair and it spiked in crazy tufts. He looked like a small animal, blinking a little in the light of early afternoon. It felt to me as if I'd come face-to-face with a stranger, or someone that I recognized from a photograph. He'd asked to see me, but once in front of me, he didn't seem to know where to start. He told me that he was having immigration troubles still—his mother had torn an important page from his passport years before. He told me that he was angry at me for abandoning him, that it made him think of all the times his mother had left him, that he didn't want me to think of him as a bad person, that the girl didn't mean anything and he never would have mentioned her but for the overwhelming value he put on honesty. That trust was the lifeblood. That he still had hopes. That he didn't want to be angry. That he loved me. "Do you hate me?"

"No," I said.

"Do you love me?"

The word bewildered me. It was like a sound fallen out of another language, one existing far away from where we had taken place. I excused myself, and went to work.

A few days after that, a friend mentioned that Corah had written an article about sex positivity. We were getting on the subway, and when I just stared at her, she went on, "You know, this whole thing about how we should love our aging bodies, and each other's aging bodies. And she talked about affairs as a way to reinvigorate the marriage."

"Oh," I said, and at the surprise in my voice, my friend glanced at me: "You can't really be surprised about that."

But that wasn't what had startled me. It was the complete absence of feeling. The name was a name, like any name. It meant nothing. It was the name of someone I'd met a year ago, in a faraway place, for a specific and inexplicable period of time. "No," I said, "I guess I'm not surprised," and then the next stop was mine, and I got off.

ON THE ONE HAND, OBSESSION is a tool. Boats are built and fleets set sail and books are written and languages are mastered because of it. And then on the other hand, when it descends like a veil, we forget that there was ever anything on the other side. We lose contact, and then context.

When I think of what I know about Assia, the list of questions is longer than the answers I've assembled. But the same could be said for Corah, or for the version of myself who spent a year living a life so far removed from who I understood myself to be, that I might as well have been on another planet. Assia never put it together, the story she needed. Neither did I—hers, or Corah's, or my own. I think we searched in the rubble in order to see ourselves reflected back—what we might be, what we could become—in ways that defied our own articulation. Assia used Sylvia as her mirror, and both Corah and I used equally unstable yet highly reflective surfaces for our own.

I think a lot about Assia's dream of the pike. It's been passed through so many filters (hearsay, a dream, a poem about a dream) that the exact truth of it has become irrelevant. The value for Ted

Hughes lay in the metaphor, and for him the metaphor was perhaps of secrets: the seeds of love, the fetus curled in the great golden eye. For me, it's neither truth nor metaphor that lingers. It's the image of a woman sitting at a breakfast table, loose hair and mug of coffee, given the license to be fascinating. Her audience is hungry, captivated; in that moment, they lean in astonished. She's woven them a story so odd and brilliant that she's captured even herself.

They lean in, and for a brief, bright, dangerous moment she sees herself reflected in their eyes—uncurled, uncurling, about to be born.

ACKNOWLEDGMENTS

The author wishes to thank the following:

My agent, Allison Hunter, for your enthusiasm and support, and for reading one story and then asking the life-changing question, "Do you have more?" My editor, Caitlin McKenna, whose unerring insights make this a better book and me a better writer. And a big thanks to the whole team at Random House, for your tireless work.

My family, for your endless curiosity, your delight in the strange, and for always marching to the beat of your own drum.

My chosen family, among them three people without whom *The Island Dwellers* wouldn't exist:

Erin Chen, for decades of thinking out loud together—you are imprinted in my creative DNA. Some of these stories were written while living together in Boston.

Marilu Snyders, for your storyteller's sixth sense and adventurer's heart—"Pretoria" is for you. Some of these stories were written while living together in Osaka.

Swan Huntley, for your insight, flair, and fearlessness—and for always finding the funny in the fucked-up. You helped me take the first tangible steps to making this a book.

I am equally blessed for: Matt Kelly and Katie Consamus, who have, at different times, created a household with me, made that household a home, and forgiven my lackluster cleaning; Emma Caraher, who shows up in far-flung cities (and sometimes countries) when I need her steady hand; Doraelia Ruiz, whose paintings are on my walls as I write; Nick Westrate and Billy Carter, who took me as family from day one; Christine Scarfuto, Kevin Artigue, and Andrew Saito, who are my siblings in theater-making and mischief; and Basil Kreimendahl, whose instinct and artistry (and carpentry) constantly inspire me. Thank you for making me a place in the world wherever you are.

My theater family, whose daring, compassion, and humor sustain me. They are many, and for this, I am lucky, but among them:

Mike Donahue—we've made many things together—plays, meals, big decisions. I'm thankful for it all, with the exception of that cassoulet. So much of what I know about storytelling was learned from and with you.

Max Posner—whether it's MacDowell, midnight on Ryder Farm, or the steps of Juilliard, thank you for our ongoing conversation about this thing of life & art & life.

Michael Yates Crowley—remember how you held my hand as I got my first tattoo? Thanks for holding my hand as I started my first novel. It's a very similar sensation.

And my thanks and love to a handful of collaborators whose work on my plays taught me about rhythm and structure in ways that directly influenced these stories: Saheem Ali, Jeremy Cohen, Kimberly Colburn, Lee Sunday Evans, Adam Greenfield, Mandy Greenfield, Dan Kluger, Marti Lyons, and my grad school mentor Alan MacVey.

To my frequent actor-collaborators: thank you for saying Yes, especially on all the projects where we got paid twenty bucks and blew it at the bar. How you bring language to life has influenced how I write.

Samantha Sherman and Renata Friedman, the other 2/3 of The P-Patrol. You are fierce, kind, and excellent.

Team UTA—Larry Salz, Geoff Morley, and the inimitable Rachel Viola. You are the answer to the question, "But how is writing a *real* job?"

Thanks to the artistic homes that nurtured and housed me, especially when I had five million bees living inside my apartment and needed a place to sleep: New Dramatists, Space on Ryder Farm, the Playwrights Center in Minneapolis, and the Lark.

Special thanks to the Playwrights of New York (PoNY) Fellowship, and its founder, Sandi Goff Farkas. Your generosity has been truly life-changing—it is directly due to you and the PoNY that I had a year of time, space, and financial freedom in which to finish this book.

The MacDowell Colony for all your magic, for the things you make possible and the people you contain, who exist nowhere else.

And to Dane Laffrey: We both build worlds for a living, but the one I love most is the one I've built with you.

ABOUT THE AUTHOR

JEN SILVERMAN is a New York–based writer and playwright, a two-time MacDowell Fellow, and the recipient of a New York Foundation for the Arts grant and the Yale Drama Series Prize. She was awarded the 2016–17 Playwrights of New York fellowship at The Lark, and is a member of New Dramatists. She completed a BA in comparative literature at Brown University and an MFA in playwriting at the Iowa Playwrights Workshop, and was a fellow in the Playwrights Program at Juilliard.

jensilverman.com

ABOUT THE TYPE

This book was set in a Monotype face called Bell. The Englishman John Bell (1745–1831) was responsible for the original cutting of this design. The vocations of Bell were many—bookseller, printer, publisher, typefounder, and journalist, among others. His types were considerably influenced by the delicacy and beauty of the French copperplate engravers. Monotype Bell might also be classified as a delicate and refined rendering of Scotch Roman.